She eyed him. "Were you always a nice guy? I don't remember that."

Hutch laughed. "Nice enough. But competitive with you. Now, I'm just relieved we're both Team Triplets."

She grinned. "Team Triplets. I like it. And I don't want my life to interfere with my time here. In fact, I just realized that for certain. I'll have my assistant, who's already got a few clients of her own and is ready to be an agent in her own right, handle that contract. I want to focus on the reason I'm here."

Chloe rubbed her eyes and her face started scrunching.

Savannah cuddled Chloe closer. "'You better watch out, you better not cry,'" she sang softly. "'You better not pout, I'm telling you why.' Though, that is what babies do, isn't it, you little dumpling."

Chloe made a little sound, a soft "ba," her gaze sweet on Savannah's face, then her eyes drooped. She let out a tiny sigh and her eyes closed, her little chest rising and falling.

"Aww, she fell asleep!" Savannah said. "Huh. I'm not too shabby at this, after all. They're all changed and ready for their bassinets."

"You really are a Christmas miracle," he said.

Her face, already lit up, sparkled even more.

Dear Reader,

Divorced dad and rancher Hutch Dawson desperately needs a nanny for his six-month-old triplets. But it's a week before Christmas and no one is available *except* the last person he'd expect to apply for the difficult job. His old high school nemesis, Savannah Walsh, is home for the holidays and makes a very poignant proposal...

Thirty-five, single and a successful businesswoman, Savannah isn't sure she even has maternal instincts, but she knows she wants a child, a family. So she offers to be Hutch's nanny for the week for the hands-on experience and training. What she doesn't tell her new boss is that she's been secretly in love with him for years...

I hope you enjoy Hutch and Savannah's story. I love to hear from readers, so feel free to email me with your thoughts about *Triplets Under the Tree*. You can find more information about me and my books at my website: MelissaSenate.com.

Warmest regards and happy holidays,

Melissa Senate

Triplets
Under the Tree

—

MELISSA SENATE

HARLEQUIN
SPECIAL
EDITION

Recycling programs
for this product may
not exist in your area.

ISBN-13: 978-1-335-59433-4

Triplets Under the Tree

Harlequin Enterprises ULC
22 Adelaide St. West, 41st Floor
Toronto, Ontario M5H 4E3, Canada
www.Harlequin.com

Printed in U.S.A.

Melissa Senate has written many novels for Harlequin and other publishers, including her debut, *See Jane Date*, which was made into a TV movie. She also wrote seven books for Harlequin Special Edition under the pen name Meg Maxwell. Her novels have been published in over twenty-five countries. Melissa lives on the coast of Maine with her teenage son; their rescue shepherd mix, Flash; and a lap cat named Cleo. For more information, please visit her website, melissasenate.com.

Visit the Author Profile page
at Harlequin.com for more titles.

Chapter One

Hutch Dawson's new nanny stood in the doorway of his home office with his squirming, screeching baby daughter in her arms. "Sorry, but this just isn't working out," she said.

He inwardly sighed but completely understood. His triplets were *a lot*. But maybe if he didn't look up from his computer screen, she'd take pity on him and go back into the living room, where he could hear his other two babies crying. It was four thirty and her day ended at five. If he could just have this last half hour to deal with his to-do list.

He had three texts from his cowboys to return. Two important calls, including one from the vet with a steer's test results. And he was in the middle of responding to his brother's passive-aggressive email about the needs of the Dueling Dawsons Ranch.

The woman marched in, holding Chloe out with her legs dangling as though she were a bomb about to explode. Given the sight of the baby's clenched fists and red face, she was about to let out one hell of a wail.

She did, grabbing on to the nanny's ear too.

Mrs. Philpot, with her disheveled bun and shirt full of spit-up stains, grimaced and pried tiny fingers from her ear. "I won't be back tomorrow." She stood at the side of his desk and held out the baby.

This wasn't a big surprise. The previous nanny had quit two days ago, also lasting two days. But Hutch had to have childcare. He had ten days to go before his ex-wife was due back from her honeymoon—he could still barely wrap his mind around the fact that they were divorced with six-month-old triplets and that she'd remarried practically five minutes later. With two of his cowboys away for the holidays, his prickly brother—and new business partner—constantly calling or texting or demanding a meeting, a fifteen-hundred-acre ranch to run and way too many things to think about, Hutch *needed* a nanny.

Chloe let out a whimper between her shrieks, and Hutch snapped to attention, her plaintive cry going straight to his heart. He stood and took his baby girl, Daddy's arms calming her some. The moment Mrs. Philpot was free, she turned and hurried from the room. By the time he'd shifted Chloe against him and went after Mrs. Philpot to talk, use his powers of persuasion, to *beg*, she had on her coat and boots, her hand on the doorknob.

Noooo, he thought. *Wait!*

"I'll double your salary!" he called as she opened the door and raced out to her car in the gravel drive.

Then again, her salary, like the two nannies before her, had already been doubled. The director of the nanny agency had assured him that Mrs. Philpot, who'd raised triplets of her own, wouldn't be scared off by a little crying in triplicate.

A little. Was there any such thing?

"They're just too much for me, dear," Mrs. Philpot called back. She smoothed a hanging swath of her silver hair back into the bun, rubbed her yanked-on ear, then got into her car and peeled away, leaving him staring at the red taillights disappearing down the long drive.

And hoping for a miracle. Like that she'd turn back. At least finish the day. Even that would be a big help.

He did not see the car returning.

The other two babies were screaming their little heads off in their swings in the living room. Hutch was lucky he was hundreds of acres and many miles away from his nearest neighbor in any direction. This morning, before his workday, before the nanny was due to arrive, he'd dared take the trio into town because he'd discovered he was out of coffee and needed some and fast. He'd taken them to Java House, and two of the babies started shrieking. Compassionate glances of commiseration from those sitting at the café tables with their lattes and treats turned into annoyed glares. One woman came up to him and said, "They could really benefit from pacifiers and so could we."

He'd been about to explain that his ex-wife had gotten him to agree to wean the triplets off their pacifiers now that they were six months old. He truly tried to adhere to Allison's lists and rules and schedules since she really was better at all of it than he was, than he'd been since day one. Even her new husband, a very nice, calm optometrist named Ted, was better at caring for the triplets than Hutch was.

He shifted Chloe again, grateful that she, at least, had stopped crying. Whether from being in her daddy's arms or the blast of cold December air, flurries swirling, or both, he didn't know. She wore just cotton pj's, so he stepped back inside and closed the door. In the living room, Carson and Caleb were crying in their swings, the gentle rocking motion, soft lullabies and pastel mobile with little stuffed animals spinning having no effect. Little arms were raised, faces miserable.

What Hutch really needed was to turn into an octopus. He could cuddle each baby, make a bottle and down a huge mug of strong coffee all at the same time. He might have been chased out of Java House but not before he'd bought himself an espresso to go and two pounds of Holiday Blend dark beans.

"Hang on, guys," he told the boys and put Chloe in her swing. She immediately started crying again, which he should have seen coming. "Kiddos, let me make a quick call. Then I'll be back and we'll see what the schedule says."

He lived by the schedule. His ex-wife was a stickler for it, and Hutch, truly no expert on how to care for triplet babies, regarded it as a bible. Between the trio's general disposition, which was *crotchety*, to use a favorite word of his late mother, and the three-page schedule, complete with sticky notes and addenda, it was no wonder Hutch had gone through six nannies in six months.

And he really was no better at caring for his own children than he was when they were born. He might be making excuses, but he blamed his lack of skills on the fact that he'd been relegated to part-time father from the moment they'd arrived into the world. His ex had left him for another man—her "soulmate"—when she was five months pregnant. He and Allison had joint fifty-fifty custody, so Hutch had the triplets three and a half days a week, which meant half the time to figure out how to care for them, to discover who they were becoming with each passing day, who liked and disliked what, what worked on which triplet. On his ex's custody days, he'd miss little firsts or milestones, and though just last week she'd FaceTimed the trio trying their first taste of solids—jarred baby cereal—it wasn't the same as being there and experiencing it with them.

With his ex away for the next ten days, Hutch was actually very happy to have them to himself. The triplets were here, in his home, on his turf. Hutch's life might have been upended by the breakup of his marriage and the loss of his father just months ago and then everything going on with the ranch, but for the next week and a half his babies would be here when he woke up in the morning and here when he went to sleep. That made everything better, gave him peace, made all the other stuff going on trivial. Almost trivial.

He hurried into his office and grabbed his phone and pressed the contact button for the nanny agency, then went back into the living room, trying to gently shush the triplets, hoping his presence would calm them.

"I'm sorry. I can't hear you over the crying," the agency director said, her tone a bit strained. He had a feeling she'd already heard from Mrs. Philpot that she would not be back tomorrow. The woman had gotten *that* call four times before.

Hutch hurried to his office, closing the door till it was just ajar. He explained his predicament. "I'll *triple* the salary of whoever can start tomorrow morning," he said. "I'll even double the salary of *two* nannies so that the big job isn't heaped on one person at such a busy time." Emergency times meant emergency measures.

"That's quite generous, Mr. Dawson, but I'm sorry to say that we're plumb out of nannies until after the New Year." His heart sank as he glanced at his computer, the blinking cursor on his half-finished email to his brother, his to-do list running in his head. "If I may make a suggestion," she added—kindly, Hutch thought, hope flaring.

"Please do," he said.

"You have quite a big family here in town—all those Dawsons with babies and young children and therefore tons of experience. Call in the cavalry."

Just what his cousins wanted to do when they had families, jobs and responsibilities of their own, and right in the middle of the holiday season. He'd leaned on the generosity and expertise of various Dawsons for the past six months. He needed a dedicated nanny—even part-time.

As he disconnected from the disappointing call with

the agency and went back out into the living room, his gaze landed on the tilted, bare Christmas tree he'd ordered from a nearby farm the other day when one of those Dawson cousins noted there *was* no tree. Not a half hour after it was delivered, Hutch had accidentally backed into it while rocking Carson in one arm and trying to push Chloe in the triple stroller since that usually helped her stop crying. Two bare branches hung down pathetically. He'd meant to decorate the tree, but between running the ranch and caring for the triplets once the nanny left, the box of ornaments and garland remained in the basement.

He looked at his precious babies. He needed to do better—for them. No matter what else, it was Christmas. They deserved *better*.

Caleb was crying harder now. Chloe looked spitting mad. Carson just looked…sad. Very sad. *Please pick me up, Daddy*, his big blue tearful eyes and woeful frown said.

"All right, kiddos, I'm coming," he said, rallying himself. He went for very sad Carson, undid the harness and scooped him out. This time, just holding the little guy seemed to help. But no, it was just a momentary curiosity in the change of position, because Carson started crying again. He carefully held the baby against him with one firm arm, then got Chloe out and gave them both a rocking bounce, which seemed to help for two seconds. Now Caleb was wailing harder.

Hutch needed a minute to think—what time it was, what the schedule said. He wasn't *off* schedule; he knew that. He put both babies in the playpen and turned on the lullaby player. Then he consulted his phone for the schedule.

> *6:00 p.m.: Dinner. Offer a jar of vegetable baby food. Caleb and Chloe love sweet potatoes. Carson's favorite is string beans. Burp each baby. 6:30: Tummy time. 6:45: Baths, cornstarch and ointment as needed before diapers and pj's. 7:00 p.m.: Story time. 7:45: Bedtime.*

It was five forty-five. Clearly the babies needed something *now*. But what? Were they hungry a little early? Had soggy diapers? Tummy aches—gas? He tried to remember what he'd read in last night's chapter of *Your Baby's First Year* for month six. But Chloe had awakened at just after midnight as he'd been about to drift off with month-six milestones in his head, and then everything went out of his brain as he'd gotten up to tend to her. The moment he'd laid her back down in her bassinet in the nursery, Caleb's eyes popped open. At least Carson had slept through.

The schedule went out of his head as he remembered he still had to return the texts from one of his cowboys and had mini fires to put out. He stood in the middle of his living room, his head about to explode. He had to get on top of everything—the triplets' needs and the to-do list.

Maybe someone would magically respond to his ongoing ad for a nanny in the *Bear Ridge Weekly*. Just days ago he'd updated the half-page boxed ad, which ran both online and in the print edition with an optional border of tiny santas and candy canes to make the job seem more…festive. He quickly typed *"Bear Ridge Weekly classifieds"* into his phone's search bar to make sure his ad was indeed running. Yup. There it was. The holiday border did help, in his opinion.

> *Loving, patient nanny needed for six-month-old trip-*
> *lets from now till December 23rd. M-F, 8:00 a.m. to*
> *5:00 p.m. Highly paid position, one hour for lunch,*
> *plus two half-hour breaks. See Hutch Dawson at*
> *the Dueling Dawsons Ranch.*

He'd gotten several responses from the general ad over the past six months, but some candidates had seemed too rigid or unsmiling, and the few he'd tried out in between the agency nannies had also quit. One lasted three days. Now everyone in town seemed to know not to respond to his ad. *It's those crotchety triplets!*

Caleb was suddenly shrieking so loud that Hutch was surprised the big round mirror over the console table by the front door didn't shatter. He quickly scooped up the baby boy and rubbed his back, which seemed to quiet him for a second. Chloe had her arms up again. Carson was still crying—but not wailing like Caleb. A small blessing there, at least.

The doorbell rang. Thank God, that had to be Mrs. Philpot with a change of heart because it was the Christmas season! Or maybe it was one of those wonderful Dawson cousins, any number of whom often stopped by with a lasagna—for him, not the babies—or outgrown baby items. They could strategize, make a nanny materialize out of thin, cold air. Mary Poppins, please.

He went to the door. It was neither Mrs. Philpot nor a Dawson.

It was someone he hadn't laid eyes on in seventeen years, since high school graduation. She was instantly recognizable. Very tall. The long red wavy hair. The sharp, assessing brown eyes. Plus, there had always been something a little fancy about her. Like the cashmere emerald green coat and polished black cowboy boots she wore.

It was Savannah Walsh, his old high school nemesis— really, his enemy since kindergarten—standing there on his porch. In her hand was the updated ad from the *Bear Ridge Weekly*.

It might have been almost twenty years since he'd seen her, but he doubted she was anything like Mary Poppins.

"You might not remember me," Savannah said in a rush of words, her heart hammering away—so loud she was surprised he didn't hear it over all the wailing. "Savannah Walsh? We were in school together." *I had an intense crush on you since the first time I saw you—kindergarten. And every year I secretly loved you more...*

"I'd recognize you anywhere," he said, giving the baby in his arms a bounce. "Even without eyeglasses."

For a split second, Savannah was uncharacteristically speechless. She always had something to say. He *remembered* her. He even remembered that she wore glasses. She wasn't sure he would. Then again, she'd been the ole thorn in his side for years, so she was probably unforgettable for that reason.

He looked surprised to see her—and dammit, as gorgeous as ever. The last time she'd seen him up close was seventeen years ago. But the warm blue eyes, almost black tousled hair, the slight cleft in his chin were all the same except for a few squint lines, a handsome maturity to his thirty-five-year-old face. He had to be six-two and was cowboy-muscular, his broad shoulders defined in a navy Henley, his slim hips and long legs in faded denim.

She'd seen him around town several times over the years, always at a distance, when she'd be back in Bear Ridge for the holidays or a family party, and anytime she'd spot him on Main Street or in the grocery store or some shop, her stomach would get those little butterflies and she'd turn tail or hide behind a rack like a sixteen-year-old who couldn't yet handle her emotions.

Amazing. Savannah Walsh had never been afraid of anything in her life—except for how she'd always felt about this man.

His head tilted a bit, his gaze going to the ad in her hand. "You're here to apply for the nanny position?" He looked confused; he'd probably heard along the way that she was a manager of rodeo performers—even had a few famous clients.

She peered behind him, where the crying of two more babies could be heard. "Sort of," she said. "We may be able to help each other out."

His eyes lit up for a moment, and she knew right then and there that he was truly desperate for help. Then his gaze narrowed on her, as if he was trying to figure out what she could possibly mean by "sort of" or "help each other out." That had always been their thing back in school, really; both trying to read the other's mind and strategy, one-up and come out victorious.

They'd been rivals whether for class treasurer, the better grade in biology, or rodeo classes and competitions. They'd always been tied—she'd beat him at something, then he'd beat her. She'd had his grudging respect, if not his interest in her romantically. She'd been in his arms exactly once, for two and a half minutes at the senior prom, when she'd dared to ask him to dance and he'd said, *Okay.* A slow song by Beyoncé. But he'd stood back a bit, their bodies not touching, except for his hands at her waist and hers on his shoulders, and he'd barely looked at her except to awkwardly smile. Savannah, five foot ten and gangly with frizzy red hair, oversize crystal-framed eyeglasses and a big personality, had been no one's type back then.

"Well, come on in," he said, stepping back and letting her enter.

The baby he held reached out and grabbed her hair, clutching a swath in his tiny fist. Ooh, that yank hurt. Rookie mistake, clearly.

She smiled at the little rascal and covered her eyes with her hands, then took them away. "Peekaboo!" she said. "Peekaboo, I see you!"

The baby stopped crying and stared at her, the tiny fist releasing her hair. Ah, much better. She took a step away.

He looked impressed. "You must have babies of your own to have handled that so well and fast."

For a moment she was stunned that she *had* done so well and she smiled, feeling a bit more confident about the reason she was here. But then the first part of what he'd said echoed in her head—about babies of her own.

"Actually, I don't. Not even one," she added and wished she hadn't. *Do not call attention to your lack of experience.* Though, really, that was why she was here. To *gain* experience. "I have a three-year-old niece. Clara. She was a grabby one too. In fact, that's why I knew to put in my contact lenses to come see you. Clara taught me that babies love to grab glasses off my face and break the earpiece in the process."

He smiled. "Ah. I thought all my pint-size relatives would have better prepared me for parenthood, but nope." Before she could respond, not that she knew what to even say since he looked crestfallen, he added, "So you said you're *sort of* here about the nanny job?"

Her explanation would take a while, so she took off her coat, even though he didn't invite her to, and hung it on the wrought-iron coatrack. For a moment all the little snowsuits and fleece buntings and man-size jackets on the various hooks mesmerized her. Then she realized Hutch was watching her, waiting for her to explain herself. Thing was, as she turned to face him, she really didn't want to explain herself. What was that saying, *all talk and no action*? Act, she told herself, like she had with the peekaboo game to free her hair from the itty fist. Then talk.

She turned her focus to the baby who'd resumed crying in Hutch's arms. Even red-faced and squawking, the little boy was beautiful. That very kind of observation was among the main reasons she was here. "Well, aren't you just the cutest," she said to the baby. "Hutch, why don't I take this little guy, and you go deal with the loudest of the other two, and then we'll be able to talk without shouting." She smiled so it would be clear she wasn't judging the triplets for being so noisy. Or him.

He still had that look of confusion, but he let her take his son from his arms. As she cuddled the baby the way her sister had taught her when Clara was born three years ago, rubbing his little back in gentle, wide circles, he calmed down a bit and gazed up at her with big blue eyes.

"You wanna hear a song?" she asked him. "I'm no singer, but here goes." She broke into "Santa Claus Is Coming to Town." "He's making a list, he's checking it twice, he's gonna find out who's naughty and nice…"

Hutch paused from where he'd been about to pluck a baby in pink-and-purple-striped pj's from the swing area by the sliding glass doors and stared at her in a kind of puzzled wonder.

But she barely glanced at him. Instead, her attention was riveted by the sweet, solid weight in her arms, the blue eyes gazing up at her with curiosity. As the baby grabbed her pinkie and held on with one heck of a grip, something stirred inside her. She almost gasped.

She'd been right to come here. Right to propose her outlandish idea. If she ever got around to it. She was stalling, she realized, afraid he'd shut her down and show her the door.

It was really her sister Morgan's idea. And it had taken

Savannah a good two hours to agree it was a *good* one. She had no idea what Hutch would think.

She glanced at the baby she held, then at the other two. "Is it their dinnertime?" she asked. "Maybe they're hungry?"

"Dinner is at six, but I suppose they could eat ten minutes early." He paused. "That sounds really dumb— of course they should eat early if they're hungry. I'm just trying to follow the holy schedule."

Hmm, was that a swipe at the ex-wife she'd heard about from her sisters? "I know from my sister how important schedules are when it comes to children," she said with a nod. She'd once babysat Clara when she was turning one, and the list of what to do when was two pages long. "I'm happy to help out since I'm here."

His gaze shot to her, and he seemed about to say, *Why are you here?* But what came out of his mouth was "I appreciate that. Their high chairs are in the kitchen."

She followed him into the big, sunny room, a country kitchen but with modern appliances. A round wood table was by the window, three high chairs around it. She'd put her niece in a high chair a time or two, so she slid the baby in and did up the straps. The little guy must know the high chair meant food or Cheerios because he instantly got happier. "What's this cutie's name?" she asked.

With his free hand, Hutch gave himself a knock on the forehead. "I didn't even introduce them. That's Caleb. I have Chloe," he said, putting her in the middle chair. "And I'm about to go get Carson." In twenty seconds he was back with a squawking third baby, who also immediately calmed down once he was in the chair. Hutch went to the counter, opened a ceramic container and scooped out some Cheerios on each tray. The babies all picked one up and examined it before dropping it on their tongues.

"Are they on solids?" she asked, remembering that was a thing at some point.

He nodded. "Jarred baby food. Their schedule has their favorites." He pulled out his phone and held it so she could see the list, then went to the cabinet and got out three jars and then three spoons from the drawer.

"Bibs?" she asked, recalling seeing it on the schedule next to dinner: *Don't forget the bibs or their good pj's will get stained.*

"Oh, right," he said and pulled three bibs from a drawer. He handed her one and quickly put on the other two. "Since you've made buddies with Caleb, maybe you could feed him while I do double duty with these two."

She smiled and took the jar he handed her. Sweet potato. And the tiny purple spoon. He sat back down and opened up two other jars, spoon in each hand, dipped and into each little mouth they went at the same time.

The kitchen was suddenly remarkably quiet. No crying.

She quickly opened up the sweet potato and gave Caleb a spoonful. He gobbled it up and tried to grab the spoon. "Ooh, you like your dinner. Here's another bite." She could feel Hutch's gaze on her as she kept feeding Caleb.

"I definitely recall hearing somewhere that you're

a manager of rodeo performers?" Hutch said, dabbing Chloe's mouth with her bib.

"Yes. I'm off till just after Christmas, taking a much-needed vacation. I'm staying with my sister Morgan while I'm in town."

"But you're sort of here about the nanny job?" he asked, pausing from feeding the babies. Chloe banged a hand on the tray, sending two Cheerios flying.

"I… Yes," she said. "I'll get this guy fed and burped and then I'll explain."

He nodded and turned his attention back to Chloe and Carson.

As she slipped another spoonful of sweet potato puree into the open tiny mouth, she wondered how to explain herself without revealing her most personal thoughts and questions that consumed her lately and kept her up at night.

She could just launch into the truth, how she'd been at her youngest sister's bridal shower earlier today, which she would have enjoyed immensely were it not for her least favorite cousin, Charlotte. Charlotte, also younger than Savannah and a mom of three, had peppered her with questions about being single—long divorced—at age thirty-five. *Don't you want a baby? And don't you want to give that baby a sibling? Aren't you afraid you'll run out of time?*

Savannah's middle sister, Morgan, happily married with a three-year-old and a baby on the way, had protectively and thankfully pulled Savannah away from their busybody cousin. And what Savannah had admitted, almost tearfully, and she was no crier, was that, yes, she *was* afraid—because she didn't know what she wanted. She'd been divorced since she was twenty-five. Ten years was a long time to be on her own with every subsequent relationship not working out. She'd put her heart into her career and had long figured that maybe not every woman found their guy.

Over the years she'd wondered if she measured her feelings for her dates and relationships against the schoolgirl longing she'd felt for Hutch Dawson. No one had ever touched it, not even the man she'd been briefly married to. That longing, from grade school till she left Bear Ridge at eighteen, was part of the reason Morgan had shown her Hutch's ad in the *Bear Ridge Weekly*.

The other part, the main part, was about the babies. The family.

She just had to explain it all to Hutch in a way that wouldn't mortify her and would get him to say, *The job is yours.*

"I have a proposal for you," she said.

Chapter Two

Savannah held her breath as Hutch looked over at her, spoonfuls of applesauce and oatmeal midway to Chloe's and Carson's mouths.

"A proposal," he repeated, sliding a glance at her. "I'm listening."

Since no words were coming out of her mouth, he turned his attention back to the babies, giving them their final bites of dinner. Then he stood and lifted Chloe out of the high chair, cuddling her against him and gently patting her back. One good burp later, he did the same with Carson.

Maybe Hutch realized she could use a minute before she blurted out her innermost burning thoughts. She definitely did, so she focused on Caleb and his after-dinner needs. She'd never been able to get a good burp out of her niece when she was a baby. Savannah was on the road so often, traveling with her clients, or at home three hours away in Blue Smoke, where one of the biggest annual rodeos was held every summer, that she didn't really see Clara as much as she wanted. Savannah had a bit of experience at childcare. But it was just that. A bit. And when it came to babies, that experience was three years old.

She'd watched how Hutch had handled burp time, so she stood and took Caleb from the high chair, put him against her shoulder and gently patted his back. Nothing. She patted a little harder. Still nothing.

Her shoulders sagged. How could she expect Hutch to give her a job involving baby care when she couldn't even get a baby to burp!

"Caleb likes three fast pats dead center on his back," Hutch said. "Try that."

She did.

BURP!

Savannah grinned. "Yes!" The little boy then spit up on her fawn-colored cashmere sweater, which probably wasn't the best choice in a top for the occasion of coming to propose he let her be his nanny till Christmas. At least she wore her dark denim and cowboy boots, which seemed perfectly casual.

Hutch handed her a wet paper towel. "Sorry."

"No worries. That I don't mind is actually an important element of why I'm here."

"Right," he said. "The proposal." He stared at her for a moment. "Let's take these guys into the living room and let them crawl around. They're not actually crawling yet but they like to try. Then I want to hear all about this proposal of yours."

She had Caleb and he took both Carson and Chloe. She followed him into the living room, and they sat down on the huge soft foam play mat decorated with letters and numbers. The babies were on their hands and knees and sort of rocked but didn't crawl. They were definitely content.

She sucked in a breath. *Okay*, she told herself. *Come out with it.* "I'm kind of at a crossroads, Hutch."

He glanced at her. "What kind of crossroads?"

"The kind where I'm not sure if I want to keep doing what I'm doing or…something else."

"Like what?" he asked, pushing a stuffed rattle in the shape of a candy cane closer to where Carson was rocking back and forth. The boy's big eyes stared at the toy.

Here goes, she thought. "I'm thirty-five and long divorced. Married life, motherhood has all sort of passed me by. I have a great job and I'm suited to it. But lately, I've had these…feelings. Like maybe I do want a family. I'm not the least bit *sure* how I feel, what I truly want."

His head had tilted a bit, and he waited for her to continue.

Why was it so hard to say all this? "My sister happened to see your ad while she was looking for a date-night sitter in the local paper's help-wanted section. She thought maybe I could get a little clarity, find out what family life is like by helping you out with the triplets till Christmas."

"I see," he said. And that was all he said. She held her breath again.

For a moment they just watched the babies, Carson batting the stuffed rattle on the mat, Chloe still rocking on her hands and knees, Caleb now on his back trying to chew his toe.

"I don't have any experience as a nanny," she rushed to say, the uncomfortable silence putting her a bit off balance. Clearly, since she wasn't exactly selling herself here. "I've cared for my niece, as I've said, here and there over the past three years. More there than here. I want to see what it feels like to care for a baby—babies. To be involved in a family."

"Like an experiment," he said.

"I guess so." Her heart sank. She was sure *experimenting* with his children wasn't going to be okay with him. Why had she thought he might consider this?

"And no need to pay me for the ten days, of course, since we'd be helping each other out." Savannah was very successful and didn't look at this as a temporary job; it was a chance to find out if motherhood really was what she wanted. For that, *she'd* pay. Her heart hammered again, and she took a fast breath to calm down a bit. "I'm sure you want to think it over." She hurried over to the coatrack and pulled her wallet from her coat pocket, taking out a business card. She walked back over and knelt down to hand it to him. "My contact info is on there."

He looked at it, then put it in his back pocket. "Can you start immediately?" he asked. "Like now?"

She felt her eyes widen—and hope soar. "I'm hired?" Had she heard him correctly?

"I can't do this alone," he said. "And I can't take off

the next several days from the ranch. I need help. And here you are, Savannah Walsh. If there's one thing I remember about you it's that you get things done. And—" He cut himself off.

Well, now she had to know what that *and* was about. "And?" she prompted gently.

"And…okay, I'm just going to say it. I used to think, man, that Savannah Walsh is all business, works her tail off, but then I experienced firsthand that you have a big heart too. That combination qualifies you for the job. And like I said, the fact that you're here. Wanting the job. Many nannies have given up. I insist on paying you, though. And a lot."

She was still caught on the middle part of what he'd said. About his experiencing that she had a big heart. There could only be one instance he was referring to— that bad day at a rodeo competition when he'd come in third and his father had gone off on him, and she, who'd come in second, had tried to comfort him. She was surprised it had stuck with him all these years later, but she supposed those kinds of things did stick with people. When you were going through something awful and someone was in your corner.

"Of course, we were big-time rivals back then," he rushed to say. "So we might not get along even now."

She smiled. "I'm sure we won't, if it's like old times."

He smiled too. "Though we had a couple of moments, didn't we?"

She almost gasped. So he remembered the other incident too. The dance at the prom. All two and a half minutes of it. Had *that* stuck with him?

"Plus, it's been a long time," she said. They were different people now; they'd lived entire lives, full of ups and downs.

"A long time," he repeated.

"I can't promise I'll be great at the job," she said, probably too honestly. "But I'll try hard. I'll be responsible. I'll put my heart and brains into everything I do when I'm with your children, Hutch."

"I appreciate that," he said. "And you have two hands. That's what I need most of all."

Happy, excited chills ran up and down her spine. "Well, then. You've got yourself your holiday-season nanny."

A relief came over his expression, and she could see his shoulders relax. He was desperate. But in this case, it worked in her favor.

"Look, Savannah," he said. "Because I know you, I mean, we go way back, and this is a learning experience for you and a severe need for me, would you consider being live-in for the ten days? The triplets are pretty much sleeping through the night, if you consider midnight to five thirty 'the night.'"

Live-in. Even better. "That would certainly show me true family life with babies," she said. "So yes. I'll just get my bags from my sister's and be back in a half hour."

"Just in time for the bedtime routine," he said. "I'm pretty bad at that. And I have a lot of unfinished business from today that I still need to get to, so having your help will make it go much faster. I can't tell you how lucky I feel that you knocked on the door, Savannah."

Ha. We'll see if you're still feeling lucky tomorrow

when it's clear I don't know a thing about babies. Times three.

She extended her hand. "And truly, I won't accept pay."

"How about this—I'll donate what I'd pay you to the town's holiday fundraiser for families who need help with meals and gifts and travel expenses."

She smiled. "Perfect."

He gave her hand a shake, holding on for a moment and then covering her hand with his other. "Thank you."

"And thank you," she said a little too breathlessly, too aware from the electric zap that went straight to her toes that her crush on Hutch Dawson was far from over.

"Well, guys," Hutch said to the triplets, each in their own little baby tub in the empty bathtub. "That is what's known as a Christmas miracle."

He still could barely believe he'd gotten so lucky— though lucky was of course relative. Savannah Walsh might not have experience with babies but she was here. Or would be in about ten minutes. To help. And, oh man, did Hutch need help.

Carson banged his rubber duckie, and Chloe chewed her waterproof book with the chewable edges as Hutch poured warm water over the shampoo on Caleb's head, careful not to let it get in his eyes. A minute ago, Chloe had dropped her head back at the moment Hutch had gone to rinse the shampoo from her hair, and water and suds had streamed down her face. She'd wailed for a good half minute until Hutch had distracted her with peekaboo— Savannah's earlier go-to. One of his cousins—Maisey, who ran the childcare center at the Dawson Family Guest

Ranch—had given him five pairs of goofy glasses to make peekaboo work even faster. He'd grabbed the plastic glasses with their springy cartoon puppy cutouts, and Chloe was indeed transfixed and had stopped crying. He had a pair in practically every room in the house.

Carson batted his hands down, splashing lukewarm water all over his siblings, who giggled.

"All right, you little rug rats, bath time is over. Let's get you dry and changed."

He lifted each baby with one hand, drained their tub with the other, then wrapped them in their adorable hooded towels, a giraffe for Caleb, a lion for Chloe and a bear for Carson. He plopped them down in the portable playpen he'd bought just for this purpose—to get all three babies from the bathtub to the nursery at the same time. It was probably the baby item he used most often; he transported them all over the one-story ranch house with ease.

He got each baby into a fresh diaper and pj's, and now it was time for their bottles. Then it would be story time, then bedtime. Hopefully Savannah really would be back to help with that.

The doorbell rang. Perfect. She was back a little early and could help with bottles. He'd gotten okay at feeding two babies at once, but he didn't have *three* hands.

He wheeled the playpen to the door, but it wasn't Savannah after all. It was Daniel, his brother. Or his *half* brother, as Daniel always corrected him. Tall like Hutch, with light brown hair and the Dawson blue eyes, Daniel lived in town with Olivia, his wife of twenty years. When he and his brother inherited the ranch from their father three months ago, Daniel had surprised Hutch by taking down his CPA shingle in town and coming aboard full-time as chief financial officer, which Hutch had been initially glad about since it freed him up to focus on the day-to-day of managing the ranch. But his brother disagreed with a lot of Hutch's plans for the Dueling Dawsons Ranch—too apt a name, as always. Hutch had been the foreman for a decade—he knew the fifteen-hundred-acre ranch inside and out—but family feuds had plagued the Dawsons on this property since his great-grandfather and great-uncle had bought the land more than a century ago. He and Daniel did not break the pattern.

The one thing Daniel did not seem interested in was pursuing the list of "Unfinished Business" that Lincoln Dawson had left tacked up on his bulletin board. There were only two items, both doozies. But Hutch intended to cross them off by Christmas. Somehow, he thought his father would truly rest in peace that way. And Hutch by association. God knew, Daniel needed some peace.

"I'm leaving for the day," Daniel said, shoving his silver-framed square eyeglasses up on his nose. "And still no response to my email about your list of costly initiatives for the ranch," he added, shoving his hands into the pockets of his thick flannel barn coat. He wore a brown Stetson, flurries collecting on top and the brim.

"I was actually in the middle of answering when disaster struck," Hutch said, stepping back so Daniel could come in out of the cold. "The new nanny quit on me."

"Another one?" Daniel raised an eyebrow, stopping

on the doormat, which indicated he wasn't staying long—good thing. "Is it you or the triplets? Probably both," he said with a nod, answering that for himself.

Ah, Daniel. So supportive, as always.

"I was just about to make up their bottles," Hutch said, angling his head toward the playpen. "If you can feed one of the babies, I can do two and we can talk."

Daniel scowled. "I'm long done feeding a baby." Hutch mentally shook his head. Daniel and Olivia were empty nesters; their eighteen-year-old son was in college two hours away near the Colorado border. "We'll talk in the morning. Or are you going to be trapped here with them and not out on the ranch, taking care of business?"

Keep your cool, hold your tongue. That was Hutch's motto when it came to dealing with his brother. His half brother.

"*Trapped* isn't the word I'd use," he said, narrowing a glare on Daniel. "And I have a new nanny already. She's starting tonight, as a matter of fact. She'll be a live-in through Christmas Eve."

"Good. Because you need to get your share of the work done."

Keep your cool, hold your tongue…

"I'll see you at 6:00 a.m. in the barn," Hutch said. "We can talk about the email and the sheep while taking on Mick's and Davis's chores."

"I don't see why cowboys had to get ten days off," Daniel groused.

Had Hutch ever met someone more begrudging than Daniel Dawson? "Because they've worked hard all year and get two weeks off. They both had the time coming to them."

"It's bad timing with our father being gone."

"Yeah," Hutch said, picturing Lincoln Dawson. He'd been sixty-two when an undiagnosed heart condition took him from them. Maybe he'd hidden the symptoms; Hutch wasn't sure, and Daniel had kept his distance from their dad as he had his entire life. Lincoln had worked hard, done the job of a cowboy half his age. He'd hated administrative work and trusted few people, so he'd offered Hutch the foreman job ten years ago, when Hutch had been fresh out of an MBA in agricultural business, about to take a high-paying job at a big cattle ranch across town. Hutch had shocked himself by saying yes to his father's offer at half the salary and fewer perks. *Maybe I'll finally figure you out, Lincoln Dawson*, he'd thought.

But he hadn't. And Daniel hated talking about their father, so he'd never been any help.

Daniel reached for the doorknob. "Six sharp."

"You could acknowledge your niece and nephews," Hutch said unexpectedly, surprised it had come out of his mouth. But he supposed it did bother him that his brother barely paid them any attention. He was their uncle.

"Don't make this something it's not," Daniel said, without a glance at the triplets, and left.

Hutch sighed and rolled his eyes. "Your uncle is something, huh, guys?" he directed to his children. "*A piece of work*, as your late grandmother would have said. Or as your late grandfather would have said succinctly, *difficult*."

His brother had always been that. When Daniel was four, Lincoln had walked away from his family to marry his mistress—Hutch's mother. A year after their marriage, Hutch was born, and Hutch could recall his brother spending every other Saturday at the ranch for years, until Daniel was twelve or thirteen and said he was done with that. Their dad hadn't insisted, which had still infuriated Daniel and also his mother; Hutch had known that from screaming phone calls and slammed doors between the exes.

What Hutch did know about his father was that he'd loved his second wife, Hutch's mom, deeply. The two of them had held hands while eating dinner at the dining table. They'd danced in the living room to weird eighties new-wave music. They'd gotten dressed up and had gone out to a fancy meal every Saturday night without fail. The way his father had looked at his mother had always softened Hutch's ire at very-difficult-himself Lincoln Dawson; Hutch had given him something of a pass for what a hard case he'd been with Hutch and Daniel and anyone else besides his wife. Hutch's mother had died when he was eighteen, and in almost twenty years, Lincoln had never looked at another woman, as far as Hutch knew. But the loss had turned his father even more gruff and impatient, and Hutch had threatened to quit, had quit, about ten times.

Your mother wouldn't like the way I handled things earlier, Lincoln would say by way of apology. *She'd want you to come back.*

Hutch always had. He loved the Dueling Dawsons Ranch. The land. The work. The livestock. And he'd loved his father. He'd been gone three months now, and sometimes his absence, the lack of his outsize presence on the ranch, gripped Hutch with an aching grief.

There were just some things that stayed with a person—the good and the bad. When Hutch's ex-wife had sat him down last year and tearfully told him she was leaving him for Ted, a distraught, confused, scared Hutch had packed a suitcase and turned up at the ranch. His father had taken one look at his face, at the suitcase, and had asked him what happened. Lincoln had called Allison a vile name that Hutch had tried to put out of his memory, then told his son he could stay at the ranch in his old room, take some time off work as the foreman if he needed, and went to make them spaghetti and garlic bread, which Hutch had barely been able to eat but appreciated. They'd sat at the table in near silence, also appreciated, except for his father twice putting his hand on Hutch's shoulder with a *You'll get through this*.

Whenever things with his dad had gotten rough, he'd remember that Lincoln Dawson had been there for him when it really mattered. He also liked how his father had bought the triplets a gift every Monday, the same for each, whether tiny cowboy hats or rattles or books, when Allison would drop them off. Lincoln would give her the death stare, then dote on the triplets, talking to them about ranch life. Then in another breath, he'd flip out on Hutch for how he handled something with a vendor or which pasture he'd moved the herd to.

He's never going to be any different, Daniel had said

a few times the past couple of years when Lincoln must have started feeling sick or weakened but had refused to see a doctor and had brushed off questions about this health. *Stop chasing his approval already.*

Hutch often wanted to slug his brother, but never so much as during those times when he'd accuse Hutch of exactly that. Chasing his approval. He'd had it— his father had made him his foreman, hadn't he? Daniel would say it was more than that, deeper, but Hutch would shut that down fast.

Five minutes later, the doorbell rang again, and he shook off the memories, shook off his brother's visit and attitude. Savannah was back. His shoulders instantly unbunched. There was something calming about her presence, a quiet confidence, and he liked the way she looked at the triplets. With wonder and affection.

He liked the way she looked, period. Had she always been so pretty? He hadn't really thought of her that way back in school, given their rivalry. But he did remember being surprised by his reaction when she'd taken his hand in solidarity after that rodeo competition their senior year. A touch he'd felt *everywhere*. His father had screamed his head off at Hutch about a minor mistake he'd made that had cost him first and second place, and Savannah had heard the whole thing. She'd walked up to him and took his hand and just held it and said, *You didn't deserve that. You were great out there as always.* The reverberation of that touch had distracted him for a moment, and he wanted to pull her to him and just hold her, his rival turned suddenly very attractive *friend*. But he'd been seventeen and humiliated by his father's tirade and wanted the ground to swallow him, so he'd run off without a word, shaking off her hand like it had meant nothing to him.

He wondered if she even remembered that. Probably not. It was a long time ago.

He went to the door and there she was, her long red hair twisted into a bun—smart move—her face scrubbed free of the glamorous makeup she'd worn earlier. She wore a down jacket over a T-shirt with a rodeo logo and faded low-slung jeans. He swallowed at the sight of her. Damn, she was beautiful.

"The doorbell reminded me that I need to give you a key," he said, reaching for her bags. He took her suitcase and duffel and set them down by the door, then reached into his pocket for his key ring and took off one of the extra house keys. "I'll give you a quick tour and show you your room, and then we can give the triplets their bottles."

She smiled and put the key on her own ring, looking past him for the triplets, first at their swings, then at the playpen, in which the three were sitting and contentedly playing with toys. "Let me at those adorable littles." She rushed over to the playpen and knelt down beside it, chatting away to the babies about how she was here to help take care of them.

As she stood and turned back to him, she seemed so truly happy, her face flushed with excitement, that he found himself touched. This was a completely different setup than he was used to; she wasn't working for him, he wasn't paying her. She was here to get experience, to have some questions answered for herself.

It occurred to him that they should probably talk about that setup—expectations on both sides, how she wanted to structure the "job," the hours he'd need to devote to the ranch, the triplets' schedule, details about each of them, such as their different personalities, likes and dislikes, what worked on which baby. They should also talk about nighttime wakings; at least one triplet woke up at least once a night and would likely wake her up. He wanted to ensure that he wouldn't be taking advantage of her being a live-in.

He suddenly envisioned Savannah coming out of her room at 2:00 a.m. to soothe a crier in nothing but a long T-shirt. He blinked to get the image out of his head. He seemed to be drawn to her—there was just something about her, something winsome, something both tough and vulnerable—and they did go back a ways, which made her seem more familiar than she actually was. But Hutch had had his entire world turned upside down and sideways and shaken—by the divorce, by being a father of three babies whom he loved so much he thought he might burst sometimes, by his father's loss and the sudden onslaught of his brother. He couldn't imagine wanting anything to do with the opposite sex.

Or maybe I could, he amended as a flash of Savannah in just a long T-shirt floated into his mind again.

Nah, he thought. He really doubted that even sex could tempt him to step back into the romance ring. Not after what he'd been through.

Suuure, said a very low voice in the back of his mind where reality reigned.

Chapter Three

Savannah liked her room. It was a guest room next door to the nursery. There were two big windows, soothing off-white walls with an abstract watercolor of the Wyoming wilderness, a queen-size bed with a fluffy blue-and-white down comforter and lots of pillows, a dresser with a round mirror, a beautiful kilim rug, and a glider by the window. Perfect for taking a crying baby into her room in the middle of the night to soothe without waking up the other two.

Hutch, with the baby monitor in his back pocket, was putting her suitcase and duffel by the closet. Being in here, her room for the ten days, with him so close was doing funny things to her belly. "This was my room growing up. The furniture was different then, but that's the window I stared out every day, wondering where my life would take me." He walked over and looked out.

He'd had a view of a stand of evergreens and the woods beyond and part of the fields.

"It took you right here," she said, thinking about that for a moment. Full circle. "Did you even consider that then? That you'd be the foreman on this ranch?"

"Absolutely not. My father wasn't the easiest man to get along with. But not long after I left for college to study agricultural business—with the intention of having my own ranch someday—I lost my mom. When my dad offered me the foreman's job, the idea of coming home called to me. She loved this ranch. I always did too."

"I grew up in town," she said. "But I've always wanted to live on a ranch. I'm a rodeo gal at heart."

"Well, for the next week and a half, you'll be woken up by a crowing rooster long before a crying baby or two or three, so that might get old fast. You should visit the barn. We have six beautiful horses."

She smiled. "I'll plan to. So what's on the schedule? I'm excited to jump right into my first official task as Christmas-season nanny."

"It's time for their last bottles. Usually I feed two at once, then the third, but now we can split that up."

"I see what you mean about needing an extra set of hands," she said. "It must have been really hard these past six months, being on your own once the nannies were done for the day. I guess you had to figure it out as you went?"

"Yup, exactly. I'm a pretty good multitasker, though, something necessary to be a good ranch foreman. You know what the hardest part has been? When I don't know how to soothe one or two or all three, when they're crying like they were earlier when the former nanny quit on me. When I don't know how to make it better and nothing works. I feel like a failure as a dad." He frowned, and it was clear how deep the cuts could go with him.

"Oh, Hutch," she said, her heart flying out to him. "I'll bet it's like that for any parent of even just one baby. They don't talk, they can't tell you where it hurts or what they want, and you love them so much that it just kills you."

"Exactly," he said. "For someone who doesn't have experience with babies, you definitely get it."

She felt herself beam. She wasn't entirely sure how she "got it"; she supposed it was just human nature to feel that way about something so precious and dependent on you.

"Let's go feed them, and we can talk about how to arrange this," he said, wagging a finger between them. "How it'll all work. I really don't want to take advantage of you being here, living here, and the *reason* you're here. It's a tough job, Savannah."

"I'm a tough woman," she said. Except she didn't feel that way here in Hutch's house, in his presence. She felt…very vulnerable.

"You were a tough girl," he said. "Kept me on my toes."

She laughed. "Well, tough might have kept me from—" Ugh, she clammed up in the nick of time. Was she honestly about to tell Hutch Dawson that she was afraid her cousin Charlotte's assessment of her earlier at the bridal shower was right, that who Savannah was made her unappealing to men? *Intimidating* and *too successful* were the actual words her cousin had used today.

Oh, please, Savannah had thought, but she'd heard that her entire life. She'd been five foot ten since she was thirteen and no slouch, literally or figuratively, so she'd been standing tall a long time. And yes, she was straightforward and could be barky, and she was damned good at her job. It was true that she could make some people quake because of her stature in the industry at this point. But that was business, and her profession demanded *tough*. She'd never gotten very far with men, though. She'd get ghosted or told it just wasn't working out after a week or two of dating.

Or seven months of marriage. *I'm not one of your clients*, her new husband had said so many times that she'd started doubting herself—who she was, particularly. *You're trying to manage me*, he'd toss at her. *Maybe if you didn't work such long hours or travel so much, I wouldn't have cheated.*

With a friend, among others, no less. Savannah hadn't been sure he had been cheating until her "friend" had confirmed it and said the same thing her husband had: *If you devoted yourself to your marriage instead of your career...* At twenty-five she'd had an ex-husband, an ex-friend, and dealt with her doubly broken heart by devoting herself even more to her career. She was in a male-dominated industry, but her voice, drive and determination had carried her to the top. She took reasonable risks, demanded the best of her clients and for them, but cared deeply about each one. Yeah, she was tough.

To a point, she reminded herself. Lately, she'd find herself tearing up. She'd been in a grocery store a few days ago, and the sight of a young family, a dad pushing the cart with a toddler in the seat, the mom walking beside him with a little girl on her shoulders and letting the child take items off the high shelves for her— Savannah had almost burst into tears in the bread aisle of Safeway.

Do I want that? she'd asked herself, perplexed by her reaction. Why else would she have been so affected? She'd written off remarriage and happily-ever-after, having lost her belief and faith in either, in the fairy tale. Her parents had had a wonderful, long marriage. One sister was happily married and the other was engaged and madly in love with her fiancé. Savannah knew there were good men out there, good marriages. But she'd always been…tough. And maybe meant to be on her own.

She didn't know how to be any different. It was her natural personality that put the fear of God into the men and women rodeo performers she managed, from up-and-comers with great potential to superstars, like her most famous client, a bull rider who'd quit fame and fortune to settle down with the woman he loved and the child he'd only recently discovered was his. She'd spent some time with the happy family the past few months, and Logan Winston's happiness, a joy she hadn't seen in him ever before, made her acknowledge a few hard truths about herself. That she was lonely. That she did have a serious hankering for something more—she just wasn't sure what, exactly. A change, but what change? She should talk to Logan about it while she was in town.

Hutch was leaving the room, so she shook off her thoughts and followed, excited to get started on her new role—for the time being, anyway. A life of babies and Hutch Dawson.

In the kitchen, she stood beside him as he made up the bottles, watching carefully how he went about it so she could do it herself. Back in the living room, he set the three bottles on the coffee table, then grabbed a bunch of bibs and burp cloths from the basket on the shelf under the table and, finally, wheeled the playpen over to the sofa.

"I'll watch you for a moment," she said, sitting down. "See how you hold the baby, hold the bottle, just so I know how to do it all properly."

"It's a cinch. Maybe the easiest part of all fatherhood—and the most relaxing, well, except for watching them sleep. There's just something about feeding a baby, giving him or her what they need, all in the grand comfort of your arms."

"I always felt that way when I watched my sister feed Clara," she said, recalling how truly cozy it looked, how content mama and baby had always appeared.

He picked up Carson and settled him slightly reclined along one arm, then reached for a bottle and tilted it into the little bow-shaped mouth. Carson put his hands on the bottle and suckled away, Hutch's gaze loving on his son.

"Got it," she said. "Should I grab another baby for you?"

"Sure. Take your pick."

"I'll save Chloe for myself since I got time with Caleb earlier." She scooped the little guy from the playpen and settled him on Hutch's right side. When he shifted Caleb just right, she handed him a bottle. In no time, he was feeding both babies.

My turn! She picked up Chloe, who stared at her with huge blue eyes. *Oh, aren't you precious*, she thought, putting Chloe along her arm and grabbing the third bottle. "Hungry?" she asked. She slipped the nipple into the baby's mouth, and it was so satisfying as Chloe started drinking, her little hands on the sides of the bottle. Savannah gazed down at her, mesmerized. When she glanced up, she realized Hutch was watching her. Her. Not how she was holding Chloe or the bottle. *Her.*

Could he be interested? Hutch Dawson, guy of her dreams since she was five, star of her fantasies since middle school? He was the one thing she'd ever wanted that she hadn't gone for, her fear—of rejection and how bad it would hurt—and lack of confidence when it came to personal relationships making her anything but tough.

"This is great," he said with a warm smile. "Having the extra two hands."

Oh. That was what the look of wonder was about. How helpful she was. He wasn't suddenly attracted to her. It wasn't like she'd changed all that much physically since high school, and he'd never given her a second glance back then.

"Having you here for the bedtime routine will be a huge help," he added. "I've really never been good at it. One of the triplets always fights their drooping eyes and fusses, then another fusses, then one starts crying… What takes Allison and Ted fifteen minutes takes me an hour."

"Allison and Ted?" she asked, glancing at him. She darn well knew who Allison was—his ex-wife. Savannah remembered her from school. Petite, pretty, strawberry blonde and blue eyed. A cheerleader. Hutch Dawson's type. They'd dated on and off but had always been more off, as Savannah recalled. She knew a little bit about the divorce from her sister. Apparently Allison had reconnected with an old flame from college on Facebook. And actually walked away from her marriage at five months pregnant. According to Morgan, Allison had been shunned by some and lauded by others—*How could you?* vs *Life is too short not to follow your heart.*

All Savannah could think was how absolutely awful it must have been for Hutch.

"My ex-wife," he said. "And her new husband. You might remember Allison Windham from school. Then she was Allison Dawson for a year, but now she'll be Allison Russo. Sometimes I can't wait until the triplets are old enough for people to stop gossiping about how I'm divorced with babies. Some folks know the sob story but most assume *I* left, even though my ex is the one living in my former house with another man. You should see some of the stare downs I get in the grocery store."

"Ugh, that's terrible," she said. "How unfair. To have your life turned upside down and to get the blame."

He shot her something of a smile. "Small town, big gossip."

"Yeah, I remember. It's one of the reasons why I was

excited to leave for bigger pastures. I do love Bear Ridge, though."

"Yeah, me too." They glanced at each other for a moment, and she felt so connected to him. They came from the same place, had the same beginning history in terms of school and downtown and the Santa hut on the town green. She'd passed it several times since she'd arrived, her heart warmed by the sight of the majestic holiday tree all decorated and lit up in the center of the small park, the red Santa hut with the big candy-cane chimney, the families lined up so that the kids could give Santa their lists.

She wondered if Hutch had envisioned himself standing with his family in line, the triplets in the choo choo train of a stroller she'd seen by the door, his wife beside him. Had he been blindsided by her affair? In any case, he must have been devastated when his ex had told him she was leaving.

She glanced down at Chloe, just a tiny bit left in her bottle, and then the baby turned her head slightly.

"That means she's done," Hutch said. "You can burp her and set her in the playpen, and then grab Carson—he's done too."

Savannah stood and held Chloe up vertically against her, about to pat her back.

"I'd set a burp cloth on your shoulder and chest," he said. "You don't want spit-up all over that cool shirt."

She glanced down at her *Blue Smoke Summer Rodeo 2019* jersey. Years old and soft and faded. She'd worn it specifically for the job—no worries in getting dirty and grabbed and pulled out of shape. But she'd still prefer spit-up on the burp cloth and not her. She shifted Chloe and bent a little to pick up a cloth, arranging it on her shoulder, hanging down on her chest.

She gave Chloe's back a good three pats and a big burp came out. "Success!" Savannah said. "What a great baby you are," she whispered to Chloe. "An excellent burper."

She set Chloe in the playpen and reached for Carson. Was it her imagination or did Hutch's gaze go to the sliver of belly exposed by her shirt lifting up as she leaned over? He handed over Carson and she repeated what she'd just done, but getting a burp out of this guy was taking longer.

How many times had she told her clients—and in talks to various groups and schools—not to think one great performance meant another? You had to work for it—always. She adjusted Carson in her arms and gave up two more pats with a bit more force, and out came a big, satisfying burp.

"I've got this!" she said, unable to contain her excitement. "I was afraid you'd regret taking me on as a student nanny, but I'm feeling a lot more confident."

He smiled. "Good. Because you're doing great."

"You hear that, Carson?" she said, running a finger down the baby's impossibly soft cheek. "I'm doing great!"

Once all three babies were in the playpen, Hutch stood. "If you'll keep watch over them, I could use a solid twenty minutes to finish up today's work—just some administrative stuff, texts and calls and emails."

"Sure thing," she said.

As he left the room, she felt the lack of him immediately.

My crush on your daddy will never go away, I guess, she said silently to the triplets as she wheeled the playpen over to the sliding glass door. There was a pretty pathetic Christmas tree with one strand of garland hanging down along with two branches. The entire tree was tilted as though someone had backed into it. She had a feeling that someone was Hutch with two babies in his arms. She'd help him get the tree decked out. Since the babies weren't crawling, there were no worries about safety-proofing for Christmas yet.

"Well, guys," she said. "How am I doing so far? Not too bad, right?"

Carson gave her a big gummy smile, two tiny teeth poking up.

I sure do like you three, she thought, giving Caleb's soft hair a caress. She'd been here, on the job, for barely an hour, and she was falling in serious like with everything to do with the triplets. And Hutch Dawson all over again.

Hutch sat at his desk in his home office, half expecting Savannah to appear in the doorway with a crying baby with a firm grip on her hair or ear and say, *Sorry, but I've already realized that this isn't the life for me, buh-bye*—and go running out the door.

But he'd gotten through three calls, returned all the texts and had made himself mental notes for tomorrow's early-morning meeting with his brother in the barn—and no appearance in the doorway. No quitting. No *crying*.

Blessed silence.

His office door was ajar and every now and then he could hear Savannah's running commentary. She'd wheeled the babies in the playpen into the nursery and changed them one by one, choosing fresh pj's, which he knew because she was chatting away. *Stripes for you, Caleb. Polka dots for Chloe, and tiny bears for Carson. Oooh, another rookie mistake, guys—Caleb almost sprayed me!* She'd laughed and then continued her commentary all the way back down the hall to the living room.

Now she was talking to the triplets about the Christmas tree and how she and her sisters used to make a lot of their ornaments when they were little as family tradition. From what he could tell, she'd wheeled the playpen over by the tree and was picking up each triplet to give them turns at being held and seeing the lonely, bare branches.

"Oooh, that's what I get for letting you get too close to my ear," he heard her say on a laugh to one of the triplets. "Strong girl," she added. "Peekaboo! I see you!"

He smiled as he envisioned her playing peekaboo with one hand to get her ear back. He'd have to tell her about the goofy glasses.

"Okay, now it's Carson's turn," she said.

This was going to work out just fine, he thought, turning his attention back to his brother's email. Ten minutes later, he was done, turned off his desk lamp and went to find Savannah and the babies.

They were sitting on the play mat, and she was telling them a story about a fir tree named Branchy who no one picked for their home at Christmastime.

"Buh!" Caleb said, batting his thigh.

Carson shook his stuffed rattle in the shape of a bunny.

Chloe was giggling her big baby laugh that always made Hutch laugh too.

Savannah turned and grinned. "They like me! Babies like me!"

He realized just then how nervous she'd probably been about how they'd respond to her. They'd managed to chase off professional nannies, including one who'd raised her own triplets. So he understood why a woman who'd never spent much time around babies would worry how she'd fare with three "crotchety" six-month-olds. She'd probably expected them to cry constantly and bat at her nose.

They did do a lot of that kind of thing. But they were also like this. Sitting contentedly, giggling, shaking rattles. If not exactly listening to her story, hearing it around them, enjoying her melodic voice.

"I'd say so," he confirmed, and she beamed, her delight going straight to his heart. "It's bedtime for these guys."

As if on cue, Carson started rubbing his eyes.

Then Caleb did.

Chloe's face crumpled and she let out a loud shriek, then started crying.

Savannah picked up Chloe and held her against her chest, rubbing her back, which helped calm the baby.

Hutch picked up both boys, Carson leaning his head

against his father's neck, one of Hutch's favorite things in the world, and Caleb rubbed his eyes.

Savannah's phone rang, and she shifted Chloe to pull it from her back pocket. She glanced at the screen. "Ugh, business," she said, continuing to rub Chloe's back as she bounced her a little. "Savannah Walsh," she said into the phone. "Ah, I've been waiting for your call. No, those terms are *not* acceptable…That's right. No again…Oh well, no deal, then. Have a nice night… What's that? You'll come up with the five thousand? Wonderful. I'll expect the contract by end of business tomorrow." Click.

He watched her turn the ringer off and then chuck the phone on the sofa.

"Sorry," she said. "I just realized I shouldn't have taken that call. I'm on duty here."

"Of course you should have taken it. Your life off this ranch still exists. You do what you need to. And that was very impressive to listen to. Hopefully you'll rub off on me and I'll be tougher when it comes to negotiating at cattle and equipment auctions."

She eyed him. "Were you always a nice guy? I don't remember that."

Hutch laughed. "Nice enough. But competitive with you. Now I'm just relieved we're both Team Triplets."

She grinned. "Team Triplets. I like it. And I don't want my life to interfere with my time here. In fact, I just realized that for certain. I'll have my assistant, who already has a few clients of her own and is ready to be an agent in her own right, handle that contract. I want to focus on the reason I'm here."

Chloe rubbed her eyes and her face started scrunching.

Savannah cuddled Chloe closer. "You better watch out, you better not cry," she sang softly. "You better not pout, I'm telling you why. Though, that is what babies do, isn't it, you little dumpling. But Santa Claus *is* coming to town, and he's making a list."

Chloe made a little sound, like "ba," her gaze sweet on Savannah's face, and then her eyes drooped. She let out a tiny sigh and her eyes closed, her little chest rising and falling.

"Aww, she fell asleep!" Savannah said. "Huh. I'm not too shabby at this after all. They're all changed and ready for their bassinets."

"You really are a Christmas miracle," he said.

Her face, already lit up, sparkled even more. He led the way into the large, airy nursery with its silver walls decorated with tiny moons and stars, a big round rug on the polished wood floor, the bookcase full of children's titles, two gliders by the window. His father had ordered the three sleigh-shaped wooden bassinets, each baby's name stenciled and painted on it. Every time he looked at the bassinets, at the names, he'd forget all the crud that Daniel kept bringing up and he'd miss his dad, his grief catching him by surprise. People were never just one thing.

Savannah was a good example of that. If he'd seen her walking down Main Street yesterday in her cashmere coat, barking a negotiation into her cell phone, he'd never imagine her as someone who'd sing Christmas carols to a crying baby, whose eyes would light up at a crabby little girl falling asleep in her arms. People could always surprise you, he knew.

"I'm praying for my own Christmas miracle that I can transfer Chloe to her crib without waking her," she said. "What are my odds?"

"She's iffy," he said. "You just never know. Carson's more a sure bet—heavy sleeper. Caleb always wakes up the minute his head touches a mattress. At my house, anyway."

Savannah glanced at him for a moment, seeming to latch on to that part about "his house." She started quietly singing "Santa Claus Is Coming to Town" again, then carefully lowered Chloe down, gently swaying just a bit. The baby's lower lip quirked, and when she was on the mattress, she simply turned her head and lifted a fist up to her ear, eyes closed, chest rising and falling.

"I did it!" Savannah whispered.

But then Chloe's eyes popped open and she started fussing.

"Scratch that. I didn't do it." Savannah's shoulders sagged.

"Told you she's iffy," he said. "She likes having her forehead caressed from the eyebrows up toward her hairline. And she likes your song. You could try both."

Savannah brightened and reached down to caress Chloe's forehead, singing the carol, and the baby girl's eyes drooped, drooped some more, and then she was asleep. "Phew," she whispered.

A half hour later, both boys were finally asleep in their bassinets, Caleb indeed taking longer than Carson. Hutch had the urge to pull Savannah into his arms for a celebratory hug, but a fist bump seemed more appropriate.

"Our work here is done," he said, holding up his palm. "I could use coffee. You?"

She grinned and did give him a fist bump. "Definitely. And we can talk about the grand plan for my time here."

As they tiptoed out of the nursery, the urge for that embrace only got stronger. Because they were Team Triplets, and it felt so good to have someone on his side, someone who wouldn't quit on him, someone he could talk to?

Or was it all of the above *and* because he was attracted to Savannah Walsh?

It was choice B that made her just as scary as she'd been seventeen years ago.

Chapter Four

In the kitchen, Hutch made a pot of coffee, then started washing the babies' bottles. He had so much on his mind—from the triplets to the ranch to some issues that he and his ex would have to deal with when she returned—that pondering any burgeoning feelings for Savannah could be easily shoved aside.

"I'll watch how you do that," she said, moving beside him. "Just in case there's more to it than dish soap and that bottle scrubber." He could smell a hint of her perfume, something more spicy than floral and utterly intoxicating. She was so close that he could turn sideways and be in kissable distance.

She had great lips.

He forced his focus back on the sudsy bottles. Why was he so aware of Savannah Walsh as a beautiful, sexy woman? He hadn't looked at another woman since the day Allison had said, *Hutch, we need to talk*, and his life had come crashing down around him. Zero interest in anything romance related. He'd built up a wall around himself, but he was too busy to even think about sex, let alone ask someone on a date. *Yeah, I'm the guy whose wife dumped him for another man when she was five months pregnant. She's married now and the triplets are six months old. Oh, that's right. I have triplet babies...* He almost laughed. Like any woman would date him in the first place.

"Only thing is to make sure to only use this scrubber for baby stuff—bottles, their little plastic bowls."

"Got it," she said as he set the bottles and nipples to dry. The coffee maker dinged, and she moved over to it. "I'll pour," she said. "Mind if I explore the cabinets and fridge?"

"This is your house too now," he said. "Till Christmas Eve, anyway." It occurred to him just then that he hadn't thought much about that. She would be living here. With him.

She opened a few cabinets and found the mugs, then got the cream from the fridge. "Oooh, is that half a pumpkin pie I see?" she asked, bent over slightly, her very shapely derriere in those faded jeans impossible not to admire.

"I'll join you in a slice," he said, forcing his gaze off her body. He sat at the table, the scents of "holiday blend" coffee and pumpkin pie and Savannah surrounding him.

She had everything on a tray and set it on the table, then sat across from him. "I can use a boost of caffeine," she said, adding cream and a sugar cube to her coffee. She wrapped her hands around the mug and took a long sip. "Ahh, heavenly."

He was looking at her lips again, he realized, and grabbed the sugar bowl, dunking two cubes into his mug and then pouring in some cream. He took a long drink, then dug into his slice of pie. "This is from the diner, which makes the best pie in town, if you ask me. Even better than the bakery, and everything there is great."

"I love diners," she said. "Burgers, tuna melts, pie, coffee. Over the years I must have been to hundreds of diners in hundreds of western towns as I've traveled to rodeos with my clients."

"You mostly live on the road?" he asked.

"Yup. I've always liked it. Hotels, B and Bs, the diners. But lately..."

"It's gotten old?" he asked.

She nodded and sipped her coffee, looking out the dark window, the stars just illuminating the barn about a quarter mile away and the fields beyond it. "Must be challenging trying to manage a big ranch like this and fatherhood. Even when you had experienced nannies."

"Even when it's not my custody days," he said. "The triplets are on my mind all the time. Last week, they had their well-baby checkups on Allison's day, but I wanted to be there, so I went. That was close to two hours that I was away from the ranch. Daniel, my brother—half brother, as he insists on being referred to as—had a conniption."

"You two run the ranch together?" she asked, taking a bite of pie.

He told her about his losing his father three months ago and Daniel surprising him by coming on board the Dueling Dawsons Ranch. But how his brother had no interest in ticking off the two items on Lincoln Dawson's list of Unfinished Business, which Hutch knew would go a long way in helping the brothers' prickly relationship.

Savannah's eyes lit up with curiosity. "What are the two items?"

He held up a finger and got up and left the room, returning a few seconds later with a piece of white paper with a short list scrawled on it in black pen. Hutch sat back down and put this paper between them. It was titled *Unfinished Business*. Underneath that: *Try to do by Christmas*.

"He ran out of time," Savannah said gently.

Hutch nodded. "He did. And I want to get the list done for him. By Christmas. Every time I talk to Daniel about it, he rolls his eyes and says the first thing is silly and the second isn't necessary."

Savannah looked at the paper. "'One, find the smoking gun—the answer—to make things right between Ernest and Harlan Dawson, the original owners of the Dueling Dawsons Ranch,'" she read aloud. "'They went to their graves at war with each other. They need to rest in peace.'" Her eyes widened. "Interesting," she said. "Do you know what the feud was about?"

"According to family lore, it was about a woman. They'd both wanted to marry the same one. Helene Mayhew. They both courted her, and she couldn't make up her mind. The day she promised to tell them which one she was choosing, she died after getting thrown by her horse. The brothers were grief-stricken, but instead of it bringing them closer, each insisted he was the one she was going to pick as her husband. They grew farther and farther apart, speaking only through the relatives and ranch hands."

"Wow," Savannah said, shaking her head. "And that feud carried on? To the next generations? How?"

He shrugged. "I know both men married about six months after Helene died. But things only got worse. Three generations later, the family curse is still upon this place. Brothers feuding."

"Might be interesting to do some digging into the past to find out what went on," she said. "Find that smoking-gun answer so that Ernest and Harlan can rest in peace."

"I've poked around my dad's old files but didn't find anything—it's full of ranch invoices and a zillion old letters. I'd moved on from that to the second thing."

Savannah glanced at the list. "'Try to bring Daniel and Hutch closer. Hell, to get along would be enough,'" she read out loud. "But your brother says that's not necessary?"

Hutch gave something of a rueful smile. "Yeah. Not happening. I've tried hard." He found himself sharing a lot of their conversation of earlier tonight, right before Savannah had arrived with her bags to save his life.

"Huh," she said. "He can't even be cordial to six-month-olds by acknowledging their presence?" She shook her head. "Sounds like he's dealing with a lot of his own stuff. And that he's baiting you. But he's here, putting his all into the ranch."

"That's true—he is here. The very place he'd refused to come to once he got old enough to tell our dad to go screw himself. That's what baffles me, that Daniel really seems to care about the ranch. I've caught him, several times, just looking out on the land with the most peaceful expression, taking a deep breath of the fresh country air. This place means something special to him. I know it. And he gave up his CPA office in town to do that work for the ranch."

"Huh. That's promising. There's hope for number two on your dad's list, then. It's possible that Daniel wants things to change—in his own life and between the two of you—but he doesn't know how to make that happen so he's coming out swinging. I've had a few clients like that early in their careers before I set them straight."

Hutch smiled. "Wow, you're good. And I bet you're right. I've thought a lot about why he's even here when he's so combative, and I know you have to be right. It's like he's trying to bring things to a head so that maybe things can change, turn around."

She nodded. "He might be working on the two of you getting closer, getting along, without even realizing it. So that you can start something new. And put an end to the name of this ranch—by finding peace for your ancestors *and* crossing off number two. You'll have to change the name to the Non-Dueling Dawsons Ranch."

He smiled. But it was much easier said than done.

"Hey, why don't you invite him and his wife over for dinner?" Savannah added. "Kill him with kindness and eggnog. Let the triplets work their charm on him. Maybe spending a quality evening at the ranch house with his nephews and niece will do wonders for your relationship. I can even do the cooking. I'm a terrible cook, except at my specialty and favorite dish—linguine carbonara. I also make great garlic bread."

He laughed. "I do love linguine carbonara and garlic bread. I guess I could invite them over. If it's a bust, I'll just never do it again."

Now she laughed. "Exactly. What's the wife like?"

"A little standoffish but nice enough. Olivia works at the library and volunteers around town a lot. The few times she and Daniel have come over, bearing gifts for the triplets, it's easy to tell she was behind it."

"Well, at least she doesn't sound difficult like her husband," she said. "We'll just get her on your side. He won't know what hit him."

He grinned. The *we* was unexpected—and a comfort, at that. He hadn't been part of a united *we* in a while. "It feels good to talk this out, Savannah. I don't really complain to my cousins about it because I don't want to talk behind Daniel's back. He's their cousin too."

She took another bite of the pumpkin pie. "Well, my ear is always available."

He smiled. "Good to know. And so's mine."

She smiled back. "I know a Dawson. I mean, I know there are a lot of Dawsons in Bear Ridge, but my former client Logan Winston quit the rodeo and bull riding at the height of his career because he fell in love with Annabel Dawson. She works at the family guest ranch. Turns out Logan had a seven-year-old he didn't know about until just last summer. Now he's one hundred percent family man."

"I did hear a little about that in this gossipy town," Hutch said. "And I've met Logan at a couple of family parties. Nice guy."

"Yeah. He's great. He hooked me up with a young replacement for himself from Bear Ridge—a nice kid, just eighteen, named Michael who came from a troubled home and needed someone to believe in him. He's already making a name for himself as a bronc rider. I can see him becoming a rising star in the coming year."

"I like that—how someone's entire life can be turned around for good."

She nodded. "If I decide to leave the management business for putting a baby to bed and carrying around a monitor everywhere I go, I know he'll be in good hands with my assistant. I wouldn't be leaving anyone in the lurch."

He glanced at the baby monitor on the table and laughed. "I go nowhere without it when they're here with me."

"You're a great dad," she said. "It's really heartening to watch you with the triplets."

"You've seen me in action for half a day," he said, though he appreciated her praise. "Trust me, I get it wrong a lot. If it weren't for my cousins, who have a lot of babies and toddlers among them, I'd have been lost the first month, when Allison would drop off the triplets and I'd be alone with them—scared to death."

"Aww, I can imagine. Plus, you must have thought you'd have a partner, a wife and mother by your side—"

"Exactly. I was blindsided. But it's been six months that I've been a dad, and though I love my children to pieces, I just don't seem to have that internal something or other that knows what cry means what and what they need. But then Ted, good old Ted, can assess a cry, whip out a bottle or change a diaper in five seconds flat. On Allison's three and a half days, when I'd drop off the triplets at her house—*their* house—I'd still be fidgeting with the five-point harness of one baby's car seat while Ted had the other two out and was playing peekaboo with them in the driveway."

Another factor in his ex's list of reasons why they should adjust the custody arrangement to sixty-forty. Not only wasn't Hutch great at triplet care, which she hadn't said directly, but he had long hours at the ranch and had to hire nannies. So why shouldn't she have the babies during that time, she'd argued a few times. Allison worked part-time as a horse trainer and also had a nanny and sitters for "date night," but she was still insistent that she have more days and time with the babies. Hutch thought they should have fifty-fifty custody, period. Yes, the triplets were with a nanny for hours when he had to work, but they were *here*, on his turf, and he could come see them on his lunch hour and short breaks throughout the day. And they were with him full-time on his days off.

"Sorry, but that actually makes me feel better," she said. "That even if I don't have maternal instincts, or haven't all these years, I can *learn* it."

"Oh, I think you do have maternal instincts," he said. "The way you've been with the triplets? I've heard you carrying on sweet, animated conversations. I've seen how gentle and affectionate you are with them."

"Thank you," she said, lifting up her mug. "I really appreciate hearing that."

She was quiet for a moment and he wondered what she was thinking. If at the end of the ten days, she would return to her life or start a new one—as a mom.

"So Ted's a nice guy?" she asked. "He'll be a good stepfather?"

"Yeah, I got lucky there. He's great. I hate to say it. But he is."

She touched his hand, a little zap traveling along his nerve endings. Suddenly, he had to get up, get a little distance from her. But they hadn't even talked about how they were going to work things with her as the nanny these next ten days.

Because they talked so easily, he realized. Because they could talk for hours.

You have to get a handle on this, he told himself. *There's a lot of stuff behind the scenes when it comes to you and Savannah—the two of you have an old history, she's familiar, she's here and helping, and she's wonderful with the triplets. The last thing you need is to get romantically involved*—sexually involved, he amended—*when it can't go anywhere because your head and heart and mind wouldn't be in it.*

"Well," he said, standing up. "Maybe we should go into my office and discuss the arrangements of the nanny position, such as hours and expectations—on both sides."

She tilted her head, clearly aware that he'd gotten all business suddenly, that he was changing things between them. Less personal, more professional. Employer, employee.

That was how it needed to be.

Savannah sat across from Hutch's desk in his guest chair, the baby monitor beside his computer, a wall suddenly erected between them. Maybe he thought he'd said too much, gotten too personal, and he wanted to remind himself why she was here, that she was the nanny, not his buddy.

It was nice to be Hutch Dawson's friend, though. She'd never been that. There had always been a distance between them as rivals and even more so between that awkward time when his father had come down on him, Savannah attempting to make Hutch feel better, and then the senior prom, when they'd danced. Also awkwardly. Now it was seventeen years later, and their history, their familiarity, was just making things comfortable between them, so of course they were talking like old close friends. She had to remember that she was here to do a job for Hutch and to learn something about herself. Not to get close to him. Old dreams died hard, though.

"The best time for me to start my day on the ranch is 6:00 a.m.," he said, taking a sip of the second cup of coffee he'd poured before leaving the kitchen. "Is that too early for you? Some of the nannies hadn't been willing to start before eight, so I did my administrative work during the early morning and can structure my time that way if it works better for you."

"Nope," she said. "I'm an early bird. Always have been. Plus, I like to catch the sunrise."

He glanced at her, then down at the list on his electronic tablet. "Perfect. So 6:00 a.m. start and now we can discuss necessary breaks and your lunch hour—"

"You know, Hutch, I'm just here till Christmas. Now, I'm usually a stickler for schedules and times, but my brief experience with the triplets has assured me I need to expect the unexpected when it comes to them. So maybe we should just keep it loose. If I need a break, I can text you. I don't need a 'lunch hour.' I'll just grab something from the fridge or pop the babies in their swings or playpen if I want to cook up something."

He was staring at her. "You're making this very easy. I'm not used to that."

She smiled. "That's the benefit of my being here as a live-in. And for me, looking at this as less a job and more a way of life is of benefit to *me*. I'll really be able to see if I'm suited to and meant for family life. Or if my heart is in the rodeo, in management, on the road."

"I can definitely give you a firm end date," he said.

Was it her imagination or had she winced at the mentioned end date? A *firm* end date. She'd just gotten started. She didn't want to think about leaving. The triplets *or* Hutch.

"My ex will be back on Christmas Eve morning," he said. "She'll have the triplets from then through Christmas Day. Then I'll have them the night of the twenty-fifth starting at 6:00 p.m. through the next couple of days." He frowned, and she could tell he wasn't happy about barely having any time with them on the actual holiday. But that was divorce for you.

She took a sip of her coffee. "That must be hard, having to give up time with your children on holidays and special occasions."

"It is. I hate it, to be honest. But Allison asked if I'd consider the Christmas schedule since she'd be gone ten whole days and would be missing the triplets like crazy. Hey, I didn't tell her to get remarried so fast and go to Aruba on a honeymoon. But I'm trying very hard to be flexible and compromise and all that horrid divorce-related stuff."

She smiled and wanted to move closer to Hutch and just put her arm around him, offer him some comfort.

He poked at the remaining bit of pie. "I'm still not used to having them part-time, and it's been that way since they were *born*."

"You don't sound angry at Allison," she said, though she probably shouldn't have. He was clearly trying to keep things more professional between them, and here she was, tossing out a very personal comment.

"Oh, trust me, I was very angry those first few weeks," he said. "But it's hard to stay mad at someone whose belly is getting bigger and bigger with your children. Who you accompany to OB appointments and Lamaze, even though she tried to switch me out for Ted. I said no way to that. We breathed *together* and it gave us more opportunity to talk, and by the time the triplets were born, I'd accepted what was. Besides, the triplets themselves took center stage, not my former marriage."

She tried to picture Hutch with nine-months-pregnant Allison at Lamaze class, knowing she was with another man, knowing he'd be a father to three babies that he wouldn't live with full-time. It had to be such a confusing time. But she supposed the only way to get through *confusing* was to come up with a new normal.

"I know you and Allison were on and off during school, but did you get married right after graduation?" she asked.

He shook his head. "I went away to college to major in agricultural business, and then I came back to the area to get my MBA. We started dating but quickly both realized it wasn't right and broke up. But when we turned thirty-four, and were both single and seeing each other casually again, she said, 'You know, we were always so good together, just no great passion. But that's not what lasts, is it? Next year we'll be thirty-five. We should just get married and have a baby.'"

Savannah gaped at him. "Wow" was all that managed to come out of her mouth. But she was thinking: he wasn't in love with Allison. He wasn't heartbroken when she left him; he was heartbroken at losing the family life she'd offered, losing half the time with his children.

He gave something of a shrug. "It sounded so reasonable. I'd had some ups and down in relationships. I was very single when she proposed that, and I thought, why the hell not? I'd always believed, deep down, that how my father was, and how he'd treated Daniel's mother and then Daniel after, had distorted my view of marriage and fatherhood. So I very quickly came around to Allison's idea."

Savannah totally got it. "That's why you weren't angry at her."

He nodded. "Then in the middle of the pregnancy, she sat me down and told me she'd reconnected with an old flame on Facebook and that it grew into something she'd never expected and had tried to stop. But that she was deeply in love when she never thought she'd have that. She was sobbing. Then I was sobbing. And I said,

'Okay. We'll work it out. But I'm their father. And we'll have fifty-fifty custody.' She said okay back, and for these six months, it's been going all right."

Savannah was shaking her head in absolute wonder. "An amicable divorce during a pregnancy. Amicable co-parenting. I'm amazed, Hutch. It's a testament to the two of you as good parents who clearly put your children first."

"And at least I like Ted. If the triplets *have* to have a stepfather, he's the one to have. The two of them got married just this morning, a rainy weekday at the town hall. The triplets were guests—in their fanciest pj's. Carson and Caleb had tiny clip-on bow ties, and Chloe wore a little spectator hat with a pink veil. I saw the pictures. And then they left for their honeymoon to Aruba."

She'd like to see those pictures of the triplets dolled up. "You must have been happy to finally have the babies to yourself."

"I was. Am. Managing that is another story, but my world feels right again, you know?"

She bit her lip. "Yes," she said. "I do know. For a long, long time, being in a rodeo arena, negotiating for my clients, traveling, looking for new talent—I always felt most myself, like I'd been born to do exactly what I was doing. And then once I stopped feeling that way…"

He nodded. "Turns your life upside down. Sideways. I'm glad you're here to figure out what you want, Savannah."

"I wish I had a crystal ball. Sometimes I think, yes,

I *do* want a baby, a family of my own, but then I try to imagine a man beside me, a husband, and I *can't*."

"Why do you think that is?" he asked.

Now *she* was poking at the remaining pie on her plate. "Maybe because I've been on my own so long. And my divorce was pretty painful—he cheated and took off with our bank account, but I quickly replenished that. None of my relationships since have worked out—two I thought were headed somewhere ended up having similar issues my marriage did." She gave something of a shrug, but her heart ached and her stomach felt like lead. "My sisters have diagnosed me with low-trust issues, and I suppose that's the case."

"Yeah, it's probably the same for me," he said. "I trust in the triplets and that's about it."

That struck her as such a lovely thing to feel that her spirits lifted. How did Hutch Dawson always manage to turn around her down-in-the-dumps moments? "Well, good."

He smiled too, and then there was that feeling in the air that they were back to spilling the most personal of their guts, and they both reached for their mugs of coffee to give themselves a little reprieve.

Suddenly, it was Savannah who needed to turn things from the personal to the professional. "It's been a long and unexpected day. I think I'll turn in, give myself time to process everything."

"Me too," he said.

But as she popped up and took her mug to the sink, an image of Hutch Dawson in bed, bare-chested and wearing sexy boxer briefs, floated into her mind and wouldn't budge.

Real professional, she thought, goose bumps tingling along her spine.

Chapter Five

When Hutch woke up the next morning at five fifteen to a cry from the nursery—Chloe, he was pretty sure—he heard Savannah's door creak open and her footsteps on the hallway floor, then her bubbly greeting to the babies. He smiled and stretched instead of bolting out of bed to tend to the triplets as he normally would.

Ah, the novelty of a live-in nanny—his babies were in good, caring hands. Hutch smiled as he listened to Savannah's usual running commentary to the triplets as she wheeled their playpen past his bedroom door and into the living room. She was telling them it was flurrying again and explaining where snow came from, that one of her cousins had moved to a state that never saw snow and how she herself would miss it, even when it piled up and became a total drag.

He got out of bed, aware that he didn't feel as stressed

as usual, to have to tend to the babies in time to make the barn at 6:00 a.m. Normally, he'd have to start his day two hours later, as most of the nannies he'd hired in the past didn't want to start *their* day at six o'clock. Since Daniel had come aboard, he did arrive at six o'clock, put in two hours of physical labor, then buckled down with paperwork. Because of that, they hadn't had to hire another cowboy to make up for Hutch's late start.

Hutch quickly showered and dressed for a morning in the barn, excited to see his babies. And their new nanny.

He found them in the living room, sitting on the play mat, surrounded by toys. No one was crying.

Savannah smiled at the sight of him. "Look who's here!" she said brightly to the babies. "Daddy!"

"Da!" Carson said.

Hutch froze. "He just said *Da*. You heard him, right?"

Savannah laughed. "I definitely did. Was that the first time?"

"Yes!" he said, rushing over to scoop up Carson and give him a twirl around the room. "It's me, Da. Da. Can you say *Da* again?"

Carson grabbed his father's ear instead. Then giggled.

Hutch did a little bit of a tango around the room. "You said *Da* and I have a witness!" He gave the baby a big smooch on the cheek. "I'd call Allison and tell her, but I'm sure the newlyweds are fast asleep in their heart-shaped bed."

Savannah smiled. "It's nice that you'd want to share that with her. You two are definitely good co-parents."

He frowned. "Well, we'll see when she comes back and wants to start talking about shifting custody to sixty-forty. She hit me with that a couple times the past month. The answer is no. Fifty-fifty."

"What's her rationale?" Savannah asked.

"That since my father died three months ago, I only take *one* day off a week from the ranch, which is a must right now. That I work full-time on two of the days I have the triplets and therefore need a nanny. I understand it—to a point. But there's more to my having fifty-fifty custody than just how many hours I can spend with my children. Besides, Allison works part-time and has a nanny too. She thinks that her new two-person-household status should be reflected in our custody agreement."

"Put that out of your mind now," she suggested. "Or it'll eat at you. And it's Christmastime." She glanced at the tree—the pathetic, tilted tree. "Maybe during your lunchtime, we can start decorating this."

"Good idea on both counts," he said. And it was. It would do no good to get worked up over something he couldn't do anything about right now. His ex was away and he had the babies with him for all these days, a blessing in itself. He needed to focus on that. And on all the other important details of his life. Like the ranch. He glanced at his watch. "Five forty-five. Time for coffee and a quick breakfast, and then I have to get out to the barn to meet with my brother."

He kissed each baby on the head, smiled at Savannah and went into the kitchen. Coffee and bagel with cream cheese downed, another round of goodbyes to the babies and his nanny, and then he was out the door.

He needed to keep thinking of her that way. Nanny. Nanny. Nanny. Not Savannah, beautiful redhead with the long, lean body and warm, smart dark brown eyes. With the sexy small beauty mark by her lips. And speaking of her lips…

The triplets had slept through the night but Hutch had woken up twice, had bolted up with the sudden remembrance that Savannah was here, in his house, just two doors down in his old bedroom. Not long after she'd left his office last night, he'd heard the shower start in the guest bathroom, and he'd imagined her standing under the spray, naked, soap on her glorious body, long red hair wet. It had taken him a while to fall asleep as he'd fought with himself to stop thinking about her *that way*.

If only he could revert back to when he was a teenager and be grumbly about his rival's existence in his world. He'd never noticed her physical appearance then. Except those last few months of school when she'd not just gotten inside his head but his heart because of how she'd come to his defense after his father had ripped into him, how comforting that had felt—for the few seconds he'd allowed it, anyway. But after graduation, she'd left town and Savannah Walsh hadn't entered his mind except for the few times he'd heard her name mentioned in line with her career. Superstar clients, hometown girl made good.

Now she'd been added to his crowded thoughts and was taking over.

With a thermos of coffee and an apple in his coat pocket, he opened the barn door. Daniel was mucking out a stall in a fleece vest, heavy jeans and dark green work boots. His brother didn't have to do physical labor or anything beyond taking care of the books, but Daniel had said he'd discovered he liked it. In the three months he'd been working at the Dueling Dawsons, he'd learned, via YouTube videos and online adult education classes at the community college in Brewer, everything from how to repair fences to the proper feeding and care of various types of cattle and horses. He was a boon to the ranch—if a pain in Hutch's side.

"Morning," Hutch called as he approached.

"I wouldn't have to do as many stalls if you hadn't given the hands time off before Christmas," Daniel complained, his trademark.

"Like I said, that was long arranged before Dad died. And I'm perfectly willing to grab a rake too," he said and did exactly that, working in the stall next to Daniel's.

Daniel went to grab more straw and Hutch was impressed that he could carry it. Three months on the ranch had definitely made his brother stronger. The former button-down-shirt-and-khaki-pants-wearing CPA with a soft belly had become lean. He spread out the straw and started lecturing about how he disagreed with Hutch's suggestion to add a herd of sheep to the ranch. Everything from they'd need to hire at least two more hands to how Daniel didn't have the time right now to build up the level of expertise needed to make sure they'd be profitable.

"Let's table the sheep for now," Hutch said. "We'll revisit it in a few months. How's that sound?"

Daniel eyed him, clearly surprised he wasn't getting more pushback, which his brother actually seemed to enjoy. Hutch went over a few more points from the email, and they came to grudging agreements, but each had gotten at least two things they wanted.

He thought about Savannah's comment—to kill Daniel with kindness and eggnog. Plus, he wouldn't mind a home-cooked meal he didn't make himself. "Why don't you and Olivia come for dinner this week? You two can meet Savannah, my new nanny and old friend. She's a whiz at linguine carbonara, apparently."

"I'll check our schedule with Olivia," Daniel said without looking up. "But I doubt she'll want to go anywhere with me," he added under his breath.

To the point that Hutch wasn't sure he'd heard correctly. "Things are not okay at home right now?" he asked.

Daniel kept spreading out the straw, pushing at it with the rake. The strain on his face was evident. Hutch had thought it was about the two of them. But there was clearly trouble in the marriage. "She suddenly wants to have another baby. We're both forty. We have an eighteen-year-old son. We're done with all that."

"Babies are pretty great," Hutch said. "When they're not screeching or destroying diapers or grabbing your ear or spitting up all over you." He wouldn't give up a moment of any of that, though. The triplets were his everything.

Daniel turned to him, his eyes all lit up. "That's it! Yes, expect us for dinner this week. Maybe tomorrow night. Olivia's just struggling with empty-nest syndrome. Once she sees how awful it is to be run ragged by six-month-olds, she'll lose interest in the idea of having a baby at our age."

Hutch sighed, loud and proud. That was not what he'd meant. "The triplets are my world. There's nothing awful about parenthood."

Daniel let out a short laugh. "Right. It's been a barrel of fun, Hutch. Who are you kidding? Every stage of parenthood was hard for me. Being woken up all night by an infant. The terrible twos. Reading reluctance in elementary school. Friends being jerks in middle school. The I-know-everything teen years. Ethan is a great kid and I'm damned proud of him, but I did my child rearing. And my focus needs to be on keeping the Dueling Dawsons Ranch profitable."

"In Dad's memory?" Hutch dared ask, wondering if such a nice sentiment could be behind his brother's motivation.

"Hardly," Daniel said. "It's half mine—and that means it's half Olivia's and Ethan's. It's their future, maybe Ethan's legacy if he wants to get involved in ranching."

"Ah," Hutch said, not surprised. And not that Daniel was wrong for feeling the way he did. Truth be told, he appreciated that his brother was a straight shooter. Hutch always knew the truth, knew where he stood.

He had no idea if Daniel was even reachable at this point, but he'd give Savannah's grand plan a try. If Daniel was being all prickly and difficult because deep down he did want to make peace with his issues with their father and have a better relationship with his brother, then Hutch was there for it.

What was that famous quote by Maya Angelou— *when someone tells you who they are, believe them the first time*? Maybe there wasn't more to Daniel Dawson.

Maybe he was just a hard case who was bitter at how his father had treated him and his mother, and who couldn't care less about becoming closer to his brother or developing family bonds with his baby niece and nephews.

Hutch had a feeling that even if he did manage to finish his father's list of Unfinished Business by finding peace for his great-grandfather and great-uncle, the original dueling Dawsons, he'd never cross off the second thing: getting closer with Daniel.

On the other hand, Daniel's mood was so improved by the notion that the triplets would knock the baby fever out of his wife that he was actually *humming* as he raked.

But the way Hutch saw it, the triplets were so lovable that the opposite was likely to happen. Maybe not for nannies whose job it was to care for them, but for a baby-wanting aunt who'd spend about two hours at dinner and then go home to her quiet house, where Chloe's, Caleb's and Carson's gummy smiles and "Da" and precious ways and baby-shampoo scents would stay with her.

Sorry, Daniel.

He almost felt bad for his brother. Almost.

Bless all the nannies that had come before her, Savannah thought as she put the last Dawson triplet next to his siblings in the playpen after their dinner. She ran back into the kitchen to grab a paper towel and wet it and run it through the glop of pureed string beans that Carson had flung at her when he threw his spoon.

It had been quite a day. A day that had started at

5:15 a.m. when Chloe had cried out, her brothers' eyes popping open with wide-awake curiosity for a new day. There had been crying jags, twice with all three wailing, and nothing seemed to soothe them. She'd get one calmed down, go to pick up another for a walk around the living room, a sway, a bounce, a Christmas carol, and the ones in the playpen or swing would start shrieking and lifting their arms. Naptime had been a doozy. It had taken forty-five minutes from the first eye-rubbing and bawling until the three were in their bassinets, eyes closed. Even recalling it made her tired.

Savannah was organized and determined, but she wasn't a superhero with the magical powers necessary to wrangle this trio into perfectly behaved, perfectly cared for little darlings. She'd done her best today and she'd give herself a C+. No one got hurt. Everyone had been fed and burped and changed multiple times. She'd played with them on the floor; she'd read them a story; she'd told them tales of her youth, riding a horse for the first time.

She'd even told them how she might have been a bigtime bronc rider herself, which had originally been her plan and goal in life. But a bunch of injuries in a row had led her to helping out her new boyfriend at the time, a fellow bronc rider who was good but had no following, and Savannah had spent her recuperation developing a public image for him, setting up his social media, getting him booked on local radio and TV spots, and even landing a sponsorship with the rodeo in Blue Smoke. Once she recuperated, her wrist and ankle healed but weakened, she'd realized her talents were in promoting, negotiating, agenting, managing. A new career was born. The boyfriend had dumped her after all she'd done for him, but she'd always be a smidgen grateful that he'd actually gotten her started in what she was born to do.

She hadn't told the triplets that last part. But talking it out, how she'd gotten her start, how she became a success, made her realize she'd accomplished every goal she'd set out for herself as a manager. She could leave that world and not feel she was missing out.

But there was a new world that felt as exciting and full of possibilities and wonder as she used to feel about her career. This. This exhaustion, the smell of green beans in her hair, spit-up on her shirt, and her ears still ringing from all the crying and shrieking… She'd had a great day. Rewarding, challenging, every minute something unexpected. She was witnessing little humans develop and grow and learn and change before her eyes. It was the most beautiful thing in the world.

And these triplets weren't even her kin. They weren't hers.

And yet she was already falling madly in love with them.

Imagine how you'll feel about your own child. Biological, adopted—either. Of course, that was scary too. All that love, all that parental devotion, her heart walking around outside her body, as the saying went. For someone who hadn't done too well with relationships, what if she'd be bad at one with her own child? She'd known a few people who didn't speak to their parents—her up-and-coming bronc rider, Michael from Bear Ridge, for instance. She also knew a few parents whose disappointment in their children, usually due to some kind of deeply troubling behavior, cut them to the quick. Being a parent was not all sunshine and roses.

She had strong feelings about the Dawson triplets and about potential motherhood after just one full day as their nanny. She'd give herself the whole ten days to really see how she felt. By then, what she wanted, deep down, would make itself known loud and clear.

Her phone pinged with a text. Hutch.

On my way home.

Her heart itself pinged. How husbandly a text that was!

By the end of her time here, maybe she would be able to envision a husband beside her, pushing their baby stroller together. *Wow*, she thought. *I am really going through something here. I feel like* I'm *changing before my eyes.*

She was sitting on the sofa and didn't think she could move, let alone get up. That was how completely physically and mentally depleted she was. She glanced at the triplets in the playpen, none crying, all occupied with their favorite toys, all clean in appearance—she'd had to change them each twice during the day from food mishaps. If she had it in her, she'd whisk them over to the play mat and read to them so that when Hutch came in, he'd see what an excellent nanny she was, full of energy, his babies engaged. But she'd never been anything but herself—and lived honestly—so she stayed put and focused on not closing her eyes because she'd fall into a dead sleep, and that would *not* be a good look for a nanny of multiples.

The key twisted in the lock, and she did perk up some at the thought of seeing Hutch's handsome face. And having him take over so that she could go shower and rest. Maybe have a little wine.

He came in and hung up his down jacket and Stetson, kicking out of his work boots. Mmm, he was sexy. He wore a flannel shirt and faded jeans, his tousled dark hair brushed back. "How'd the afternoon go?" he asked, coming over and picking up each triplet for a cuddle and kiss before putting them all back in the playpen and dropping down on the sofa beside her.

He'd checked in several times during the day and had come in twice, once to have a quick lunch—he'd had to put off the tree decorating till later—and play with the triplets and another time to give her a break. She'd fallen into a deep sleep right on the living room sofa until he'd had to leave for a meeting.

"It was a good day," she said. "Tiring but good. Carson's favorite Christmas carol is 'Frosty the Snowman.' Every time I sang it he'd stop and stare at me with those big eyes. And Chloe does not like banana baby food anymore, even though it was on the list as a favorite. She knocked the spoon out of my hand so hard it landed on my bare foot. Pureed bananas between the toes." She laughed, but at the time, squishy wet glop on her feet and Carson's string beans in her hair and Caleb's little fist pound sending his five Cheerios flying had been quite the twenty minutes.

He looked at his babies in the playpen, then at her.

"Thank you, Savannah. From the bottom of my heart, thank you. I got more accomplished today than I have in a while because I just felt good about them being with you. Someone I know and trust."

"Ha, you trust me? A total novice."

"Look at them," he said.

"Well, they're alive." She grinned. "Ah, okay, I will give myself a little credit for taking good care of them. They're changed and ready for playtime and then bottles, then bath, tummy time, story time, and then bed. Wow, that's a lot still left."

"I've got it," he said. "You go put your feet up. Want me to make you a sandwich? I have roast beef, turkey, provolone. And sourdough. And a really good mayomustard combo with dill something."

"I would love a turkey and provolone with the mayomustard with dill. And a Coke."

"Two of each coming right up. I'll eat while I play with them on the mat."

When he wheeled the playpen of needy heart-tuggers away with him into the kitchen, she let out a sigh of *Ahh, I'm off duty* and did put her feet up. She could fall asleep right here, her head against the soft, cushy back pillows, but she wanted that sandwich and needed that crisp, caffeine-filled Coke.

In a few minutes he was back with a tray—the sandwich, the Coke in an ice-filled glass and a small plate of two chocolate chip cookies. Her heart runneth over.

"Thank you," she said. "This looks heavenly."

He smiled and headed back to the kitchen, wheeling the playpen over to the mat and then going back for his plate. She wanted to join them, to eat with Hutch, but she really couldn't move a muscle. She ate and drank and thought about her day, every now and again looking over at the group of people—one very tall, three very little—over by the sliding glass door, the swirling flurries beyond, the majestic evergreens illuminated by the outdoor lights.

This was family. Right here, right now. And her heart pinged again.

And I want in.

This family. Them.

She froze and sat up and stared at the second half of her sandwich. She was clearly delirious from her long day to have had such a thought. Hutch wasn't on the market, not with his recent divorce and the loss of his dad and the challenges with his brother. His head was deep in his very busy life. Not a new relationship with his old school nemesis turned novice Christmas nanny.

And the three Dawson babies weren't hers. They were his. And his ex's.

You're just in fantasyland, Savannah. Christmas wish land. Get back to the reality. Of course the triplets tugged at her heartstrings. They were babies and she'd cared for them all day. They'd sneaked into her heart.

Along with their handsome father.

Keep your head on straight, she told herself, biting into her sandwich. She took a long drink of the Coke. *You're here to find out what you really want, what's next for you. And you're clearly discovering your own family is exactly what you want.*

You're the nanny, she told herself. *Just remember*

your place here. With that, she eyed the pathetic Christmas tree on the other side of the sliding glass door. A project to take her mind off Hutch—and those sweet babies.

"Hey," she said. "Maybe after the triplets are down for the night, we can finally fix the tree and decorate it. It's looking kind of…"

He looked up from where he was flying a stuffed bunny around where the triplets were sitting. "Sad and lonely?" he said with a smile. "Sorry I didn't have time during lunch to work on it. I've been meaning to get to it for a couple of weeks now. There's a box of ornaments and Christmas stuff in the basement."

"Now we know what we're doing tonight," she said. If *I can stay awake past eight o'clock.*

But now that she thought about it, decorating the Dawson Christmas tree did seem like an awfully cozy thing to do, given how careful she needed to be with her burgeoning feelings for this family.

Two hours later, the triplets fast asleep, Hutch brought up from the basement two boxes marked *Christmas*—one of ornaments and one of decorations. He set them on the console table next to the two cups of eggnog. He and Savannah had decided if they were going to decorate for the holidays they should do it right—eggnog, Christmas carols coming from the speaker on the mantel and Santa hats, which he'd found stuffed in the box of decorations.

"I'm surprised I remember all these ornaments," he said, poking through that box. "Trimming the tree used to be a big family tradition, and we'd all take a side and put up our favorite ornaments. But after my mom died, my father ordered a boring artificial tree with garland and white lights and the box stayed downstairs." He pulled out a misshapen Lucite red star with a tiny copy of his sixth-grade school picture inside. "Ha, the awkward stage memorialized forever?"

"Hey, I was there," she said, stepping closer to look at the photo. "You had no such stage. Me, on the other hand? I could have won first place for Most Awkward. I was five-ten at thirteen."

"Me too," he said with a grin. "I remember we were always paired in any kind of height-related lineups." An image of Savannah in middle school floated into his mind. If anyone had told him then that one day she'd be his Christmas miracle…

She pulled a little nutcracker out of the box, her gaze soft on it as if she was deep in a memory. "My mom collected nutcrackers, from tiny ones like this to two that were six feet tall and flanked the front door of our house every Christmas season." She bit her lip. "We lost her this past January, and my dad had a great suggestion that we each add a new nutcracker to the collection in her memory. I happened to find a great one she would have loved in the holiday section of the grocery store—isn't that funny? Three ninety-nine and absolutely perfect."

He gave her hand a squeeze. "I'm sorry about your mother. I still can't really wrap my mind around the fact that my father is gone."

Savannah squeezed his hand back. "It's so hard, isn't

it? One minute they're there as they've always been and then…" The sadness on her face, in her eyes, had him wanting to hug her again. "I'm seriously grateful for my sisters. When the three of us are together and either Morgan or Cheyenne gets quiet, I always know it's because they're thinking about our mom. Then one of us will bring up a sweet memory, and we start bawling. It helps."

"Daniel and I definitely won't be crying together over our dad," he said, looking at the still-tilted tree. "He did come to the funeral, his wife and son with him, and to the house after, but they left pretty quickly. He'll never forgive our father for being who he was. But I grew up with our dad and Daniel didn't, except for a few years of Saturdays."

"He had a very different experience," she said. "But who your father was—that seems to be something you two agree on, no?"

Hutch nodded. "Lincoln Dawson was a hard case. Not easy to get along with. No patience. He did have his good points, though, personally and professionally. He was a good rancher. A good businessman. People respected him even if they didn't like him."

"What about you?" she asked, taking a sip of the eggnog.

"I loved him and sometimes I even liked him." He smiled and shook his head, and told Savannah about how just a month before he died, his father bought the triplets baby cowboy hats and plunked them on their heads, then took a photo. A couple of weeks later, he saw his father sitting on the porch having coffee and looking at that photo with rare delight in his expression.

"The triplets meant something to him, and that meant something to me."

"Aww," she said. "I'm glad you'll get to tell them that story someday about their grandpa."

He nodded, about to say something else when his phone pinged with a text. His brother.

We're on for dinner tomorrow night. 7? Do me a solid and skip the triplets' nap tomorrow so they're wired and screaming messes when we arrive.

Hutch frowned and rolled his eyes and held up the phone so Savannah could read the text.

"Wait, what?" she said. "I'm confused. He's accepting your dinner invitation, I assume, but he wants the triplets to be screaming messes?"

He told her about the conversation in the barn. About his sister-in-law's longing to have a baby now that she was an empty nester. And Daniel's been-there-done-that complete lack of interest.

Savannah raised an eyebrow. "And what if his big plan backfires? What if the triplets, even screamy, make her want a baby even more?"

"It could happen," Hutch said. "Stranger things have."

She smiled and nodded. "I think you said Daniel is five years older than you, so forty. With an eighteen-year-old son—he and his wife started their family young."

Hutch took the packet of small tools from the box and found scissors, giving the two broken branches a snip. Even that helped. Then he straightened the tree. "Daniel and Olivia were high school sweethearts. They eloped to Vegas when they were eighteen. I remember them coming to the house to tell us, and the first thing my dad said, 'Shotgun wedding, right? Guess we can expect a grandchild in seven, eight months.' Olivia turned red and my brother grabbed her hand and stormed out. I was thirteen and had no idea what just happened. Ethan was born when I was seventeen, so it definitely wasn't a shotgun wedding."

"I'm curious," Savannah said. "What kind of father is Daniel?"

He paused with a string of multicolored lights in his hands. "Definitely devoted. There a hundred percent and always has been, even if he complained a lot and still does. Ethan's a great kid—young man."

"Huh. I wonder why he's so against having another? Though I guess I can see his side too. Maybe he's been looking forward to his new chapter—taking up new hobbies, traveling."

Hutch almost snorted. "Daniel? He's a homebody and a creature of habit. He likes numbers and ranching and that's about it."

"How's their marriage? Any idea?"

"They've always seemed like a happy couple," Hutch said. "I personally wouldn't want to spend so much time with him, but hey, lid for every pot."

She smiled. "Dinner should be very interesting."

Hutch laughed. "That's for sure." He wrapped the strand of lights around the tree. "I wonder about starting all over again with a baby if I had a grown child. I guess I can see his side too. I mean, I can't imagine ever wanting to get married again. Not with that big fiasco." He finished winding the lights and told himself to get off the subject, which would just affect his mood if he kept talking about it. Right now was about tree trimming and eggnog and Christmas carols, not how his cruddy divorce turned him off the idea of ever trusting another person. Not just with himself now—with his children.

He glanced at Savannah, and she seemed to be studying him. She was probably thinking: *same here*. She'd said as much about how her divorce had affected her. No wonder she was so easy to talk to; she understood him.

"Marriage, divorce, remarriage, stepparents," he went on, "even when it's amicable it's complicated and hard. No way would I actually make any of that happen *on purpose* for me or the triplets by getting married again. The divorce rate is what it is."

"What if you fall in love with someone?" she asked.

This time he did snort. "This thing," he said, giving his heart a slap, "is closed for business. I've got my kids and the ranch. I'm all set. I'm done with love, except when it comes to the under-twenty-pounds set."

She was quiet for a moment. "I don't know, Hutch. I feel like I said that exact thing the past ten years since my divorce. I'm not sure being so absolute did me any good. It's like I told myself nothing would work out and it didn't." She gave a small shrug. "I used to think I just haven't met the right guy. But I'd think he'd have made his appearance if he existed."

"Well, I'm the last person to be having this conversation with. I'm terrible at love and romance. It's why I'm divorced with three six-month-olds."

"You two got married for practical reasons, though," she pointed out.

"And Allison broke our bargain. Split up our family when the babies weren't even born yet. But it also happens when people *are* in love and happily married—someone falls for someone else, and wham, heartbreak. Divorce. Dishes being thrown at someone's head. Just like it happens when you make a practical arrangement at thirty-four with someone you're dating and like very much."

"I wonder if that's what I'll end up doing," she said, her face kind of crumpling.

He paused with garland half draped around the tree. "What do you mean? Doing what?"

"I'm thirty-five. Maybe I'll start dating a nice enough guy, and I can propose that we get married and have a baby since it's not going to happen in the fairy-tale way." She bit her lip, defeat all over her beautiful face.

"Savannah, just because I went that route doesn't mean you will."

"But I do want a baby. I do want a family. I know that already. Just from being here a day and a quarter. From the day I spent with the triplets."

It occurred to him that she must have known for a while, deep down, that this was where her heart was taking her, and last night and all day today had cemented it for her. "Wow," he said. "Maybe you should call Daniel and tell him his plan is going to backfire if just a day with the triplets brought you to this huge life revelation." He smiled. "I'm happy for you, Savannah."

"I'm suddenly going to meet the love of my life at

thirty-five and magically get pregnant? Everything is up in the air. And what if I do make some practical deal to get the family I long for—what if he ends up meeting his soulmate and leaves us? I'd have to be half happy for him and then I'd half hate him. My baby's father." She threw up her hands. "What am I even saying?"

"I understand, Savannah. Completely." And he really did. Hell, she was using his life as an example.

She looked at him, her usually sharp brown eyes so unsure. "I just hate how nothing is guaranteed. *Nothing.* Even the most fundamental things."

If he wasn't mistaken, her eyes were misty now.

She was standing so close to him. And beautiful Savannah Walsh, unsure and kind of trembly, was his undoing. He turned and put his arms around her. "I think you can have everything you want, Savannah. You're you. You're a mover and shaker."

She offered a small smile. "Helpful in business. Not in matters of the heart."

His lips were on hers before he could even think about it, before he could tell himself this was a very scary idea that would lead nowhere good. Bed, maybe. But after that? Complications. Both of them were knee-deep in *complicated* right now.

Pull your lips away right now. Do not deepen this kiss. Do not wrap your arms tighter around her. Do not put your hand in her silky red hair. Do not inhale the scent of her spicy perfume.

But he did deepen the kiss. Her moment's hesitation, instead of snapping him back to reality, made him hope and pray she'd kiss him back—and she did.

And then he was all in. The feel of her against him, her large, round breasts pressing on his chest, her hair in one fist, his mouth exploring hers. She felt so good. *He* felt so good.

She pulled back a bit, a bit breathless as he was. "The ornaments will never get on that tree at this rate," she whispered, taking a step away from him.

He missed her the second she was out of his arms. But at least one of them was responding to reason.

"You're right," he said. He wagged a finger between them. "Bad idea. Right?"

She was in a vulnerable place right now. Changing her entire life. And he was the opposite—his life was set on a course. The triplets and the ranch. Nothing else.

"Really bad," she confirmed.

He gave her something of a smile. "We'll pretend it never happened."

"Now, *that* is a good idea," she said. "Never works. But still a good idea. For now."

His mind stopped on that *For now.* That was what he was afraid of. He could still feel the imprint of her lips on his. He could still smell her perfume and shampoo. He wanted more. And not only just now. He'd want more again and again.

Uh-oh.

Chapter Six

The next morning was all about small talk. From Savannah: *I think I'll try applesauce for Chloe's breakfast and see if she'll like it.* From Hutch: *The Christmas tree looks amazing—thanks again for your help.* No talk at all about the kiss.

That was for the best, Savannah thought as she sat at the kitchen table, the triplets in their high chairs. The kiss happened around 9:00 p.m. and it was now almost 6:00 a.m. She still hadn't processed it. That he'd kissed her. That of course she'd kissed him back.

That after all these years, he was attracted to her. Oh, how that warmed her middle school heart.

But Savannah wasn't fourteen. Or the eighteen-year-old who'd left Bear Ridge knowing she'd never get Hutch Dawson, that he'd never be hers.

She'd always been aware that she'd given up. She'd

moved on. Sometimes, you had to, and you had to know when to do so.

Then last night, he passionately kissed her. When moments before she'd said that she wanted love and romance and family and wasn't sure she'd get it. When moments before *he'd* said he didn't want any of that.

So he was attracted to her but had he also been responding to what she'd said? Maybe he'd just felt close to her because the triplets who had scared off professional nannies from an agency had made her want her own family, her own baby. They'd just been talking about how his brother fully expected them to rid his wife of her longing for a new baby at forty. Here she was, feeling the opposite. Yes, she was pretty sure he had felt close to her, and attracted, and he'd kissed her. That was passion *and* emotion.

For a split second, while his lips were on hers, while she'd been pressed against his hard, muscled chest, while she could feel his erection hard against her upper thigh, she'd only focused on her wild attraction to him. A second later, she'd thought, *Maybe I can finally have Hutch Dawson, the old dream. Maybe...*

But he'd said what he'd said. About being done with love and romance. Done with marriage. He had his family.

And so she'd stepped back, out of that dreamy embrace. She had to proceed with a balance of heart and head.

Now, as she bit into a slice of sourdough toast with butter and strawberry jam, the triplets enjoying their Cheerios, which meant she had a good five minutes to drink her coffee in peace, Hutch filled his thermos with coffee, made himself a bagel with cream cheese and sat down beside her. He ate quickly, telling the babies all about his day, what was on the agenda. Then he stood and kissed each on their head.

"I'll check in about breaks, and I'll come in for lunch so you can put your feet up," he told Savannah, grabbing a granola bar and apple.

"Actually, it's probably better if I *don't* have time to myself to think today," she blurted out, then felt her cheeks warm.

He smiled. "I know what you mean." He looked at her a good long moment, and she knew he was thinking about the kiss too. He headed to the door, and she tried not to watch him slide into his heavy rancher barn coat, his scarf and Stetson and boots.

He would pretend the kiss never happened, like he said they should, but he'd still *think* about it today, she figured. Just as she would.

The idea that kissing her, having her in his arms, would break into his thoughts while he was out on the range or in the barn brought a smile.

"Need me to pick up anything in town for your famous linguine carbonara for tonight's big dinner with my brother and his wife?"

She took a fast sip of her coffee. "Yes, actually. I checked the fridge and cabinets. Looks like you have everything except for prosciutto and Italian bread."

"I'll get both," he said. With a last somewhat awkward smile, he was gone.

She grabbed her phone and texted her sisters in a group chat.

Can either or hopefully both of you come to the Dueling Dawsons Ranch this morning? I might have kissed Hutch last night.

She waited.

Three dots appeared, then disappeared.

Three more appeared.

I'll be there in twenty minutes, Morgan said. Clara's on a sleepover and I'm not picking her up till 8. She added a puckered lips emoji followed by an exclamation point.

I'll be there in fifteen-ish, Cheyenne texted. I'd stop for coffee and breakfast sandwiches for us but I have to hear about this kiss so have coffee ready!

Savannah grinned and texted back. Will do. I have ham and cheese croissants.

I have? She might be a little too comfortable in this kitchen.

"Guess what, peanuts," she said to the triplets as she put her phone down. "You're going to meet my sisters!"

"Da!" Caleb said, little fists landing on the tray of his high chair.

She was about to grab her phone and text Hutch that now *Caleb* had said *Da*, but he'd said it to her and not to Hutch, so it wasn't quite the same. And she didn't need to be texting him right now. They both needed a breather.

Last night, after that breathtaking kiss they would

somehow pretend never happened, they'd finished decorating the tree, which did look very festive, sipped their eggnog, and then they both made excuses for turning in—Hutch to his office, Savannah to her room.

She'd been beyond exhausted at that point, but sleep had eluded her for a while. She'd taken a shower, regretting that she was washing away her Hutch-touched-and-kissed body and lips, but that was probably for the best. And then she'd lain in bed under the fluffy down comforter and stared out the window at the stars for a while, thinking. Actually, not thinking. *Feeling.* She'd let it all come, and the next thing she knew, a cry had woken her, the sky half-dark at just past 5:00 a.m.

Just as Savannah finished her first cup of coffee and had gotten up to grab the jars of baby food, she heard a car pulling in and a car door open and shut. Then another car was arriving. Good, both her sisters were here at the same time.

She hurried to the door, and there they were, both looking very curious. Thirty-two-year-old Morgan, her auburn hair in a long ponytail, held a Tupperware container. "I come bearing the last three muffins I made yesterday. Cinnamon chip."

Cheyenne, twenty-nine-year-old strawberry blonde bride-to-be, smiled. "I come bearing nothing but my nosiness. Tell us every detail, Savannah."

Savannah led the way into the kitchen, where the triplets were in their high chairs. "Morgan and Cheyenne, meet Caleb, Chloe and Carson Dawson. They're six months."

Both her sisters gasped and oohed and aahed and gushed at the triplets as they took seats at the table.

"They're so beautiful!" Morgan said, making silly faces at the babies, who were staring at the guests.

"And well-behaved," Cheyenne added. "They're totally content right now, no fussing, no crying. These darling babies scared off several nannies?"

"You came in at a *really* good moment," Savannah said as she grabbed two mugs and poured coffee for her sisters. She told them about tonight's dinner and Hutch's brother's big plan to use the screechy triplets to knock the baby fever out of his wife.

"Ooh, that'll be interesting," Cheyenne said. "I wonder if it'll work. I mean, *I* have baby fever, and every time I see a baby screaming its head off in the grocery store or a toddler pitching a fit over being told no to candy, I think 'Aww, I can't wait.' Seriously."

Savannah laughed and poured herself a second cup. "That's kind of what happened to me."

Both sisters' eyes widened. "You made a decision?" Morgan asked.

Savannah sat down and took the lid off the container of muffins. "It's more like the decision made itself known. A feeling came over me, a knowledge—an *acknowledgment*, I guess. I think I've known for a while now that I want something else, but I was scared about admitting it. Being here made it impossible to deny. I want a family."

Both sisters leaned over to squeeze Savannah into a hug.

Morgan put a muffin on each sister's plate. "And this

kiss you mentioned will get you there! Nine months?" she asked with a wink.

"We're already pretending it never happened," Savannah said with something of a frown. She took a quick sip of her coffee, then opened Caleb's jar of oatmeal cereal and slipped a spoon in.

Her sisters looked at each other, then back at her.

"Okay, hold on a sec," Cheyenne said. "Let's each feed a triplet so all their mouths are occupied and no crying can interrupt the story. Gimme a spoon and the jar this cutie likes," she added, gently caressing Chloe's soft brown hair.

"Ba!" Chloe said, moving the last Cheerio on her tray and then giggling.

"And I'll feed this sweetie," Morgan said, scooting closer to Carson.

Savannah let out an appreciative sigh. "The cavalry. Thank you." She slid the other two jars and spoons over to her sisters, then inched the spoonful of oatmeal toward Caleb. "Ooh, Caleb, look what I have for you. Yummy oatmeal cereal! Your favorite breakfast!" He opened his bow-shaped mouth, her heart doing little flips. Yes, she wanted this. Caleb took the bite, his blue eyes happy.

"Wow, Savannah, you're really good at your new job," Morgan said, gesturing at Caleb. "I wasn't sure what to expect, if you'd need a basic tutorial on baby care, if you'd be running around ragged, trying to feed one baby, calm down another and change yet another. But you've clearly got things under control."

"Yesterday had its major share of shrieking and fussing and throwing things," Savannah said. "I had a glop of string bean puree in my hair and bananas between my toes. But I should toot my own horn a little—I've already figured out tricks and how to be fast with diapers and little things each likes and doesn't like."

Cheyenne was looking at her in amazement. "I'm so happy for you, Savannah. Whodathunk? Now back to the pretending the kiss didn't happen. What the heck?" she asked, giving Chloe another bite of her applesauce.

"You know Hutch is divorced," Savannah said. "And you know the basic story, that his wife left him when she was five months pregnant for her soulmate. They're on their honeymoon right now. So Hutch is not exactly a champion for love and marriage and happily-ever-after. He was blindsided. He's not bitter, but he says he's done with all that. Plus he lost his dad recently and his brother slash partner is a piece of work and he's got the ranch to manage. Kissing me while decorating the Christmas tree last night wasn't on his to-do list."

Morgan laughed. "But that's how the best things happen. Spontaneously."

"It was spontaneous, all right," Savannah said. "And granted, I'm the one who pulled away—out of fear, mostly. But he immediately said we should just pretend the kiss never happened. And then this morning, we were small-talking. There was definite distance in the air between us."

"Except you *live* here," Morgan said. "And tonight you're making dinner for his brother and the wife? Helping with a family issue? Oh, I'd say the distance is as manufactured as the idea of pretending the kiss didn't happen."

A big blast of hope flared in Savannah's chest. "Yeah, I know," she said with a big smile, which faded quickly. She gave Caleb another bite of his oatmeal. "But Hutch's life is very complicated. I really don't think he wants to add anything to the mix."

"It's already been added," Morgan pointed out.

Savannah took another sip of her coffee just as Caleb's face started to crumple. "Aww, what's the matter, little guy? You have a burp in you?" She placed a burp cloth on her shoulder, then lifted him from the high chair and settled him against her, giving his back a few good pats. He let out a monster burp, his face brightening again.

"Wow, you are good!" Cheyenne said.

"Do you think it's because I have a serious crush on their dad and therefore I have a serious crush on them?" Savannah asked. "I mean, if I were babysitting random triplets, would this be working out so well? Or is it because they're Dawsons?"

"Babies are pretty powerful little creatures," Morgan said. "Even screechy strangers in grocery store carts shrieking their heads off. It's just kind of what babies do. And you really seem to know how you feel."

"And maybe these next days till Christmas will actually go on forever," Cheyenne said, giving Chloe her last spoonful and then lifting her up for a burp.

"What do you mean?" Savannah asked.

"I think she's saying you might never actually leave this house," Morgan said. "The kiss *did* happen. And where there's one kiss, there's much more."

A warm, fuzzy feeling settled in Savannah's heart. But it soon dissipated. As much as she might want a future with Hutch and these triplets, that wasn't going to happen. Hutch wasn't *there*. He wasn't open to a relationship or anywhere near ready. And it wouldn't be fair for this attraction brewing between them, quite possibly out of need on both sides, to add pressure at a complicated time.

But it was sure nice to think about.

That night, while Hutch played with the triplets on the mat in the living room, chatting away about how Uncle Daniel and Aunt Olivia were coming over in ten minutes, Savannah was at the stove, making her one specialty, linguine carbonara. The pasta was awaiting the pot, the prosciutto for the sauce was chopped in its little bowl, and she was slathering the Italian bread halves with butter and layering on the garlic. Everything was prepped. All she needed was the doorbell to ring so she could get everything going and hopefully the timing would work to get everything on the table within fifteen minutes.

And sorry, Uncle Daniel, but Savannah hadn't skipped the triplets' naps so that they'd be screechy messes right now. They'd had their moments of fussing today but had generally been wonderful. Whether one baby or even all would throw a tantrum during dinner was anyone's guess, but it was unlikely since they were all content right now, and during dinner they'd sit in their high chairs at the table with their handfuls of beloved Cheerios and do one of their favorite things: stare at people around them.

There was the doorbell. She could hear Hutch telling Carson and Chloe that he was tucking them in their swings for a minute and would be back. Savannah turned on the oven to preheat and the burner under the pan of olive oil and headed out into the living room to greet the guests.

Hutch stood in the entryway with Caleb in his arms. "Daniel and Olivia Dawson, you know this little guy, of course, and this is Savannah Walsh, an old friend from my school days and the triplets' temporary nanny till Christmas."

There were handshakes and pleasantries and the hanging up of coats and hats.

"Hello, sweetheart," Olivia said to Caleb, her gaze tender on the baby. She was petite with straight light brown hair to her shoulders and hazel eyes.

Daniel barely looked at the baby, turning his attention to Savannah. She could see the resemblance between him and Hutch. "I was telling Olivia that you're a rodeo manager—you used to manage Logan Winston, right? He was my favorite bull rider. I still can't believe what I've heard, that he quit the rodeo to be a stay-at-home father."

"I think it's wonderful," Hutch said, leading the way into the living room. He set Caleb on the play mat, then got his siblings from their swings and put them beside him.

"Aww, do you like puppies?" Olivia asked Caleb, sitting down close to them and smiling at Chloe, who was shaking her rattle with the puppy ears.

Daniel sat down on the club chair by the fireplace,

not a glance at the triplets. "Logan Winston was a national star, though. And he just walked away from fame and fortune and living the high life to deal with homework and soccer games in the pouring rain." He shook his head. "I don't get it."

"I don't want to gossip," Olivia said, "but I did hear from one of the Dawson cousins that he'd just found out he had a child. He'd missed out on the first seven years and didn't want another day to go by without his boy in his life. That's lovely."

Chloe stared at Olivia with her big blue eyes, and Olivia brightened. "Would you like to sit on my lap?" she asked. "You would? Oh, good." She reached over and scooped up the baby girl, settling her down. Chloe grabbed her ear. "Oooh, some grip," she said, squeezing a toy to get Chloe's attention. It worked—she got her ear back. Olivia laughed. "Aren't you so precious?" she said, giving her a nuzzle on her head.

Daniel frowned.

Savannah mentally shook her head. Hutch hadn't been exaggerating about Daniel in any regard. "Well, if you'll give me ten minutes, I'll have dinner on the dining room table."

"Can I help with anything?" Hutch asked her.

"Nope. I've got it, but thank you." She disappeared into the kitchen, ears peeled toward the living room. She put the linguine in the boiling water and got the carbonara sauce going.

"Then again," she heard Daniel say, "as you said, Logan Winston did miss the first seven years of his son's life. He had zero experience with being a dad. So I guess

I can see why he went all in. It's not like he already had kids and had been there, done that."

"I'd think discovering he had a child would be special and life-changing either way," Olivia said. "Now, Hutch, tell me about the triplets. What's new with them? Milestones?"

"As a matter of fact, Carson said *Da* for the first time yesterday. And they're all on solid foods now—jarred baby food, cereal, strained fruits and veggies. They still get bottles before bed. And they're sleeping through the night."

"Must have been rough waking up like ten times a night till just recently," Daniel said with a note of triumph in his voice. "I remember how hard those days were."

"Well, there are lots of phases," Hutch said. "And I'm happy to go through them all."

The oven dinged and Savannah turned it off, gave the linguine carbonara a final stir and then slid the pasta into a serving bowl. It smelled and looked great, if she did say so herself. She put the garlic bread in a ceramic basket, then went into the living room. "Dinner's ready," she called out.

Hutch picked up two babies, and Olivia picked up Chloe, snuggling the girl against her.

"I just love that baby-shampoo scent," Olivia said. "I forgot how much I've missed that."

Savannah noticed Daniel frowning again. She almost felt sorry for him. This was *not* working out like he'd hoped. He'd probably be even more prickly and grumbly toward Hutch after this.

"You can't have another baby out of the blue just

because you miss the smell of baby shampoo!" Daniel snapped, his outburst making everyone stop in their tracks for a second.

Olivia lifted her chin. "It's more than that and you know it. But this is not the time or the place," she said, forcing a smile as she glanced sheepishly at Hutch and Savannah.

Chloe started fussing, waving her arms around. She let out a sharp cry.

"Yup, that's what babies do," Daniel said with relief in his voice. "Cry their little hearts out. Just when you're about to sit down to a nice dinner with family."

Olivia glared at her husband and gave Chloe a bounce, patting her back with a "there, there."

Hutch put on a pair of very silly plastic eyeglasses with springing cartoon monkeys popping from them, and Chloe stopped crying. Olivia slid her into her high chair at the table, and the baby girl seemed content to pick up a Cheerio and stare at it. Carson and Caleb were beside her, munching and staring too.

The adults all sat and dug into the linguine carbonara, everyone seeming relieved to be occupied with something other than one another or conversation.

"Mmm, this is really good," Daniel said, fork digging into his pasta. Whether trying to get back in everyone's good graces—though he didn't seem the type to care about being *out* of them—or because it *was* good, she wasn't sure.

Savannah smiled and swirled a forkful. "I'm glad to hear that. It's my one specialty. Because I love it so much."

"So, Savannah, you're just here until Christmas?" Olivia asked, reaching for the basket of garlic bread.

She nodded. "That's the plan, but we'll see." She didn't want to think about leaving Bear Ridge or the Dueling Dawsons Ranch. Just like her sister had basically said this morning. *Maybe you'll never leave Hutch's house...* "To be honest, I think Logan Winston might have rubbed off on me, because I, too, am thinking about changing my life."

"I am too," Olivia said softy.

Daniel narrowed his eyes at his wife but didn't say anything.

"You very recently did just that as well, right, Daniel?" Savannah said, not sure if she should have.

"I suppose," he said, breaking a piece of garlic bread in half. He took a bite. "Although if our father hadn't died, I'm not sure I'd be working for the ranch."

"You were thinking about it, though," Olivia said. "Even before."

Daniel shot a sharp gaze at Olivia, and it was clear he hadn't wanted that to be public knowledge. Or maybe just not for Hutch to know.

"Really?" Hutch asked. "You were thinking about joining the ranch for a while? I had no idea."

Daniel seemed to calm down some. "I suppose I was. The Dueling Dawsons Ranch was my first home, you know." He seemed about to elaborate but then bit into the garlic bread and looked down at his plate.

Savannah thought about what Hutch had told her, that Daniel and his mother had lived on the ranch, in this house, until he was four. But when the affair with

Hutch's mother was discovered, Daniel's mother took her boy and moved out in an angry huff. She'd gotten quite a good settlement in the divorce, although the iron-clad prenup ensured the ranch stayed with Lincoln. Daniel had begrudgingly visited his dad, stepmother and half brother until he was a young teen, was pretty much ignored by his father otherwise, and refused to come anymore. Hutch had shared all that with her, and it seemed like a long-ago story of family strife in explanation for why Daniel had never wanted to be close to his father or brother.

But looking at Daniel now, the flesh-and-blood man, she could easily see that he still carried scars from his childhood. He wasn't the easiest person to be around, but she found herself understanding him a bit better.

"Then you should relate to the fact that I might want a change in *my* life," Olivia said, strain in her voice as she pushed pasta around with her fork.

Daniel slid a sheepish glance at his wife. "We could start going to the movies every Friday night like we used to."

"That's not quite what I mean," she said. "But I would like that."

Daniel seemed very relieved that he'd said something right and kept his eyes on his plate, inhaling his pasta and another piece of garlic bread.

Savannah could see everyone needed a break from the heavy conversation, so she asked a general question about the ranch, the acreage and how big the herd of cattle was. Daniel answered, animated and full of interesting stories about the Dueling Dawsons. She could tell he really did love the ranch. He'd probably always wanted to be part of it but had felt uncomfortable about his place until he was legally handed half of it.

Finally, plates were empty, coffee and the homemade pecan tart Olivia had brought consumed, the babies were ready for their bottles, and both Daniel and Olivia looked exhausted. They said they'd better get home since they both had early wake-ups tomorrow morning. Olivia started clearing the table, but Savannah told her she and Hutch would take care of it.

All three babies started crying as the adults stood, Daniel brightening as if he finally got his wish. Olivia looked tenderly at each baby. "I could stay and help with them," she offered.

"No worries," Hutch said. "We've got it. If it were just me, I'd take you up on it. But I have supernanny now."

Savannah felt herself beam. "I'm hardly that," she said, but the compliment had gone straight to her heart.

Hutch scooped up Chloe and Carson, Savannah plucked up Caleb, and they put them in the playpen in the living room, then walked their guests to the door.

As the babies wailed in the playpen, Daniel had a big smile on his face. "Ooh, that's loud," he said, covering his ears.

"They're just tired from a long day," Olivia said, looking forlorn.

Savannah would call her tomorrow and invite her over again. *Just* her.

Finally, the guests were gone and Hutch and Savannah hurried over to the playpen to tend to the crying triplets.

"So who won the night?" Savannah asked, honestly having no idea.

"Definitely no one," he said.

"I think the triplets did. In cuteness," she added with a smile.

He smiled too. "That. Dinner. Was. Exhausting."

"It was. But I feel like I took a master class in your brother and sister-in-law." She told him her plan to invite Olivia over. "She just seems to need a pal to listen to her. I get the feeling she doesn't open up easily, and I already know all their business."

"I think that's a nice idea. Okay if *I* avoid Daniel tomorrow like the ole plague?"

"I'm pretty sure he'll find you and grumble," Savannah pointed out. "At least he can't be mad at you about the triplets. They did act up a little."

Chloe lifted her arms, and Hutch reached in the playpen for her.

"Let's do bottles and get these guys ready for bed," Hutch said, kissing his daughter's soft cheek. He let out a yawn. "I have to say, those two adults exhausted me more than the triplets ever have."

Savannah smiled. She had no trouble believing that.

And as she lifted up Carson, rubbing his back as he flailed his arms, she realized just how deep she was falling into this family. And wanting to belong.

Chapter Seven

Hutch's eyes popped open in his dark room at the sound of a cry. He was in bed, remnants of a dream about Savannah flitting away. He glanced at his phone on the side table: 1:12 a.m. Another cry. Two different cries.

He listened for the sound of Savannah's door and her footsteps, but he didn't hear her. And now he couldn't hear much over the wails coming from down the hall. He sat up and stretched, giving the triplets a few seconds to soothe themselves back to sleep. Which they rarely did.

After they'd gotten the trio to bed last night, he'd wanted to do something nice for Savannah since she'd not only made that great dinner but had been subjected to his brother for two hours. He'd suggested running a pampering bubble bath for her—particularly because she'd been a huge help with the triplets' baths earlier.

Not a drop of water had splashed on the floor. Savannah had said a bubble bath sounded wonderful, and as he'd turned on the water and poured in the scented bath beads, all he could think about was joining her in the tub, soaping her luscious naked body. He'd had to splash his face with cold water to try to get the images out of his head.

She'd taken her bath alone and had knocked on his office door a half hour later in the white terry guest robe, her red hair damp down her shoulders, to say thank you and good-night and that she'd handle the wee-hour wakings since "I don't have to be in the barn at 6:00 a.m., doing manual labor and dealing with a persnickety brother, particularly after that get-together."

He could not appreciate this woman more. She had to be exhausted after another very long day with the triplets and cooking, and then she'd insisted on helping him clean the kitchen. He'd told her he'd take the night wakings, but she'd insisted. How he'd wanted to scoop her up and carry her to her room, lay her down on the bed and just sleep beside her.

Which made his attraction more than just physical. That was a problem.

He had to stop thinking of her in any way other than his temporary nanny. They weren't going to get together. He would *not* lie beside her in bed, holding her hand and chatting about the awkward dinner with his brother and wife. And there most certainly would be no sex. Nothing to add any more complications to his life. He had a very lucky thing going here and messing that up, the way sex and romance always ended badly, would hurt everyone, but especially the triplets. They—he—needed Savannah.

He figured she was so zonked that even a herd of stampeding buffalo wouldn't wake her, and sometimes the triplets did sound like that. He got out of bed and headed into the hallway, not bothering with a shirt. Chloe had stopped crying, but Caleb still was. Or was that Carson? He was so tired himself he wasn't sure. He stopped in the doorway of the nursery, surprised to see Savannah already inside. She was standing by the bassinets and holding Caleb, patting his back and singing the same mangled line from a Christmas carol as she rubbed Chloe's forehead, the little trick he'd told her about.

"Dashing through the snow in a something, something sleigh, something, something, something, laughing all the way… Hee, hee, ha ha."

He couldn't help laughing himself, and she whirled around in surprise.

He almost gasped.

She wore a T-shirt and yoga pants. But the T-shirt was thin and a little sheer, and he could see the outline of her full breasts. It took everything in him to drag his eyes off her body. The pink yoga pants clung to her tall figure. He swallowed, realizing that looking at her beautiful face, into her brown eyes, was having a similar effect.

She was staring at him too. Her gaze was a few inches down from his face, on his shoulders, then lower to his bare chest.

Was it his imagination or did she swallow too, the

tip of her pink tongue barely peeking out to moisten her lips…

"He's better now," Savannah said, cuddling Caleb to her as the baby's eyes drooped.

The words got him moving and he went to check on Chloe, who was fussing, her eyes fighting sleep, but then she turned her head, little fist shooting up alongside her ear, and she was once again fast asleep.

Savannah gently lowered Caleb into his bassinet. "Fingers crossed," she whispered. The baby went in silently.

"Success," he whispered back.

They stood just inches apart. If he turned, if he looked away from Caleb and up at Savannah, he'd be in kissing distance and he didn't think he could come up with small talk to make this moment go away, to clear his head of the very X-rated thoughts. He wanted Savannah—hard.

"I've got a problem," he said, his gaze intent on her.

"Oh?" she asked.

He took her hand and led her out of the nursery and into the dimly lit hallway. "I'm so attracted to you that I'm going to spontaneously combust if I don't kiss you again. If I don't *more* than kiss you again. I meant what I said about pretending the kiss didn't happen, but that only worked in theory."

"Same here," she whispered. "I thought about the kiss a lot *all* day. It definitely happened."

Dammit. He was hoping she'd say something that would have the same effect as cutting off their kiss had last night. One of them had to move away from this very dangerous territory they were stepping into.

"I did too," he said. "But sex would seriously complicate things, Savannah. I'm... I don't know what I am, but I'm—" He searched his brain for the right words but stopped when he realized she was smiling.

"I'm flattered," she said.

"But..." he prompted. "You have to come out with the *but* so we can both go back to our separate rooms and not ruin this perfect arrangement—perfect for both of us."

"Who says sex would ruin it?" she asked, her brown eyes steamy on his.

"What happens after, though? In the middle of the night when one of us wakes up and—" He shut up again.

"And can't handle it?" she asked, finishing his question.

"Yes. Exactly."

"Hutch," she said softly, stepping even closer to him, and there wasn't a lot of room left between them. If she even leaned toward him, her breasts would touch his chest. And he'd be a goner. "You've been through a lot recently. *A lot.* I know that. And as for me, I'm going to be making some big life changes. Maybe what we both need is to just let go and enjoy each other and not have any expectations. Nothing changes in the middle of the night. Nothing changes in the morning. Sex between two adults who could seriously use some release."

The problem was that Savannah Walsh was already too good to be true. His miracle nanny when he desperately needed help this week. And now she was proposing they have no-strings sex when he desperately wanted her—*without strings*? Could there be two Christmas miracles in the same time frame? The same *week*? His life so far had shouted loud and clear that there were no miracles.

"You're sure?" he asked, searching her eyes for any hesitation, any vulnerability. "I can't mess this up, Savannah. You're the best thing that's happened to this house in a long time."

She gave him a tender smile, then cupped her hand on his cheek. "I won't let you down with the triplets. You've got my word. No matter what. I'm here till Christmas."

What if I let you down, though? he thought.

Then she did it. She leaned forward. Before her lips even got close, her lush breasts in that thin T-shirt brushed against his bare chest and he pulled her to him, his mouth covering hers, his tongue exploring, his hands in her hair, up under the T-shirt. Just the feel of her skin almost undid him.

"Savannah," he whispered.

She took his hand again and led him to his bedroom. Invitation proffered. Thought left his head as pure sensation took over his body.

He picked her up and kissed her, passionately, as he walked over to the bed. He laid her down and stretched over her, leaning up on his forearms, kissing her, looking at her beautiful face, his hands moving under the shirt to those incredible breasts. She was arching her back and pressing up against him, driving him wild with need and desire. He peeled off the T-shirt and took in how sexy she was, his hands and mouth roaming all over, down to her breasts and stomach and lower until her breathy moans had him barely on the edge of control.

As he kissed his way back up her torso and neck, she inched down his sweatpants—he wore nothing underneath—and he kicked them off. He couldn't get her yoga pants off fast enough. The white cotton undies with tiny flowers had him grunting. Sexy as they were, off they had to come.

Suddenly they were naked.

She flipped him over and straddled him, her turn to work her way down his body, her hands and tongue and lips covering every inch of him. When her palm made contact with his erection, he closed his eyes and seized up every muscle in his body, forcing himself to hold on. He reached a hand over to his bedside table and pulled open the drawer, grabbing a condom from the box he kept there.

"I like that the box hasn't been opened," she whispered.

He smiled, but when she grabbed the condom and scooted down his body so she could roll it on him, he almost lost it.

He flipped her over and looked at her beautiful face before he thrust inside her, Savannah moaning and arching up to meet him, rocking against him. He felt so connected to her, so truly one.

He grasped both her hands in each of his and slid them up on the bed, her grunty moans getting louder, his thrusts getting harder. She started moving a bit sideways and he realized she wanted to be on top, so he turned them over, Savannah straddling him, the moonlight casting a glow on her red hair as it shook over her shoulders, her breasts right there for him to relish.

He couldn't get enough of her, never wanted this to end, but once she started moaning hard, her head thrown back in her ultimate pleasure, he knew he had moments to go before he exploded.

And then she crashed down on him, her face in his neck, breathing as heavily as he was, and he let himself go. Once he could catch his breath, he wrapped his arms around her.

"That was amazing," he whispered.

"I agree," she whispered back and snuggled even closer against him.

He had no idea what the bright light of morning would bring, but right now, she was his, and he was hers.

Savannah woke in the dark, sure that glorious sex with the man of her fantasies had all been a dream, but no, there was Hutch lying beside her. He was asleep, his head turned slightly away, his chest rising and falling, the down comforter pulled up to his pecs.

She'd been in love with Hutch Dawson forever. Puppy love since age five. Teen love since middle school. And full-out love-love since her senior year of high school. Seventeen years later, the fantasies that had stayed with her had become reality. She'd never experienced anything like lovemaking with Hutch. He'd been all in— wildly passionate yet looking tenderly into her eyes. A few times, she'd felt the depth of his feelings until she realized that depth was about desire, not love. But in those moments, those several moments, she'd relished the way he'd made her feel.

A baby cried out. Sounded like Caleb again.

Hutch bolted upright.

She was so startled she sat up too. "I'll go."

"That's okay. I'll go," he said quickly, pulling on his sweatpants. He gave her an awkward smile and touched a hand briefly to her cheek, then left.

Had he gone to get away from her?

Yes, the tiny devil on her right shoulder said.

No, the little angel on her left shoulder said louder. *He's just being thoughtful and wants you to stay in bed and relax.*

Maybe a little of both.

A minute later, there was silence again. She waited a few more minutes, anticipating Hutch's return, but he didn't come back. *Jeez, calm down. Give the guy a little time.* That seemed to be both angel and devil.

She glanced around his bedroom, which she hadn't been in until last night. The queen-size bed with the wrought-iron headboard dominated the room. Silver shag rug that had felt amazing on her feet was underneath. A large dresser with a square mirror, a tray on it with a candleholder, a dish containing some coins. Above the headboard hung an abstract watercolor of cattle that she liked very much. And there were two bedside tables, her side with a lamp and box of tissues, his with a few books stacked. The top one was: *What to Expect the First Year*, an illustration of a mom holding a baby on the cover. There was a bookmark half-

way through, sticky notes poking out. Below that book
was: *The First Time Father*.

Her heart pinged. *God, I love you, Hutch.*

Her eyes widened and she bit her lip.

She did love him, no surprise there, but now the words
were echoing in her head, her heart, and she was scared.
She wasn't supposed to be, though. Based on her big
statement last night about how things would be between
them in the middle of the night and in the morning. No
expectations. Just some much-needed good sex. An or-
gasm.

She let out a deep breath, telling herself to get herself
together. He'd be back any minute, and she didn't want
to be caught with a conflicted expression on her face. Or
even worse: a moony, *I love you and have forever* look.

Thirty-five minutes since he'd left, still no Hutch.
Even she, still a novice, never took that long to get one
or all the triplets back to sleep.

Her heart plummeted to her stomach.

She'd never been one to "wait and see," so she got up,
put her T-shirt and yoga pants back on, and slipped out
of the room, practically tiptoeing down the hall to the
nursery.

She took in a breath to brace herself and pushed open
the door. All three babies were in the bassinets, sleeping soundly.

And Hutch was sitting on the glider, holding a stuffed
bunny against his chest, his gaze out the window at the
dark night, his mind so elsewhere that he hadn't noticed
her in the doorway.

Crud.

She quickly backed away. She needed to leave him be with his thoughts. Even if they were: *Whoa, that was a mistake. A hot mistake, but a mistake.*

You were the one who assured him there would be no expectations, she reminded herself again. *Not in the middle of the night, like now. Or tomorrow morning. So no feelings hurt, Savannah*, she ordered herself.

That wasn't working. A burst of sadness spread in her chest. Her fantasies would not be coming true. Because when it came to Hutch Dawson, those fantasies were always about winning his heart, not just his attention. She'd never had that and she never would. She really had to accept it.

If you thought you were joining this family, you were wrong. Unless it's to be the permanent nanny while Hutch remains a man alone, not open to romance or love.

She headed back to her own room, still able to feel the imprint of his lips on hers, his arms around her.

Savannah got into bed, pulled the down comforter up to her chin and stared up at the ceiling, awareness overtaking her that this had been Hutch's childhood room. While she'd been endlessly thinking about him as a teen, imagining her first kiss—their first kiss— he'd been right here, doing his homework at the desk she figured had once been by a window or reading a textbook on this very bed.

At least one of your dreams came true. You not only kissed Hutch Dawson, you slept with him.

Yeah, but I have other dreams now. Big dreams. And they all involve him.

She turned on her side and closed her eyes, but she knew sleep wouldn't be coming so fast.

Why did love have to hurt so damned much?

Hutch woke up in the nursery in an uncomfortable angle on the glider, daylight peeking past the blackout curtains at the window.

He looked at the clock on the wall. Just past five. The triplets would wake up any minute, and Savannah would come in. He wondered if she knew he'd gotten up to tend to Caleb and had ended up staying in the nursery for a bit and falling asleep. Maybe the triplets would wake her up, and she'd assume he'd gone to them now. He didn't like the idea of her thinking he'd abandoned her in the middle of the night. But he supposed he had.

Last night, Caleb long asleep, Hutch had told himself to get up and go back to his room, back to beautiful Savannah in his bed, but his body had felt like lead and he couldn't make himself move from the glider chair. Sex with Savannah had been as amazing as he'd said. Too amazing. Hot and passionate—but there was a connection between them he hadn't expected.

A connection he didn't want right now. Friendship, yes. But the fledgling feelings he had for Savannah weren't welcome. His life and future had been upended not too long ago, and he was just getting used to this new normal. He might want Savannah, he might feel a lot for her, but the idea of starting a relationship? No. His trust level was too low, his energies needed in too many other places. Romances started out all fun and hot, and then they quickly turned serious and expectations developed.

She would *need* from him, and he wouldn't be able to give. Then they'd argue. Angry words, slammed doors.

No, thanks.

Start as you mean to continue, he thought, recalling a favorite old adage of his mother's. He'd already blown that, though, by sleeping with Savannah.

They would simply rewind. They'd talked about this, right? How they'd both needed last night, the release, and now they could move on, father of triplets and nanny. Nothing more. Friends. They could enjoy the holiday season.

Everything would be okay with Savannah.

Chloe cried out, and he realized he was so deep in his thoughts that he hadn't noticed her getting fussy. Savannah came rushing in—the terry robe covering the T-shirt and yoga pants—and he could tell by her expression, which was *forced pleasant*, that she knew he'd slept in here last night. He also knew she'd say nothing about it or she'd say, *No expectations. We're good. I'll go put on a pot of coffee and take a quick shower, if you don't mind getting these guys changed.*

Interesting that he knew her that well so fast.

"Can I ask you a question?" she said, reaching in Chloe's bassinet and picking her up. She cuddled the baby against her, caressing her hair.

Uh-oh. That had the sound of a real question. Not about coffee or grabbing a shower. "Sure."

She lifted her chin. "Did you sleep in here because coming back would have been too much? Because you needed to keep things separated come morning?"

Savannah always just said it. He admired that. A straight shooter who asked.

"I was in here and got to thinking," he said. "Over-thinking. And I guess I fell asleep. But yes," he admitted. "I'm not in any position to start something, Savannah." He shook his head. "Scratch that, since it's a little late for that. We did start something. We just can't see it through."

"I know," she said. "I mean, I'll be looking to find my Mr. Right, someone who wants love and marriage and to start a family."

"We're okay, then?" he asked stupidly.

"Yes," she said, forcing a bit of cheer in her voice. "I needed last night. You did too. Now it's a new day. We both have things we want to accomplish and that's where our heads should be."

Yes. For him, that meant taking care of the ranch. Figuring out how to work better with his brother. Building his list of arguments about why custody would remain at fifty-fifty when Allison and Ted returned from their honeymoon and she brought all that up again. Having the triplets full-time the next bunch of days, well, with another set of hands, was a big help in solidifying why keeping it equal was important to him.

"I'd like to take a quick shower while you get these dumplings up and changed," she said.

I really do know this woman, he thought, kind of amazed that she'd gotten inside him so quickly. She needed a little space, breathing room, ten minutes to herself now that they'd had this conversation.

"Of course," he said.

She gave him an awkward smile and hurried from the room.

He had no idea how this was going to work, but it had to. He needed Savannah as his nanny. But he also had feelings for her as a woman and it was no use denying them.

Chapter Eight

Well, she'd called that one, Savannah thought as she
ate the last bite of her peanut butter toast at the kitchen
table. At least things were okay between her and Hutch.
They'd talked about it. They'd moved on. New day.

Right, sure. Hutch had left the house forty-five minutes ago, and her heart was still sore. His reaction hurt,
even though she understood where he was coming from,
why he had that wall built up around himself. Sure, it
would be nice if he would look at what was between
them the way she did—the heady rush of feeling excited
about someone, thinking about them, wanting them.
But that wasn't where he was, and she had to honor
and accept it.

Do not take it personally, she told herself. But hadn't
she been taking his rejection of her personally since the
first time he'd snarled at her in kindergarten?

Savannah finished her coffee and smiled at the triplets in their movable playpen, parked against the counter. They were occupied with their teething toys at the moment.

"You know what we need?" she asked them.

No one looked her way.

"A change of scenery," she said. "All in agreement, raise your hand."

No hand rose, but Savannah knew it was a good idea. The weather was decent—midforties and sunny—which for Wyoming in December was another miracle. She was going to dare take the triplets to town.

She grabbed her phone and texted Hutch.

I'd like to do a little holiday shopping in town, show the triplets the Santa hut. Can I take your SUV with the car seats?

He responded within minutes. Sure. Keys are on the peg by the coatrack.

It suddenly occurred to her that she'd never gone *anywhere* with the triplets, not even outside. Getting them into their seats in Hutch's SUV would itself be an undertaking.

This is actually doable right? she texted.

He texted back a smiley face with a cowboy hat. Honestly, it's hit or miss. Bring pacifiers, a baggie of Cheerios, their bottles, baby food and toys. Don't forget spoons. Their baby bag has diapers and wipes and a changing mat.

Huh. Maybe she'd stay home.

Except she could not spend another second in this ranch house without feeling like the walls were closing in on her, thanks to her own thoughts.

I'm game. I could use a change of scenery.

Ugh, why had she texted that? She'd been here, what? Two days?

Any problems, text me. I'll drive right over.

A half hour later, the triplets were changed and bundled into their fleece snowsuits, the baby bag was packed, and she was ready to maneuver the monster triple choo-choo-train stroller out the door and over to the SUV.

I've ridden bucking bulls. I've stared down misogynistic good ole businessmen. I can absolutely take three six-month-olds into town.

She plopped each baby into the stroller, Caleb, then Chloe, then Carson. They truly did look like they were taking a choo-choo-train ride. She wheeled them out the door and down the side ramp to the vehicle. She got each baby in a car seat and buckled with a little fussing, but nothing big. They clearly liked the idea of a change of scenery too. The stroller had a foot press that magically folded and collapsed it, and she lugged the thing into the cargo area.

By the time she got behind the wheel, she felt like she'd had an entire day's outing.

"Okay, cherubs, off we go to town!" She sang an off-key Christmas song as she drove down the long drive toward the service road. "Frosty the Snowman was a something, something soul. With a button nose and a something, something and two eyes made out of coal." She'd have to google the words to Christmas songs and commit them to memory.

So far, so good, she thought, looking in the rearview mirror and wishing she could see the triplets' faces, but their seats were rear-facing. No one was crying or fussing, though; Hutch had mentioned they liked the movement of the car.

Twenty minutes later, she pulled into a spot at the town green, where a line of people with children waited in front of the adorable red wood Santa hut, lots of folks walking around. The town's holiday tree was nearby, festooned with garland and lights. She'd seen the tree at dusk when it was all spectacularly lit up.

She opened the cargo area and lugged out the stroller, using the same pedal to open it. She made sure it was snapped securely into place, set the baby bag in the basket underneath, and then took out the triplets one by one and settled them into the seats.

Huh. She wasn't half bad at this.

"Ooh," she said to them. "Look at the Santa hut! And the Christmas tree. So pretty!"

She dashed her head around to see if they were look-ing. They couldn't be less interested.

"A little shopping, then," she said, turning the stroller toward the shops. The town green was right in the cen-ter of the small but bustling downtown. Better to hit up the general store and gift shop before the lunch crowd descended, especially with this giant contraption to weave around aisles and people with puffy coats and shopping bags.

She smiled and waved at folks she remembered from having grown up here. She was pretty sure she saw a couple of Dawsons—one in a police uniform—going into the diner across the street.

"Savannah Walsh," said a blonde woman with two teenagers flanking her as she approached from the opposite direction. "Mandy Howell Green. We were in school together."

As if Savannah could forget. Mandy was one of the golden girls, cheerleader, prom court, boys falling over themselves to date her. In middle school, Savannah, who'd been about becoming her best self and shooting for the stars, had decided to emulate Mandy's look to up her game in the boy department. She'd raided her sisters' closets for a cute and figure-revealing outfit to wear the next day. But everything she tried made her feel weird and not like herself and she'd gone back to her rodeo clothes, which involved western-style shirts, non-designer jeans and cowboy boots. She'd dressed like most boys did.

"Hi, Mandy, how nice to see you again." Savannah smiled at the two teens, who were glued to their phones.

Mandy made a gushing face at the stroller. "And how nice to see that you finally got yourself married and became a mama! And triplets! IVF? My cousin Patricia did IVF and it took three years, but she has gorgeous twins."

Ugh. She'd never liked Mandy Howell.

"Actually, I'm babysitting," Savannah said, lifting her chin. "I'm the triplets' Christmas-season nanny while I'm in town."

"Oh," Mandy said. Something dawned in her eyes. "Ah, these are Hutch Dawson's children! I've seen the ad. Poor guy." Her gaze went to Savannah's bare left ring finger. "Well, if you have any free time this week and want to be fixed up, my cousin Dylan is recently divorced and could use a date."

"Mom, could we go?" one of the teens whined.

Mandy gave her a "poor you" tight fawning smile and continued down the street.

"Double ugh," Savannah whispered to the triplets. "People like that never change. You just gotta ignore them."

Finally got married and became a mama... IVF... Poor guy.

"Especially when they live to say super beyotchy things like that!" she added.

She shook it off. Mandy Howell could not get her down. Savannah had a plan for the life she wanted. She'd go after it.

But you don't always get what you want, she thought a bit dejectedly as Hutch's gorgeous face floated into her mind. *And when you don't get what you want, you move to plan B.* That was what she would work on now.

That settled, she felt instantly better. Until she spotted someone else she knew who appeared to be surreptitiously crying on the bench at the edge of the town green. Was that Olivia Dawson sniffling and dabbing at her eyes with a tissue?

As Savannah got a bit closer, she saw that it *was* Olivia. Her brown hair in a low ponytail, she wore a cream wool hat with a camel-colored peacoat.

The moment Olivia detected someone coming along the sidewalk, she straightened up and lifted her chin. Had Savannah not noticed her thirty seconds ago, she wouldn't have known the woman was upset in the slightest.

"Olivia?" Savannah called.

Olivia turned and shot up from the bench. "Oh, Savannah. Nice to see you again. I just got out of a volunteer training session at the animal shelter. I'll be walking dogs."

From what Hutch had told her, Olivia was busy with her volunteer commitments in addition to her job at the library. She seemed to be trying hard to fill up her spare time.

Olivia bit her lip. "Sorry about all that arguing last night. Who'd think that two forty-year-olds would be fussier than three babies," she said, putting on a smile as she knelt by the stroller to give each baby a kiss on the head. "Were we awful guests?"

Savannah gave her a commiserating smile. "Not at all. And no worries. Seems like we're all going through some changes."

"Especially the triplets," Olivia said, gazing sweetly at the babies, then stood up. Savannah had the feeling she was a little embarrassed about last night and wanted to get off that subject fast. "Every time I see them, they've changed. I swear they're bigger than they were last night."

"Is that why pushing this thing is such a chore?" Savannah asked with a grin. "I'm so glad I ran into you because I planned to call you today."

"Did I forget something at the ranch house?" Olivia asked, looking confused.

Savannah shook her head. "No, nothing like that. I just thought it would be nice for us to get together."

"I'm okay really, but I appreciate it. Don't mind us. Daniel and I are just…" She burst into tears and covered her face with her hands.

"Hey," Savannah said gently. "Why don't we go to Bear Ridge Coffee and find a table in the back and have some girl talk."

"I'm only accepting because you're leaving town in a week and you'll take my secrets with you," Olivia said in a half-joking, half-serious way.

Savannah could see the relief on the woman's face. Olivia had likely been keeping her marital issues to herself and her husband. Savannah wondered if she had any girlfriends—anyone to talk to. Savannah had a few friends in her home base, Blue Smoke, more like acquaintances, really, but she'd shied away from friendships after learning that her ex-husband had cheated with a friend. She'd probably have worked harder at friends if she didn't have two excellent sisters.

Olivia was looking off in the distance. She seemed to be staring at the Santa hut. Her face all but crumpled. "I just can't believe my baby is eighteen and away at college. That he's not coming home for Christmas. He met someone special and told me over Thanksgiving that he'd be going to meet her family. It'll be the first Christmas I don't see him."

Savannah glanced at the line of families waiting their turn inside with Santa. Lots of moms and little kids.

"I used to take him to see Santa here every year," Olivia said, her eyes misty as they started to walk. "And now, he's not even coming home."

"Aww, I'm sorry," Savannah said, putting a hand on Olivia's arm. "That's gotta be so hard."

Olivia sniffled. "One minute, they're in elementary school, and then…" She trailed off, taking in a resigned breath.

"I guess I'll be starting all that," Savannah said as they stopped at the crosswalk. "I came home to Bear Ridge for the holidays to really figure out what I want and I've realized it's motherhood."

Olivia brightened. "How exciting! Gosh, I was such a young mother. I wonder what it would be like to be a new mom at my age—forty."

"I'll be honest," Savannah said. "Daniel did mention to Hutch that there's been talk in your house about having another child—even before it came out at the dinner."

Olivia's smile faded and her shoulders sagged. "A few days ago, I was so sure that's what I wanted, that a new baby would make everything okay again. And when I talked about it with Daniel, he was so against the idea that I dug in my heels. But…"

"But what?" she prompted gently.

They crossed the street, the coffee shop just down the sidewalk.

"I just don't know what to do with myself, I guess," Olivia said. "My life was so intensely focused on raising a child, and just like that," she added, snapping her fingers, "he's gone and doing his own thing, as Daniel puts it."

"Daniel must miss him too."

Olivia nodded. "I know he does, but it's different somehow. Maybe my whole identity was too wrapped up in being a mom. I don't know. I've been throwing myself into all these volunteer jobs to keep busy. But Daniel just goes happily off to work at the ranch and then comes home, content as can be. Ethan calls or texts every few days with a quick something and Daniel's just hunky-dory with that. And then Daniel disappears onto his computer for the online courses he's taking in ranch this or that. We barely spend any time together. I thought…" She trailed off again with a sigh.

Ah, Savannah was beginning to get the bigger picture. Olivia's life as she'd known it had come to a halt with her son out of the house. And her husband, in his own new role, had learning the ranching business as his new focus. Olivia likely felt unmoored and alone.

"*Do* you want another child?" Savannah asked as they arrived at the coffee shop.

Olivia bit her lip again. "I want…" She looked at the triplets in the stroller. "I do miss those days," she said, kneeling down and running a finger along Caleb's cheek. "So much. But… I don't know."

"I understand. I took some time to really think about what was bothering me, what felt missing. I wasn't sure if it was motherhood. But signing on to be Hutch's temporary nanny made me realize it was. Among other things but—"

"Other things?" Olivia asked, standing up straight again. "I couldn't help but notice you didn't mention wanting a *husband*. Just motherhood."

"I've been in love with the same man since I was five," Savannah admitted, feeling vulnerable and hoping she hadn't made a mistake in telling Hutch's sister-in-law. Not that she'd named names. But it had to be obvious. "But I need to let that go. It's not going to happen."

"Ah, so I wasn't wrong," Olivia said, pulling the door open wide so that Savannah could push the stroller through.

"What do you mean?"

"I was pretty sure from the way you look at Hutch, the way you talk to him, the way you just are with him, that you have feelings for him. But he's the same with you, and the two of you aren't a couple, as far as I know, so I figured I was imagining it. Or that everyone is just a lot sweeter to each other than Daniel and I are." She frowned.

Savannah's mind had hooked on to a couple of things Olivia had just said—not only that it had been obvious she was in love with Hutch but that he might have feelings for her too. But she didn't want to think about everything the two of them had talked about in the middle of the night and this morning. It was a lot easier to focus on Olivia's love life than her own.

Savannah wheeled the huge stroller over to a table at the far end of the shop, which wasn't very crowded, something she was grateful for since she and Olivia could talk without being overheard. "Maybe with Ethan away and not coming for Christmas, this could be a great time for you and Daniel to find your way back to each other. Put the romance back, as they say."

From the look on Olivia's face, Savannah knew she'd

hit on the heart of the issue. Olivia seemed to feel disconnected from her husband just when she needed him most. And she was finding ways—talk of a new baby, throwing herself into volunteer work—to fill the holes in her heart.

Savannah set the parking brake on the stroller and plopped down on a chair, lowering hoods and unzipping snowsuits. "Omigosh. It's another Christmas miracle. Caleb and Carson are both asleep! And look at Chloe. Those eyes are drooping fast."

Olivia smiled. "And she's out. Wow, all three at once. We can definitely continue our girl talk."

Savannah was glad that Olivia was amenable to that; she hadn't been sure if the woman would feel comfortable opening up to her, but they did seem to be hitting it off.

"If you know what you want, I'll go order for us," Olivia said.

"I'd love a mocha with whipped cream. And any type of scone—berry, cinnamon chip. I'm easy."

Olivia smiled. "Be right back."

Savannah glanced around. Two young mothers with babies napping in their strollers were in the front of the shop by the big window. The women looked exhausted but exhilarated at the same time. *I want to be a mother*, Savannah knew with absolute certainty, a warmth spreading in her chest.

Olivia returned to the table with a tray. "I stole your idea and got a mocha too. Plus a white chocolate coconut scone for you and a blondie for me."

"Mmm, treat therapy. Just what the doctor ordered."

Olivia laughed. "Definitely."

They sipped and shared their confections. This was so nice, being in the coffee shop with a new friend.

"So I guess it's just bad timing for you and Hutch?" Olivia asked, and Savannah almost choked on the bite of scone. She'd known they'd be really talking, but she wasn't quite ready for such a *real* question.

But Olivia had gotten it exactly right. "I think that *is* the problem. Maybe if I'd come along a year from now, when Hutch had had time to deal with the divorce, when the triplets were a bit older, when he felt more solid in his life..."

"Love is love," Olivia said. "Bad timing, crazy life—attraction and feelings can't be ignored."

Olivia had *that* right too, and Savannah felt herself brighten a bit. Because Savannah and Hutch had made love.

"Hutch has made it clear he needs to ignore that, though," Savannah said, her heart plummeting. "That he just can't jump into something, no matter how wonderful, with all that's going on in his life. I completely understand. Even if I wish it could be different."

"I've known Hutch a long time, Savannah. I might not know him well because he and Daniel have never been close. But even I can see that man has strong feelings for you."

I thought so too. But maybe he doesn't. Maybe last night really was just about sex for him. "I can't pin my hopes on him suddenly wanting to add a romantic relationship to the mix, though," Savannah said.

Olivia sipped her mocha. "I get that. But he's probably just protecting himself. He was blindsided by the divorce. And he's dealing with a lot. Maybe what he'll discover this week is that what you bring to his life is *good* and not more chaos."

"I don't know about that. He seems to think romance and relationships lead to arguing and breakups instead of happiness and bliss."

Olivia took a sip of her mocha. "I wouldn't give up on him just yet."

"I couldn't if I wanted to," Savannah admitted. "I'm here till Christmas."

That was coming right up.

"You know, Olivia, I saw the way Daniel looked at *you*. Underneath his grumbles, that man is in love with his wife."

Olivia gave a little shrug. "He has a funny way of showing it—"

Another old classmate of Savannah's stopped by the table, bending down to see the triplets.

"Aww, they're so adorbs!" the woman said. "IVF?" she whispered to Savannah.

Jeez, what was it about multiples that made people think they could ask the most personal of questions?

"Oh, wait," the woman continued. "I'm forgetting that *you're* a triplet. I remember your sisters."

Savannah smiled and was about to correct her—not only weren't these babies hers, but she most certainly wasn't a triplet—but before she could, the woman waved at someone, offered a quick "Well, it was nice to see you," and finally left.

"I can't believe people feel free to ask the most intrusive questions. You know how many people asked

Allison about that?" Olivia said. "I remember at her baby shower she actually told one woman off. Then it turned out the woman had been trying for two years to get pregnant and wanted to try IVF so was more asking in that vein—she burst into tears, and instead of opening presents, Allison wound up comforting her. The shower was almost ruined."

Savannah shook her head. Her own choices, which she'd be making soon, would invite the same kinds of curiosity and questions. That was part of life in a very small town; people felt they knew you and could be buttinskies, even if they didn't know you were not a triplet yourself.

"And here I am, about to ask a personal question," Savannah said. "But feel free to tell me to mind my own business."

"Shoot," Olivia said.

"Were you and Allison close? As sisters-in-law?"

"Nah," Olivia said. "Mostly because Hutch and Daniel weren't close. We did all the obligatory events, but she and I never did this." She pointed at the coffees and treats. "I liked her fine, but I'll tell you, I've never forgiven her for what she did to Hutch. Daniel might have issues with the man, but I think Hutch is a wonderful person. I always see him trying. With Daniel. With the triplets."

If only he'd try with me, Savannah thought. "You were saying Daniel has a funny way of showing how he feels?" Savannah asked. "Pokes at Hutch but won't talk to him. Is he the same with you?" Savannah saw that for herself last night.

Olivia sighed and nodded. "He assures himself that he's right and I'm wrong, states his case, and then since he feels better, he goes back to his basement man cave and takes his online classes and studies. That's on top of working long hours for the Dueling Dawsons. We barely spend any time together. Or talk anymore. And when I try to, he says things are good and that he can't understand why I'm complaining. It just shuts me down."

"Well, you don't give up on getting through to that man," Savannah said. She sipped her mocha for caffeine fortification. "One thing that might draw Daniel out is for him and Hutch to get closer. They'll have to really talk, deal with their past. We should push them together socially."

Olivia brightened again. "I think that's a great idea. They do argue a lot, though."

"Maybe we can sow some seeds," Savannah said. "Get them talking about things that might lead to a better understanding instead of the way they stick to their point of view."

Olivia held up her mocha. "Count me in."

Savannah grinned and clinked. "I may not win that man over, but if I can lead him to his brother and a good relationship there, I'll feel good about that." And hey, maybe she'd help along Lincoln Dawson's list of Unfinished Business while she was at it.

As Savannah broke off a piece of her scone, she realized something else. Now that she'd decided to pursue motherhood, she'd do that here. In her hometown. With her family surrounding her.

She noticed her old classmate Aimee Gallagher—

actually, she was Aimee *Dawson* now—at the counter and excused herself for a moment to say hi and make plans to get together soon. Aimee had ended up snowbound in her home during a freak October blizzard with Detective Reed Dawson, a distant cousin of Hutch's, and the newborn baby who'd been left in his care. Now they were married and Aimee's dream of becoming a mother had come true too.

Yours will too, she told herself.

Yup, Savannah had friends here and family. She wouldn't be leaving Bear Ridge. She'd leave Hutch's house, yes. But she was staying in town for good. She'd buy herself a home and settle down.

She sipped her mocha and wondered what that would be like. If she had a baby and ran into Hutch in the park with the triplets by the playground, which was broken into age ranges. Would she be over him by then?

To help move on from Hutch Dawson seventeen years ago, she'd started over somewhere else.

This time, she was coming home for good.

Chapter Nine

All day, a number of stark truths had let Hutch know he was kidding himself about his relationship with Savannah. From the moment he'd left the house this morning, sure in his bones that he'd done the right thing by telling her they had to be platonic, thoughts of her—lovely welcoming thoughts—had been humming in the background. Thoughts about how truly great it was to have her around. How he trusted that his children were safe and happy in her care. How they talked so easily about such personal, fundamental subjects. How their chemistry could not be denied nor their passion for each other.

When he thought of her beautiful face, their night together, how they simply meshed, goose bumps had trailed up and down his spine, along his forearms and the nape of his neck. He'd liked walking and riding around the ranch with those goose bumps accompanying him.

You don't feel so alone, he'd realized with a start.

And when he'd come home a half hour ago, anticipation of seeing her, being with her, talking to her, telling her a funny story about a bull, sharing in caring for the triplets with her, he'd realized his feelings for her were too far gone to ignore. Last night and early this morning, he'd planned to try to do just that, but now, as he watched her lift Carson from his high chair to burp him after dinner, her fuzzy green sweater lifting to reveal a creamy expanse of skin, he knew there was no ignoring what this woman was coming to mean to him.

Scary but true.

"I ran into Olivia today at the town green," she said, putting Carson in the playpen and picking up Caleb for his burp.

Hutch grabbed a burp cloth and settled Chloe against his shoulder, giving her back a few good pats. "Oh yeah? She seem okay?"

"Not at first. But we took the triplets to the coffee shop, where they immediately conked out, and we had such a good talk. I really like her, Hutch."

"So did the trio scare her off from the idea of having another baby?" he asked.

"It seems to me that what she *really* wants is to reconnect with her husband. Now that they're empty nesters and Daniel is so consumed with the ranch and his on-line classes, she's been trying to fill herself up, fill the void, but I think she's realized it's her relationship with Daniel that needs a little revitalizing."

"Ah, that makes sense. And knowing Daniel, whenever she tries to talk to him about how she feels, he's dismissive and says everything is fine and goes back to his computer." They both got good burps from the babies held and put them beside Carson.

"Exactly. I might be poking my nose where it doesn't belong, but I'm hoping we can help somehow. I'm just not sure how." She seemed to be really thinking about it.

"Same here." Before he could stop himself, he found words forming and coming out of his mouth. He knew all about feeling disconnected from a spouse. "My ex-wife told me that one of the reasons she felt justified in breaking up our marriage was because I didn't even know she'd been carrying on an emotional affair for months with another man. 'That's how disconnected we were,' she said. I thought it was a crappy thing to say to me, but I suppose if I looked at it from her point of view, she was right. I didn't notice because I *wasn't* really all that engaged with her—except when it came to the pregnancy."

"You know, Hutch, this might sound a little Dr. Phil-ish, but you've really put in the work. I mean, in looking at what went wrong and all that. I think that's really commendable. I also think it's why you're not bitter and are able to have an amicable relationship with Allison."

"I just thought about it a lot," he said. "I'm not sure that counts as working on it."

She smiled. "It does count. Now, me, on the other hand, I was bitter for a long time. After I found out my ex-husband was cheating—and with a friend—I really closed up. I didn't trust anyone for a long time. Maybe

I still don't. It's why I appreciate how honest you were with me this morning, Hutch."

What if I realized how stupid I was being, though? he thought. *What if I realized how lucky I am to have you in my life?*

"You're just so easy to talk to," he said. "I don't talk about this kind of thing with anyone. Ever. Until you came along."

She smiled. "I feel the same way. Like I can tell you anything."

He reached for her hand, the contact with her skin as usual sending good chills along the nape of his neck. She pulled away quickly, and he realized she was protecting herself. He knew right then that he had to be careful with her feelings *and* voicing his every thought. He'd told her they had to be platonic, that he wasn't anywhere close to ready, which was true. But here he was, willing, *needing* to jump in anyway. He wanted to take her into his arms and just hold her.

Should he hold off on making any pronouncements? Give it a day or two? They didn't have all that much time, though. Christmas was in a week. She'd be leaving his house, his guest room and very likely his life if he didn't fix what he'd mangled this morning. She wanted to start her own family—which meant looking into all the options for doing so. Like falling for someone else. There were plenty of single men in Bear Ridge. And plenty of dating apps. He scowled at the thought of her kissing anyone but him.

Just as he moved closer to her, Carson batted Caleb on the arm, and Caleb let out a shriek and started bawling.

"Now listen here, little guy," he said to Carson, as Savannah picked up Caleb to soothe his tears. "No hitting. Got it, bub?"

Hutch got a "ba" in response. Caleb was reaching down toward the playpen, so Savannah put him back. Carson waved around a rattle toy, and Caleb giggled. Chloe ignored them both, biting on her little chew book.

Savannah seemed grateful for the interruption. She'd used the opportunity to move a few feet away from him and his hand squeezes. "I've been thinking about something ever since Olivia and I parted ways this morning. I might not know how to bring her and her husband closer together, but I do have an idea for bringing you and Daniel closer. And that may in turn make for a warmer, fuzzier Daniel—and husband."

"Yeah, how?"

"You want to take care of your father's Unfinished Business list before Christmas. Maybe if you two work together on the first item, finding the smoking gun that will put the past to rest for Ernest and Harlan Dawson, the second item—you and Daniel making peace—will take care of itself."

Huh. She had a point. And he was glad she'd brought up the list; fulfilling his father's wishes was important to Hutch and doing so came with a deadline. He'd had so much going on that the list had kept moving farther and farther down in priority.

"And it *is* Christmastime," she said. "That's gotta be working its own magic on Daniel. Or it'll help, anyway."

"What would I do without you?" he asked—about to close the distance between them.

Then he found himself freezing. What he'd just said might be taking his feelings a bit too far. Farther than he was ready for.

She was staring at him, head slightly tilted.

"You're a gift," he added before he could snatch it back from his mouth. "That's what you feel like to me. A gift."

A small gasp escaped her pink lips. Savannah wasn't easy to surprise, but he knew he'd just accomplished that.

He moved closer to her. "I know what I said this morning. I wish I could stand by it. Because I *am* worried about stretching myself too thin and then failing everyone and everything important to me. You, the triplets, the ranch. Even Daniel."

"But?" she whispered, taking a step closer herself.

"But there's just something very special here. Too special to pretend otherwise."

"I completely agree," she said softly, her arms sliding up around his neck. "Maybe we just need to take it day by day. No rushing. No labels. Just...*feeling*. We'll go with what we're feeling. If it's too much and you need space, take it. Same for me. I've never been scared of anything but you, Hutch Dawson."

"Oh yeah? So my mother was right? You had a big crush on me?"

This time she gasped loudly. "What? Your mother told you I had a crush on you?"

He nodded, the memory making him smile. "After I beat you at the 4-H fair competition our junior year. You were so furious and so happy for me at the same time. I couldn't understand it. I remember leaning over to my mom and saying, 'I'll never understand that girl.' And she said, 'Oh, I think I understand her perfectly. She has a huge crush on you.' I remember shaking my head and saying, 'No way. Savannah Walsh hates my guts.' And my mother chuckled and said, 'Nope. Quite the opposite.'"

"Your mother was right," she said. "I had a whopper of a crush. For a long, long time."

"Why didn't you ever say anything?" he asked.

"Oh, right. Like I could have told you. You wouldn't have gone for me then."

He cupped a hand to her soft cheek, her red hair falling down around it. "Actually, that time you tried to comfort me when my father screamed his head off at me after the rodeo competition? I saw you in that moment, Savannah. Really saw you. I wanted to just grab you into a hug. But I was so shocked by how I felt and so stung by how my father had acted that I just huffed off."

She touched a hand to her heart, and he knew he'd touched her. "And then we had that awkward dance at the prom," she said, swaying her sexy hips.

He swayed with her. "Very awkward. We were both awkward."

"Yup. I was so scared of how I felt about you. And maybe you were too."

He nodded. "Fast-forward seventeen years later. Little has changed." He laughed. "That's sad."

She smiled at that. "Except we made love. And now we're sort of dancing in your kitchen, no awkwardness this time around, with the triplets as witnesses that it's all really happening."

He leaned down and kissed her.

"I have big plans for you after we get these three to bed."

"Does it involve getting *us* to bed, I hope?"

"Oh, yes, it does."

She smiled and he pulled her close, resting his head atop hers. How could he ever have thought he could ignore *this*?

A cry woke Savannah. She slowly opened her eyes to find Hutch doing the same. They faced each other in his bed, barely an inch apart, and though she felt unsure of how he'd react in the morning, she couldn't help but smile.

Last night had been something.

First, he'd said he didn't know what he'd do without her.

Then he'd called her a gift.

Then he'd said he couldn't ignore how he felt about her after all.

Then they'd made amazing love. Twice. Once last night, and once in the middle of the night, after they'd both tended to Chloe, who'd woken up just after 3:00 a.m. with a little gas. A few "bike" pumps of her little legs later, she was back in her bassinet, and they were back in his bed.

She'd actually given herself a little pinch to make sure this wasn't all a dream.

Right now, Hutch was not looking at her with horror. He was not reaching for his clothes and racing from the room. He was smiling too, his gaze soft and tender on her.

Her heart almost burst with happiness.

"Why does five fifteen come so fast?" he asked, pulling her against him. "It's so warm and comfortable under this blanket and still dark out, and I can think of more enticing things to do than change diapers before the crack of dawn."

She laughed. "Right?"

Chloe cried out again. Then Carson did. And when Caleb added to the fussing, they kissed each other and flung off the comforter.

"I'll go," she said. "Hard as it is to leave this bed. I'll meet you downstairs for coffee and bagels."

"You sure?"

"Yup. I've got it," she said, every cell in her body tingling.

She enjoyed the eyeful of him walking naked to the en suite bathroom. She grabbed her yoga pants and T-shirt and slid them on, then went into the nursery and got the triplets out of their bassinets and into the playpen. She picked them up one by one for fresh diapers and cornstarch and cuddles. Once they were all in the playpen again, she stopped by the guest bath to wash her face and brush her teeth, and when she looked at herself in the mirror, she had to admit her eyes were bright, her skin was positively glowing and she looked radiant. She looked *happy*.

"Oh, my dears," she whispered to the triplets, grabbing hold of the push bar on the playpen and wheeling them down the hall and into the kitchen. "Today is going to be a good day."

"Ba!" Carson said. "Ba-ba!"

Ma-ma, she mentally rhymed, feeling her cheeks flame. She bit her lip, wondering just where this new beginning with Hutch might go. Might she find herself stepmama to these precious babies? That would make her very happy. Perhaps she and Hutch would have a baby of their own. Of course, Hutch could not possibly want another child so fast, and that was fine.

Oh, Lordie, she was getting way ahead of herself. She and Hutch were not getting married. She was not having his baby. They were dating. Testing the waters. That was all. And that was as it should be. For both of them.

She smiled with anticipation and put each triplet into a high chair, then set a handful of Cheerios on the trays.

Twenty minutes later, Hutch came in looking absolutely gorgeous, his dark hair damp, his blue eyes happy and twinkling like hers had been in the mirror. She'd put the bagels in the toaster oven when she heard the shower stop running, and now it pinged. He came up behind her as she was about to grab two plates and wrapped his arms around her.

"I missed you when I was in the shower," he said.

Oh, Hutch, you're going to make me cry.

"I missed you too," she said, turning around and kissing him. "One of these days, maybe we'll be able to coordinate the two of us in the shower."

"I'd like that very much. Probably will have to be a night shower with a baby monitor on the sink counter to ruin the moment at any second."

Savannah laughed. Even two minutes in the shower with Hutch sounded very good to her. "Butter or cream cheese?" she asked, upping a thumb toward the counter where the bagels were awaiting.

"I wish I could have you again," he said.

Savannah grinned. "Me too. That's what tonight is for."

"Sounds good to me. Anticipation. All day. That'll get me through this morning's barn chores with Daniel. And I'll have cream cheese." He moved to each triplet and kissed their heads. "Wow, you already fed them?" he asked, eyeing their empty food jars on the table.

"And burped them," she said.

"I did say you were a gift. To me *and* them. You're five times faster and better at everything concerning caring for them than I am."

"Hey, you're the one who taught me everything I know about triplet rearing," she reminded him. "So don't sell yourself short, mister."

His eyes lit up and she could see how touched he was—and that he'd realized it was true. He *had* taught her everything she knew about caring for the babies. He'd always been a better father than he'd given himself credit for.

He smiled and pulled her into a hug. "How about I take you out to dinner tonight. Just the two of us. I can ask Olivia if she'd like to babysit."

"Oooh, I like the sounds of that. And I'm sure Olivia would love to."

"We'll keep it quick and simple," he said. "The brick oven pizza place? Or the Mexican café? But when my ex is back, I'll take you out for a real night on the town. That's a promise."

"I'll hold you to it," she said and kissed him.

She couldn't be happier right now.

When Carson started fussing, Hutch put on his goofy glasses and played a round of peekaboo.

God, she loved this man. Loved, loved, loved.

She froze again at the stark truth. Then she thought, oh, what the heck. She did love him. He wasn't denying his feelings, so she wouldn't deny hers. Especially to herself.

She practically floated to the refrigerator, aware of how at home she felt here. And how maybe her sisters had been right when they'd said that Savannah could end up *never* leaving. Her heart did a set of little flips at the thought.

Chloe let out a loud sound, happy at least, and Savannah stopped her daydreaming and set out the cream cheese and knives while Hutch poured the coffee and put the bagels on plates with a bowl of red grapes.

They sat and ate and told the triplets what they planned to do that day.

This is what family life is like, she thought. *And I want in.*

Chapter Ten

"Savannah must really hate her job," Daniel said as nonchalantly as if he were talking about the weather.

Hutch glanced up from the guest chair in the barn office. Daniel sat behind the desk; he'd insisted on having an office in the main barn, heated and with a small coffee station, since Hutch had his in the house and Daniel didn't want to share that. The two of them had started the morning in the barn for chores, then had ridden out on the range to move the cattle with the help of one of their cowboys who was part-time today. Hutch and Daniel had been in here for the past hour, going over inventory.

Now that they were almost done, Hutch had one more thing for the agenda—his father's file labeled Family Feud, which apparently had been passed down from generation to generation. Christmas *was* coming and Hutch did want to cross off the first thing on his father's list of Unfinished Business. Especially since the second seemed impossible to achieve, no matter how optimistic Savannah seemed about it.

"Savannah does not hate her job," Hutch said. "In fact, she seems to love it. So much that she's decided to have a child."

He wondered if she'd be okay with holding off on that. With three six-month-olds, he wasn't about to have a fourth baby anytime soon. One day, yes. But not in the near future.

Oh, heck. Three, four, was there really a difference? He smiled at the thought of a red-haired baby in his and Savannah's future. Perhaps next year, when the triplets were a year and a half, he and Savannah would add that little ginger to the family. Surely they made quadruplet strollers.

So now he envisioned a future for them? And a baby?

Okay, he must be falling hard for this woman, because he couldn't possibly be thinking along these lines. But there they were, flying all about his head and heart.

"All I know," Daniel said, "is that ever since Olivia ran into Savannah in town yesterday and they went for coffee and 'had a great chat,' my wife has not said one word about having another baby. After a few weeks of Olivia talking about little else. So Savannah must have said something to turn her off the idea. I owe your nanny big."

Hutch mentally rolled his eyes. As usual, Daniel was off the mark, only seeing things from his perspective. But maybe Savannah had been right about the possibility that working on number one of their father's Unfinished Business list would help with number two—stopping *their* long-running feud. Which would make for a kinder, gentler Daniel, who would then be a better husband. *Everyone* would be happier. Especially at Christmas.

"Anyway," Hutch said, holding up the legal file he'd brought from his father's desk drawer in the home office. "I think we should work on Dad's list."

Daniel scowled. "We don't have time for that."

Interesting that his brother knew exactly what Hutch was referring to. Daniel could have said *What list?*, which would be characteristic. That told Hutch that the list was in the back of his brother's mind too. Maybe *both* items.

"Unfinished business—with a Christmas deadline," Hutch said. "We should *make* time. Let's split up the file and see if we can find anything about the original feud that would help us get to the bottom of it."

"We know everything there is to know. The brothers wanted to marry the same woman. She couldn't decide between them. The day she finally planned to tell them her choice, she died after her horse threw her. The end. Nothing much to it."

"A lot much to it," Hutch said. "If we can find out more about why things went so south *after* she was gone, after Ernest and Harlan married and had children, we could bring them peace—and fulfill Dad's first wish."

"It's not a wish. It's just a thing he meant to do."

"By *Christmas*. That makes it a wish. And because he died before he could do it himself, it's a dying wish."

"Oh, please," Daniel said.

"Can you just take half the file?" Hutch asked.

"I don't have time for this," Daniel grumbled, eyeing the file as if it were a dirty diaper.

"Just go through some of it," Hutch repeated, taking out half for himself and handing Daniel the rest of the file. "Poke through it. Look for anything that jumps out. Personal letters, anything mentioning Helene. Or Ernest's and Harlan's wives and children."

Daniel let out a resigned sigh. "The feud ended with Lincoln Dawson. He was an only child. Though I suppose he did duel with you and me and everyone he came into contact with."

Except my mother, Hutch thought. He'd rarely heard them argue about anything.

"What about us?" Hutch said. "We seem to be keeping it alive and well."

Daniel shot him a glance, his expression changing for just a moment. Then Daniel the Scrooge was back. "Fine," he snapped, taking the file and opening it. He flipped through some papers. "Nope, don't see anything." He closed the file and dropped it on the desk.

"Gee, thanks," Hutch said. He grabbed the file and shoved his half into it and stood.

He was sick of Daniel Dawson. Their feud would end by Christmas? In less than a week? Right. *Sorry, Dad. There doesn't seem to be enough Christmas miracles for that one.*

As he was about to leave, he heard Daniel groan.

"Something wrong?" Hutch asked.

"Olivia just texted me that we're babysitting the triplets tonight. How'd you rope her into that? We *just* saw them."

"I want to take Savannah out for a quick dinner as a thanks for all she's done for me and your niece and nephews. We won't be more than a couple of hours."

Daniel tilted his head. "You and Savannah are dating, or is it not like that?"

"It's like that," Hutch said, finding himself smiling.

"Wow. Good for you," Daniel said—earnestly. "Olivia likes Savannah. And it was very obvious the triplets do too."

Was this Daniel actually showing support? Being on Hutch's side? Would wonders never cease...

Daniel took a sip of his coffee. "And if Olivia does still have any of that baby fever, surely having to babysit the triplets with just the two of us will knock any remnants right out of her."

Hutch shook his head on a smile. He should have figured.

They'd decided on Margarita's Mexican Café, which was a fun, colorful restaurant on Main Street, dimly lit enough to be romantic, but fast-moving enough that Hutch knew they'd be in and out within an hour. Which was perfect for tonight. This date was meant to be a little something to mark their new beginning and to thank Savannah for being there for him and for the triplets. But when his ex was back and he had a night to devote to Savannah, he'd take her out for a very special evening. As for tonight, after dinner they could stroll around and admire the Christmas lights on all the shops and the holiday tree on the town green.

He and Savannah had a table for two by a window decorated with twinkling white lights. He could barely take his eyes off her long enough to look at the menus they'd been given. She wore a long sparkly silver sweater and black leggings with her sexy knee-length boots. Her silky red hair was loose past her shoulders, her brown eyes twinkling in the candlelight, and she looked so beautiful that sometimes he found himself staring. Googly-eyed and moony-eyed over Savannah Walsh from middle school. He smiled at how surprising life could be.

Hadn't he just this morning been imagining a little ginger baby joining the family?

What did it mean that he *could* imagine it—another baby on top of triplets?

It means your feelings for this woman go deeper than you may realize. Just another Christmas miracle. Maybe the good man above had decided Hutch had had enough heaped on his head and deserved a little extra happiness.

"I've never been here," Savannah said, swiping a tortilla chip in the dish of salsa between them as she scanned the menu. "My sisters rave about it."

"I come here for lunch as often as I can. I love their enchiladas. And the quesadillas. And the burritos."

Savannah laughed. "Not the tacos?"

"Actually, I'm trying to decide between the carne asada soft tacos or the enchiladas. Maybe enchiladas suizas."

"I'm getting the special burrito."

"Excellent idea," he said, closing his menu. He picked up his water glass. "To us," he said. "To you. To the triplets. To Olivia and Daniel for babysitting."

Savannah grinned. "I'll drink to all of that." She clinked.

The waiter came over and they ordered, and while they awaited their entrées, they talked and laughed and munched on the tortilla chips. The waiter was back in no time with their steaming dishes, and they both dug in, sharing from each other's plates. Hutch had stolen a kiss across the table, almost getting suizas sauce all over his shirt.

Just as the waiter came over to clear the table, Hutch's phone rang. He checked the screen—Olivia's number. Uh-oh. He held up a finger to the waiter, who moved on to another table, and answered.

"Hey, Olivia," Hutch said. "Don't tell me my brother is complaining up a storm and wants us to come home immediately." *Please no*, he thought, glancing at Savannah, who was looking at him curiously.

"Hutch, actually, Chloe is burning up with fever," Olivia said, sounding like she was trying to control how frantic she was. "Her temperature has been a hundred and four for the past hour and baby fever reducer hasn't helped. I just got off the phone with her pediatrician and she said to bring her to the ER at the Bear Ridge Clinic. Daniel and I are about to load the triplets in your SUV. You might even beat us there since you're already in town."

Hutch's stomach dropped. Chloe was sick? Burning up with fever?

And he'd been here. On a date. Eating enchiladas. Fantasizing again about having a baby with Savannah. Getting all soft-hearted about a tiny ginger Dawson.

He'd been doing all that—instead of being with his children. His sick child.

He felt sick.

This time, his nanny hadn't even been with Chloe because she was here with him. On that date. The sitter—albeit his sister-in-law—had called the doctor. The *sitter* was taking Chloe to the ER. If no-nonsense Mrs. Philpot hadn't quit on him days ago, it might have been her taking care of Chloe. A practical stranger to whom Chloe was just a job. That had his gut aching.

Yes, Olivia was family and cared about his daughter. He was grateful for that. But still.

Hutch should have been there.

Hutch should be rushing her to the ER.

This was all wrong. "We'll head over right now."

"See you soon," Olivia said.

Soon. Like that was good enough. He was Chloe's father. He was responsible for her. Particularly this week when his ex was away. He was Chloe's sole parent right now. And he *hadn't* been there for her.

He pocketed his phone and signaled the waiter for the bill, his heart thrumming.

"What's wrong?" Savannah asked, concern in her eyes.

"That was Olivia. Chloe's burning up with fever. They're taking her to the Bear Ridge Clinic's ER." His stomach was twisting. "We have to go."

"Of course," she said.

The waiter came with the bill and Hutch handed over enough to cover it and a tip, then stood. Savannah did too. They rushed out to her SUV, which they'd taken instead of his with the three car seats in the back, just in case of emergency.

At least he'd gotten *that* right.

Please let her be okay, he prayed heavenward toward the bright stars in the night sky. *Please.*

Chapter Eleven

Olivia was holding Chloe in her arms, gently rubbing her back, when Savannah and Hutch arrived at the clinic's ER. Daniel was sitting with the stroller, Caleb and Carson fast asleep.

"No one's seen her yet?" Hutch barked, taking his baby daughter from Olivia and looking toward the reception desk. Though maybe he should be glad he'd gotten here in time. He would have hated rushing into the exam room. *Sorry, Doctor, but I was on a date with my daughter's nanny and that's why I'm late.* His stomach twisted again.

"They said it wouldn't be too long," Olivia said.

Without even touching her forehead, Hutch could feel how hot Chloe was. She was a tiny baby with a high fever. Why wasn't she being called in? There were two others in the waiting room, a middle-aged couple. At least the place wasn't packed. Hutch went up to the reception desk. "I'm worried about my baby daughter," he told the woman sitting behind the Plexiglas shield. "Will it be much longer?"

"Both ER doctors are with patients right now," the woman said. "It shouldn't be more than fifteen minutes until a nurse can come get the baby settled in a room. Hang tight, okay? In the meantime, please fill out this paperwork." She handed Hutch a clipboard with a pen dangling from a little cord.

Hutch shot Olivia, Daniel and Savannah a frustrated glance.

Savannah rushed over. "Here, let me hold her while you fill that out," she said.

He didn't want to hand his daughter over. He wanted to hold her, protect her, relieve her fever. But he had to fill out the damned paperwork.

He let Savannah take Chloe and dropped down on a chair with the clipboard, writing so fast that no one would be able to read his chicken scratch.

"Does she still feel as hot?" Olivia asked Savannah.

He glanced up. Savannah nodded and paced the room, gently rocking Chloe in her arms.

"One minute she was fine," Olivia said, "and the next Chloe was fussing. I was reading the triplets a story while they were in their swings when I noticed her face seemed a bit red, and she started crying, and nothing I did could soothe her. When I went to pick her up, it was such a shock how hot she was."

High fevers could be dangerous.

I should have been there. Instead I was on a date.
A damned date.

Hutch shook his head at himself, ashamed. Disappointed. What the hell was wrong with him? First he hired a full-time live-in nanny for ten days. Then he went on a date with that nanny? His priorities weren't where they should be.

He was furious at himself.

A few minutes later, a door opened and a nurse came out. "Chloe Dawson?" she called, her gaze going to the baby in Savannah's arms.

"Oh, thank God," Hutch said, hurrying over to the reception desk to give back the paperwork.

"Okay, great, both mom and dad are here," the nurse said. "Right this way," she added to Savannah, gesturing toward the doorway.

"She's not her mother," Hutch said to the nurse. "I'm her father. I've got this," he added to Savannah, barely looking at her as he took Chloe from her arms.

The nurse looked embarrassed. "Oh, sorry about that. Well, right this way, Dad," she added, walking down the corridor.

Hutch followed, cuddling Chloe against him, the door closing behind him.

Savannah felt her cheeks flame as hot as the baby had been against her. What the hell? She knew Hutch was worried, but what was that all about?

The door had practically closed in her face. Savannah on one side, Hutch and Chloe on the other. He'd been so quiet on the ride from the restaurant to the clinic, his expression strained as she'd driven as fast as she could without risking being stopped by a cop. She'd tried to say something comforting, that she was sure Chloe would be just fine, but he hadn't responded.

Olivia popped up and came over to her. "He's just scared," she said. "Don't take anything personally when it comes to a scared parent."

"She's right," Daniel said from his seat by the stroller. "When Ethan was a baby and had a sky-high fever, Olivia told me to get the thermometer from the bathroom and I couldn't find it. Man, did she let me have it. I felt like a terrible father, but I knew it was the fear yelling at me, not Olivia."

Olivia went back over to the chairs and sat beside her husband, touching his arm. "I remember that. I had to find the thermometer myself with sick Ethan in my arms." She shook her head with a little smile. "I was so furious I told you that some people weren't cut out for parenthood. I cringe at how mean I could be in those times. I knew you loved Ethan as much as I did."

Daniel patted her hand. "It's one spouse's job to get mad and the other's job to keep the peace. Whose job it is shifts, depending on the situation."

Olivia smiled and squeezed her husband's hand. "That's true." She looked up at Savannah, who'd moved over by a window and was staring out at nothing in particular. "Hey, you okay? Hutch didn't mean it like it sounded."

He did if Olivia and Daniel had taken it the same way Savannah had.

Savannah *wasn't* the mother. She was the nanny. She

MELISSA SENATE   173

wasn't family. When it came right down to it, she was
an outsider. And she'd been left outside.

No, they're right, she told herself as chills ran up her
spine. *He's just scared. Bite and bark is all it was.*

Then why had it cut her to the core?

For the next half hour, she went back and forth like
that. Finally the door opened and Hutch came out, Chloe
in his arms. She looked less red, but definitely very tired.

Savannah hurried over to them, Olivia and Daniel
behind her with the stroller. "What did the doctor say?"

"Chloe's okay," Hutch said. "Dr. Guzman says that
babies can spike high fevers without being sick, and
since she's not showing any other symptoms, it's possible she won't develop any and that it might not be a
virus. She said I should just keep an eye on her and
limit activities."

Savannah's shoulders sagged with relief. "I'm so glad."

"Me too," he said. "I'm sorry for how I acted before,"
he added, his expression contrite. He paused, then whispered, "But we should talk at the house."

Savannah's shoulders went right back to hunched.

Hutch watched Chloe sleep in her baby swing in the
living room. It was set to gently rock and played a soft
lullaby. Her brothers were beside her, wide-awake and
each chewing on a toy. He was keeping an eye on changes
in their fussiness or complexion, but so far, all three
were fine. Chloe's fever had come down, and she seemed
comfortable.

Hutch was anything but.

Savannah sat on the sofa, folding a load of the triplets'

laundry. She'd been quiet since they'd gotten back to the ranch. He'd hovered over Chloe and she'd fed the boys. She'd barely glanced at him in an hour.

"Am I fired?" she blurted out, standing up and facing him, blue-and-yellow-striped fleece pj's in her hand. "Just tell me. And by fired I mean from all aspects of your life."

He stood up too. His head felt both empty and crammed at the same time.

"You said we needed to talk, Hutch. That always means something serious is coming. It's been an hour and I need to hear it."

"I meant what I said about you being a gift." He moved over to the chair across from the sofa and sat down. She sat back down on the sofa. She looked worried and miserable, and he hated himself for putting that on her face.

"But?" she prompted.

"But I'm not the father I want to be. Need to be. What the hell was I doing out on a date when I already have full-time live-in childcare? I spend far too much time away from my children, Savannah. I work too many hours when I have three babies depending on me. This whole time I've had them to myself I was completely reliant on childcare when *I* should have been the childcare."

"You do have to work, though, Hutch. Millions of parents have to work."

"Right," he said. "But I knew my ex was leaving for ten days. I should have made arrangements to take that time off from the ranch. I could have hired someone to cover for me. I should have relished the chance to have the triplets to myself for over a week—especially leading up to Christmas."

Savannah leaned forward. "You're being too hard on yourself. Your father died three months ago and left the ranch to you and your brother. Daniel unexpectedly came on board. It wasn't as simple as taking time off."

"I need to be harder on myself, actually," he said, the ache in his gut worsening. "I need to make changes. I know now why I didn't before. And it kills me."

She tilted her head. "Why?"

"Because I was too damned scared to be alone with them for longer than fifteen minutes. Scared to do something wrong. Here I've been worked up about my ex asking for more than equal custody time when I can't even handle my fifty percent." He stood up and paced to the sliding glass door, looking out. "And us. I prioritized my love life instead of being home with my children. After a whole day away from them at work. I needed to be away from them another two hours? To have enchiladas? That's *wrong*."

He was aware of Savannah getting up and coming over to him. She pressed herself against his back and wrapped her arms around him. It felt so good. And again: so *wrong*.

He turned around and stepped back. "I thought I could do this, Savannah. Have everything. But I'm stretched too thin. You want to know what I was thinking when I had no idea that Chloe was burning up with fever?"

"What?" she asked, and he could tell she was bracing herself.

"I was thinking—for the second time today—about

having a red-haired baby. That's what a craptastic father I am. I can't handle the ones I have, but I'm jumping into a new relationship with a woman who wants a baby and envisioning a child with her? What the hell is wrong with me?"

Savannah stepped back as if he'd slapped her. "Hutch, listen to me. *Please.* I get that you're disappointed in yourself. Your baby got sick—it happens. No one is just one thing. You're a father, but you're also a rancher, a foreman, a brother, a cousin, a man—and yes, *my* man."

He shook his head. "Everything I said to you this morning, I meant. I thought I could do this and I can't. I'm sorry." He turned away for a moment. "I've got just days until my ex comes back. I'm going to take that time off from the ranch and focus on my children full-time. I won't need a nanny."

Her eyes misted with tears, and he felt as though someone had punched him hard in the stomach.

He looked directly at her and reached for her hand. "You know what you want, Savannah. I know what I want. Right now, those two things aren't meeting." He'd tried to say it gently. But it had to be said. He had to let her go. She had to let him go.

She opened her mouth to say something, then clamped it shut. "I'll go pack." She hurried away.

He hung his head. This was supposed to fix things, fix where he'd messed up with his priorities. But he could add hurting Savannah to the list of things he'd gotten very wrong.

Chapter Twelve

Savannah had let herself cry for a good hour in her SUV while parked on a side street in town before she drove to her sister Morgan's house, her suitcase and duffel in the trunk. Morgan had called Cheyenne, and they'd both run out when Savannah had arrived in the driveway, helping their red-eyed, tear-streaked sister into the house and onto the sofa with a chenille throw and a cup of honey-lavender tea and a box of tissues. She'd told them everything, this time not leaving out a single detail.

"I'm so sorry," Morgan said, rubbing Savannah's shoulder. "And I'm sorry for Hutch. The man doesn't realize that you make his life easier, not harder—and I'm not just referring to you being his nanny."

"I know. It's hard to be mad at him because his life is just so hectic right now. I knew what I was stepping into. And I did it anyway."

Cheyenne squeezed her hand. "I get it. The man told you he was daydreaming about the ginger baby you two would have. If he actually said that aloud, imagine what goes on in his head in private, Savannah. It's clear he has serious feelings for you."

Her knees had wobbled when he'd said that. She thought, in that moment, that it meant he had really fallen for her, that he could see a future with her. But he was so torn up about his priorities, which she did understand, that he was resolute about ending things between them. This was the second time he'd told her he *couldn't do this.* "Feelings he is set on ignoring," Savannah said, taking a sip of her tea.

Morgan raised an eyebrow. "I don't know how possible that'll be. I mean, it doesn't work that way."

"It'll have to for me, I guess," Savannah said. "If he's telling me there's no us, no future, at least for now, I need to respect that and make my own plans. Because he was right when he said that I know what I want. I want a baby. And yes, a husband. I want love. I want the whole happily-ever-after forever thing. I thought it didn't exist, but it clearly does."

"You could give it time," Morgan said gently. "Give Hutch time, I mean."

Savannah bit her lip. "I don't know. To put my life on hold for something that isn't a sure thing when I don't have time on my side…"

Part of Savannah wanted to wait. But part of her had a sinking feeling that Hutch Dawson would be closed to her, closed to anyone, for a long time. He wanted to be a good dad and that would now be his focus. He'd

work on how to balance being the father of baby triplets with running a working ranch. Those were his priorities and rightfully so.

Not his love life.

Her heart ached deep in her chest, and to ward off the
fresh round of tears, she took a long sip of her herbal tea,
which was soothing.

"Did I mention my husband's lawyer is long-divorced,
no kids?" Morgan said. "He's a good guy. And that he
casually let slip to Evan at the firm holiday party last
week that he wants children?"

"Ooh," Cheyenne said. "He sounds promising, Savannah. Even just to meet someone so you know there
are men out there who might pique your interest."

"Good-looking too." Morgan grabbed her phone and
swiped, stopping on a blond man in his forties with
round Harry Potter glasses and kind pale brown eyes.
He had nice teeth and a dimple in his cheek. "His name
is Andrew."

Savannah tried to imagine sitting across from another man at a candlelit table like she had just hours ago.

But maybe saying *yes* would help. To put herself out
there. To try. To see.

"You know what? Set me up," Savannah said. "I could
cry for the next few days, bawl my eyes out on Christmas and then plan on a New Year's Eve on the sofa with
a quart of ice cream and rom-coms, or I can be proactive. I've always been proactive."

"That's my girl," Morgan said.

"And you know," Cheyenne added, "if you want to
look into all options regarding motherhood, you could

make an appointment with a reproductive clinic and with an adoption agency."

Savannah felt herself brighten a bit. "I will absolutely do that. I want to know all the pathways to motherhood. Maybe trying to find love first isn't necessarily the answer."

Except her time with Hutch and the triplets had shown her just how much she wanted to share in the trials and tribulations of parenthood with her life's partner, her love by her side.

Morgan picked up her phone again and was texting away. She waited a moment, and it pinged. She glanced up at Savannah. "Free for a blind date the day after tomorrow at 1:00 p.m. for lunch?"

Savannah inwardly sighed. This wasn't exactly what she wanted. No, that was in a ranch house twenty minutes away from here. But she couldn't have that. "Yes," she said.

Morgan smiled. "One p.m. at the brick oven pizza place on Main Street. He said he'll be wearing a red-and-green-striped tie with tiny Santas on it."

"I already like him," Savannah said, trying for a smile.

But she was about as ready to date as Hutch was. She had no idea if this was the right thing to do—to steam-roll ahead as if her heart wasn't smashed to bits. As if anyone could fill Hutch's shoes. As if she didn't already miss the triplets so much her heart felt shredded. Saying goodbye to them, wishing them Merry Christmas early, had been so damned hard.

She sipped her tea and dabbed under her eyes with

a tissue, then let her sisters lead her to the guest room where she could spend a little time under the covers and think. Or not think at all.

Two days later, Hutch woke up still in a funk. His first thought when he opened his eyes was about Savannah. That she wasn't here. That he'd sent her away.

I won't need a nanny.

He felt her absence so acutely. From the moment she'd left the day before yesterday. He wondered if the triplets had too.

The past two nights, Hutch had to force himself not to think about Savannah and what had happened between them so that he could be present for the triplets. That was why he'd smashed his own heart—and hers—wasn't it? So that his love life, whether problems or being on a date, wouldn't interfere with being a good dad.

He'd turned down Olivia and Daniel's offer to come over and help with the boys so that he could focus on Chloe, but once her fever broke it hadn't spiked again. Daniel had been surprisingly okay with the news that Hutch was taking off from the ranch until his ex returned to town and would personally hire, from his own bank account, a cowboy willing to work the next bunch of days.

As he let his baby girl take it easy in her swing, he'd played with Caleb and Carson on the play mat, told them stories about Christmases past, then got them bathed and into their bassinets. Of course, all that had taken quite a while, and there'd been spit-up and a wet bathroom floor and he'd actually gotten sprayed by Caleb when Carson had distracted him with a fussy shriek from the playpen after he'd changed him. But Hutch had coordinated pretty well, surprising himself with just how competent he'd gotten at taking care of triplets on his own.

He glanced at his phone on his bedside table. Just after 5:00 a.m. He'd woken before any of the babies. But a minute later, Carson cried out and Chloe let out a "ba!" so he flung off the blankets and went into the nursery. He'd started his new life when he'd sent Savannah away. Focusing on being a father. The best parent he could be.

He took Chloe's temperature—normal. Still, because he just wanted a clean bill of health from her pediatrician, Hutch made an appointment for a quick visit. And given today's forecast, high forties and sunny, he thought he'd show the triplets the holiday tree afterward and the Santa hut and maybe catch a glimpse of Santa inside.

His phone rang, and he snatched it up as if it were going to be Savannah, anticipating hearing the sound of her voice, but of course it wasn't her.

It was Daniel. Couldn't he wait till at least sunrise to call? "Olivia asked me to check in about Chloe," his brother said. "How is she?"

Hutch had to smile. Daniel had to make it clear he wouldn't have called unless his wife made him. "She seems completely fine. She'd been fussy on and off all day yesterday, but right now you wouldn't even know she'd ever been sick. I guess it was a fluke fever, like the doctor said it could be. I'm taking her to see her doc at noon, though, just to have her looked over. I'm sure she's perfectly fine, but I just want to hear the doctor give her a clean bill of health. Then I figured I'd take the triplets to see the tree. Walk around a little. Supposed to warm up this afternoon."

"Well, like I told you, no worries about the ranch," Daniel said. "I made some calls and found two hands who are off this week from their usual gig but want the extra pay, so I'll be meeting them at the Dueling Dawsons at six."

"I'll pay them out of my personal account," Hutch said.

"That won't be necessary, but I appreciate the offer. There'll be times I'll need time off, I'm sure. It'll balance out. Oh, and I have an appointment with the feed store later this afternoon to get a ten percent discount for switching our business to them. I want to rectify Dad not shopping local all these years. I feel okay about getting into town once the new guys are settled. I can meet you at the doctor's office and watch the boys while you're in with Chloe."

Hutch almost fainted. He was about to make a quip but went for earnest instead. Because he was actually quite touched. Even if his sister-in-law was behind it, Daniel always did only what he wanted.

"That sounds great. Why don't you meet me at the doc's office at just before noon, then?"

"Will do," Daniel said.

Huh. His brother offering a favor—again. First he'd gone with Olivia to the ER and kept watch over the stroller with the boys while Olivia had been trying to

soothe screeching, feverish Chloe. Then he'd offered
to stick around with Olivia at the house to watch the
boys while Hutch hovered over his daughter. Now he
was coming to the pediatrician's office.

Maybe Olivia was working on her husband. Or maybe
when it came right down to it, his brother would be there
for them. Daniel had been, to a degree, when Hutch's
marriage had ended in one conversation, but their dad
had said a couple of things that had rubbed Daniel the
wrong way when his brother had come over to the ranch
to check on Hutch, and he hadn't been around much after
that, except with Olivia to bring lasagnas and bagels.

Hutch wasn't sure how much more change he could
take. But this, with Daniel, was another of those Christmas miracles he was damned grateful for.

Savannah spent the morning looking at town houses,
condos and single-family homes for sale in Bear Ridge
with a Dawson real-estate agent. Danica Dawson was
married to Ford Dawson, a police officer with the Bear
Ridge PD—a second cousin to Hutch and one of the
owners of the Dawson Family Guest Ranch. But Savannah had her own in with the Dawsons apart from
Hutch, so she didn't feel funny about calling Danica this
morning about viewing some properties. Savannah's old
friend Aimee had recently married a Dawson. And Savannah's former client, star bull rider Logan Winston,
was now married to a Dawson. Logan would always
feel like family, so technically, the Dawsons were already "her people" and not just Hutch's.

There was a little rationalization going on there, but

half the town were Dawsons, and she couldn't cut them all out of her life because they were Hutch's territory.

"Well, I've shown you four great homes this morning," Danica said, tucking a swath of her long blond hair behind her shoulder. "What do you think?"

I think I don't want to live alone anymore. I think I don't want to buy a house on my own. I think I want to move into Hutch's ranch house on a permanent basis and be a stepmother to the triplets. And then have that red-haired baby he'd been thinking about.

Savannah ignored the ache in her chest. "I loved the end-unit town house."

It would be perfect, like her Blue Smoke condo, were she just thinking about herself and a baby. A big two-bedroom. That gorgeous stone fireplace. A fenced-in backyard so she could finally adopt that dog she'd been thinking about for a while. As she'd walked through the town house, she could see that second bedroom as a nursery. And she wouldn't be living there alone if she did bring a child into her life.

The problem was, her taste of family life, the big gulp she'd taken of love, made it very clear she wanted a home for herself, her husband and their child. And date or no date this afternoon, she couldn't see herself falling for anyone else so fast.

"But today's my first day out," Savannah added. "I'd like to think about it now that I've seen what's available." Savannah had told Danica she wasn't sure what she was looking for—a two-bedroom condo or a big house with four bedrooms, so Danica had shown something in every category. The four-bedroom Craftsman had a master suite, a guest room on the first floor, and two bedrooms with a cute Jack and Jill bathroom upstairs. For her *two* children.

You never know, Savannah. You'll go on this date with Andrew the lawyer with the cute Santa Claus tie and maybe he'll make you laugh and be a rodeo fan and you'll unexpectedly be attracted to him and want to see him again. It's entirely possible. And then you'll date for three months and you'll both be so in love that he'll propose, and within a few years, those two bedrooms will be filled with your two kids.

She sighed.

She wanted a family, yes. But now that her heart was taken by someone, it was impossible to think of family, husband, baby in the abstract anymore.

She wanted to be part of Hutch's family. She wanted to marry Hutch. She wanted to have a baby with Hutch.

This was the problem with being a doer. She'd felt compelled to do something rather than be taken over by sadness about what she couldn't have. So now she had this date at the brick oven pizza place when her heart was taken by someone else. When she'd cried all day and all night yesterday, after sobbing the entire night before. Maybe she should cancel. It was hardly fair to go on a date and waste a perfectly nice man's time.

Except she *did* believe in you-never-know. Maybe Andrew and his Santa tie would make her forget all about Hutch Dawson.

Not that time and distance had. Even after seventeen years.

"Sounds good," Danica said. "No pressure." Her

phone pinged. "Ah, the husband texting me with a re- minder that we're due for my prenatal checkup in fif- teen minutes."

"Oh!" Savannah said. "Congratulations." She'd had no idea Danica was pregnant. She was tall and model slim and so pretty that Savannah thought she just nat- urally glowed.

"What's amazing is that I wasn't even sure I'd ever be a mom—if I even wanted that. But I fell in love and suddenly everything clicked into place."

Huh. Savannah certainly understood that. The same thing had happened to her.

Another thing she was sure of was that she was say- ing goodbye to her career as a manager of rodeo per- formers. She'd already made the necessary phone calls; her clients would either move to her assistant, who Sa- vannah had promoted to agent in her own right by simply saying so, or they'd sign with managers on Sa- vannah's level. Michael, her rising star from Bear Ridge, was sticking with Lizzie, and Savannah saw great things for them both.

She was more than ready for this new phase of life. Even if it didn't start off in a blaze of glory like her rodeo management career had.

But as they said their goodbyes and Savannah walked along Main Street, she suddenly was not really sure about buying in Bear Ridge. The permanence. Even though her family was here, maybe she'd be better off staying in Blue Smoke. Try harder to join the community, make friends. Hutch wasn't in Blue Smoke. There weren't

Dawsons on every corner there, reminding her of him. Of his family.

Of the triplets.

She glanced at her watch. She had a date to get to.

She had ten minutes to get to the restaurant. If it wasn't rude to cancel this late, she would.

A date was the last thing she wanted. Because even if there was the remote possibility that she'd like the guy and want to see him again, she'd have feelings for Hutch gnawing away at her heart, mind and soul.

Chapter Thirteen

Hutch's mood had improved a tiny bit because Chloe's pediatrician had given her that clean bill of health. Fever gone, color good, eyes bright. Daniel had stayed with Carson and Caleb in the waiting room, reading to them from *Wyoming Rancher* magazine. Now they were headed down Main Street, Hutch wheeling the giant stroller. They'd part ways at the town green—Hutch would show the triplets the tree and Daniel would go to his appointment at the feed store.

"Want to hear something great?" Daniel said. "Ethan told me during our weekly talk yesterday that he's thinking of switching his major to agricultural business. Turns out my going on and on about the ranch the past few months has gotten to him. Wouldn't it be something if he came to work at the Dueling Dawsons summers and then came on board full-time when he graduates?"

Hutch smiled. "That would be really wonderful. Ethan's a great guy. Smart, mature and a good sense of humor. Gets that from his uncle Hutch."

Daniel raised an eyebrow. "Yeah, not."

Something was definitely different about Daniel, just slightly nicer. Less ready to pounce, accuse, blame, complain. Whatever it was, Hutch would take it.

Hutch was about to ask what area of ranch management Ethan was interested in when he saw something—a flash of long red hair—that had him stop dead in his tracks.

Just up ahead, Savannah, midlaugh, was coming out of Gennaro's Brick Oven Pizza, a tall, well-built blond man beside her, saying something. She touched his arm, and now he laughed.

They sure looked chummy.

And given her cashmere coat and the high heels instead of her down jacket and brown cowboy boots, plus the red lipstick, Hutch didn't have to be a detective to know she was on a date.

His heart plummeted to his stomach. He felt like hell.

And she and the blond guy were headed straight toward him. Savannah hadn't seen Hutch yet because she was too busy laughing again over something her date said. And touching his arm again.

Hutch wanted to roll over the man with the huge stroller, knock him down like a bowling pin. Not that he would.

Savannah's gaze suddenly landed on Hutch and she

stopped as dead as he had just a few feet away, the man beside her looking at her with concern. Hutch wheeled the stroller along as though this was no big whoop, his brother beside him muttering "Oh jeez" under his breath.

Hutch decided to paste a smile on his face and just keep walking, but Daniel stopped.

"Hi, Savannah," Daniel said. "Nice to see you again."

She looked mortified. "Nice to see you too." She glanced between the brothers, then quickly at her date. "Well, we'd better mosey," she added.

"Daniel Dawson," his brother said, sticking out his hand toward the guy.

"Andrew Rand," the blond guy said. "Savannah and I are on a first date, if you were wondering how we knew each other. I'm hopeful there'll be a second." He swept his gaze on Savannah, a kind of warm interest in his eyes.

The guy was smooth, Hutch would give him that.

"And this is my brother Hutch," Daniel added. "Savannah was Hutch's nanny for these little folks until just recently."

Savannah paled a bit.

Hutch almost choked on nothing.

"Yup, heard all about her being a nanny to six-month-old triplets," Andrew said. He came around to the side of the stroller and peered in. "They sure are beautiful babies. I'm in the market myself," he added, sliding a glance at Savannah. "Never thought I'd hear myself say that, but, well, here I am."

Ugh, Hutch thought. The guy seemed…nice. Savannah couldn't be interested in him, though, could she?

He was the right age, from the looks of him.

Had his act together, also from the looks of him.

Wanted a baby and actually said so in front of people.

Savannah couldn't look more uncomfortable, which gave Hutch some relief, not that he wanted her to be miserable. But if she were comfortable and happy and hunky-dory, he'd...

He'd what? Know she was gone? Lost to him? He'd already taken care of that himself.

But he was jealous as hell, and it was his own damned fault.

"Well, bye!" Savannah said in a faux-cheerful voice, and the pair started walking again.

Hutch pretended to fuss with the stroller sun shield so he could see where the happy couple was headed. They stopped at a black BMW, the date opening the passenger door for her.

Daniel also turned, then looked at Hutch. "We told Savannah not to take how you acted the other night in the ER personally, but I guess we were wrong."

"Meaning?" Hutch said. He was in no mood to talk about this with Daniel, who wasn't exactly a master at relationships.

"Meaning you clearly ended things with her. Or she wouldn't be on a date with a very successful attorney. I had a feeling you were headed in that direction after the way you shut Savannah out in the ER."

Hutch scowled. He hated thinking of that. Remembering how he'd acted. How she'd looked. "How do you know he's an attorney?"

"He has his own firm near where I used to have my CPA office. Nice car."

"Whatever," Hutch muttered.

Daniel shocked him by putting an arm very briefly around his shoulders. "You okay?"

Hutch was vaguely aware that Daniel had asked him a question but Hutch couldn't focus on anything but the thought of Savannah in that BMW, heading God knew where. The successful attorney's condo for some afternoon delight?

"Guess not," Daniel said.

Hutch glanced at Daniel. "Sorry. Just a little preoccupied. I suppose I'm not okay."

"So do something about it."

Hutch shook his head. "This is exactly why I ended things. So I *wouldn't* be preoccupied. So I'd focus on the triplets, on being a good dad. That's what should matter most to me. That's all that matters."

Daniel was eyeing him. "Would have been nice if our own father shared that sentiment."

Hutch sighed and nodded. "Yeah, I know."

"Guess we both became good dads anyway, though," Daniel said. "Role model–schmole model."

Hutch stared at him. "You think I'm doing okay as a dad?"

"You broke up with a woman you're in love with, didn't you? A really good babysitter, too, so yes, your priorities are in the right place. Your children come first with you. That makes you a great dad, Hutch."

"So I did the right thing," Hutch said, his chest aching, his head beginning to pound.

Daniel shot a glance at him. "I don't know about that. You don't have to be alone to be a good dad. You just have to *be* a good dad."

"I can't be a good dad if I'm on dates while my children are burning up with fever and someone else has to rush them to the ER."

"I'll be honest with you, Hutch. That you put your children first over your love life goes a long way with me. Our father didn't do that. He dumped my mother for yours. He dumped me for the ranch. Everything else came first with him. He was better with you because you were right there, but not by much."

"Yeah, I'd have to agree with that," Hutch said.

"I'm just saying if he'd been a good father to either of us while we were growing up, I would have forgiven him for falling in love with another woman who wasn't my mother. You know?"

Hutch nodded. "Yeah, I hear you." But he didn't want to hear anything. His hands tightened on the stroller. He had to clear his head, push everything away. He just wanted to focus on the triplets right now. Show them a great day. Christmas trees and Santa and beautifully decorated shop windows and doors.

Daniel was about to say something, but they'd reached the corner where Hutch would head across the street to the town green and Daniel would go to the feed store.

"You'll figure it out, Hutch," Daniel said and continued down Main Street.

"I have," Hutch called after him, but Daniel had already ducked into the feed store.

I'm doing what feels right to me.

He crossed the street and wheeled the big stroller up the path toward the Santa hut so the triplets could get a glimpse of Santa when the door opened. Surely with Christmas carols playing from a speaker and chatting up the triplets about the big day coming up, he wouldn't have time to think about Savannah. On her date.

Or anything his brother had said.

Except thinking about Christmas reminded him that his ex would be back Christmas Eve morning. She'd have the triplets from then until the evening of the twenty-fifth, when she'd drop them off at the ranch for a few hours so he could spend a little of the holiday with them.

You'll have them ten whole days prior, Hutch, Allison had said when they were making the arrangements about her return. *Surely you can understand why I should have them for most of the holiday.*

He didn't understand, really. He could have insisted they split Christmas Eve and Christmas Day, maybe. But she was about to get married and going off on her honeymoon and he would have them for ten days all to himself, so he'd relented.

The words *flexible* and *compromise* made him want to throw something.

Welcome to the two-house Christmas.

He'd be alone for Christmas.

Bah humbug.

Savannah sat with her sister Morgan at her dining room table, wrapping presents while her husband and daughter were out doing some last-minute Christmas shopping for Morgan herself. There was a plate of home-

made Christmas cookies and two cups of eggnog to for-
tify them for the stack of fifteen or so gifts left to wrap
and place under the spectacular tree.

"So if Andrew asks you out again, you'll say yes?"
Morgan said, spreading a piece of tape along the seam
of the book she'd just wrapped.

Morgan had been after her since Savannah had gotten back to the house a half hour ago. She had spent the
afternoon in the shops, driving around town and visiting all her old haunts. She'd parked in the high school
lot and tried to conjure up that girl she'd been, to tell
her she'd finally done it, gone for Hutch Dawson with
everything she had, but that girl was long gone. She felt
like a very tired adult.

"We ran into Hutch and Daniel and the triplets on our
way out of the restaurant," Savannah said. "What the heck
were the chances of that, and whammo—we walked right
into each other."

Morgan's eyes widened and she put the tape dis-
penser down. "What happened? That must have been
so awkward."

"Very. And weird. Hutch's brother made a point of
introducing himself and Hutch when I was trying to
get away fast, and Andrew mentioned that we were on
a first date and that he hoped there would be a second."

"Wow," Morgan said. "He said that? He must *really*
like you."

"We did have a nice time. Talked easily, lots of laugh-
ter. Had a few things in common. He likes the rodeo, and
I'll forever be a big fan." She sighed.

"But…Hutch," her sister said.

"Yeah. And running into him and the triplets just sort of cemented how strongly I feel about them all. I'm just going to have to put off dating and motherhood for a bit. Until I'm myself again. Until I somehow get Hutch Dawson and the triplets out of my dumb heart."

"Aww, your heart is not dumb. It's open and hopeful and huge. That's good, Savannah." Morgan laid a hand on her arm, her brown eyes compassionate.

"Merry Christmas to me," Savannah said in a sing-song voice. She took a long sip of her eggnog, hoping it would put her back in the Christmas spirit. But she could add *heavy* to that open, hopeful, huge heart.

Savannah's phone rang, and the dumb part of her hopeful heart wanted it to be Hutch. But it was Olivia Dawson.

"Hi, Olivia, how are you?"

"To be honest, I don't know," Olivia said. "Guess who took his first motorcycle ride and is now waiting to get stitches in the ER? Ethan."

"Oh no!" Savannah said. "Is he okay?"

"He's fine. He managed not to break any bones, thank heavens. But Daniel and I are going to drive the two hours to baby him, and that means we can't watch over the ill mare we'd planned to keep an eye on all night in the barn." She let out a sigh. "It was supposed to be our romantic evening—even in a barn, even with a sick animal, but I'd been really looking forward to it. Just the two of us, talking, you know."

"Oh, I'm really sorry," Savannah said.

"This is where I'm hoping you come in. Daniel's called at least four of his cousins at the Dawson Family Guest

Ranch to see if they can keep watch, and no one's free tonight. Sick kids, Christmas choral concerts at school, unbreakable plans. The two new hands can't do it. That leaves Hutch, even though he's supposed to be off till Christmas Eve, but he can't very well be on duty *and* take care of the triplets."

Savannah swallowed. "So where exactly do I come in?"

"He'll need a sitter—overnight. He'll have to go out to the small barn twice during the night to administer medicine and stay a bit to monitor Daffodil."

"Of course I'd be happy to help out," Savannah said. "But I don't know that Hutch will *want* me there. Do you think I should offer? Or wait till he asks?"

"Good question," Olivia said. They were both quiet for a few seconds as they thought about that.

Savannah's phone pinged with a text. Hutch. "Did you hear that ping?" she said to Olivia. "It's Hutch texting. I think he's asking."

"I'll let you go, then. Thank you, Savannah. You're the best."

She disconnected from Olivia and clicked on the text from Hutch.

Got a minute? Can I call you?

Sure, she texted back.

Her phone rang and Savannah grabbed it. Hutch told her everything Olivia had already.

"I know it's a lot to ask," he said, "especially given... everything, but I could sure use your help."

"I'll absolutely be there at seven. And I'm just glad I get to hang with the triplets one more time. I have Christmas gifts for them that I was gonna drop on your porch. Now I can hand them over in person."

"I can't thank you enough, Savannah. I'll see you soon."

Goose bumps, chills and tingles lit up every bit of skin, every cell in her body. She should not be looking forward to tonight. She should be worried that it would make her heart hurt worse, be a reminder of everything she wanted and couldn't have.

But all she saw was a chance to make Hutch see he couldn't live without her.

Ha. She had no idea where that confidence came from. Life, maybe. Or just from wishful thinking.

"Okay, I caught like five percent of all that," Morgan said.

Savannah filled her in.

Morgan smiled. "Oh yeah. I'd say you might not be leaving that ranch in the morning."

Somehow, hearing her sister say it made her realize she very likely would be. But she had a shot and she was taking it.

Chapter Fourteen

Hutch knew that his stubborn nature could get in his way—he'd been working on it for years—but when it came to a sick horse needing him and his children needing a sitter when he'd be occupied, he wasn't about to mess around. Daniel had told him he'd called multiple Dawsons at the guest ranch, and they were all unavailable tonight to keep watch over Daffodil—who'd been their father's favorite horse. The cowboys both had plans their families "would kill them" if they broke. That left Hutch—and Savannah as backup with the triplets.

He'd felt like hell asking her for a favor when he didn't deserve anything from her. But she'd immediately said yes.

"Bet you guys are happy that Savannah's coming over," he said to the triplets, who were in their swings on the play mat in the living room.

"Ba!" Carson said, waving a hand.

Caleb chewed on the edges of his chew book. Chloe was chewing on her giraffe rattle.

He'd checked on Daffodil just five minutes ago and noted on the checklist the vet had tacked up to the stall door that the mare looked comfortable for now. One of the new cowboys had been grooming her this afternoon with his leftover sub sandwich half sticking out vertically from his coat pocket—all kinds of meats and onions, garlic and a bunch of condiments—and before he knew it, Daffodil had been munching away on it, wrapper and all. They'd watched her for signs of colic, and within two hours, she was showing it—and a bad case. The onions and garlic were the biggest danger and could cause all kinds of misery to a horse's digestive tract.

Since there would be downtime during the night and he wanted to fill it with anything else but talk of them—or her date—he'd set out on the coffee table board games, a deck of cards and the file from his dad's office labeled Family Feud. Maybe he and Savannah could go through it and see what they could find about what made the feud blow up.

It was just a few minutes till 7:00 p.m. when he heard her SUV pulling in. He'd thought of her too much since running into her earlier. And afterward, while he'd been showing the triplets the tree and walking along Main Street to point out the beautifully decorated shop windows, he'd kept having the unnerving sensation that something was missing.

Savannah herself.

That had thrown him even more off balance than

seeing her on a date had. He'd just need a little time to get over Savannah and what was between them, and as long as he kept his attention where it needed to be—on his children—he'd keep doing just fine.

Given that his focus tonight would be on Daffodil and the triplets as well, he'd have no time to notice how beautiful Savannah was or how much he'd missed her today. They'd have no time to talk about anything more in-depth than the weather or what a horror show colic could be.

The moment he opened the door to Savannah on his porch, however, he froze like he had when he had seen her today on her date. It wasn't just that she was beautiful and sexy and how much he adored her long red hair. The jolt he felt was in his chest, in his head, in his heart. This woman meant something to him, something big and special, and having her right here, an evening with her anticipated, was an unexpected relief. Despite him being the one who'd let her go.

"I come bearing gifts and something of a picnic dinner," she said, holding up the two big bags in her hands. "Turkey clubs, fries, two sodas and homemade Christmas cookies from my sister's house."

"Sounds perfect," he said, wishing he could draw her into a hug.

"I'm excited to give the triplets their gifts. And I have a little something for you."

"I have a gift for you too," he said.

She bit her lip and seemed a bit subdued for just a second, then adopted a cheerier expression. "So where are we on the triplets' schedule? They ate?"

"They ate, had their baths and bottles. I changed them. All that's left is story time and then bed."

"You left the easy stuff for me."

"That's the new Hutch Dawson," he said. "I want to take care of them."

She winced a bit, and he felt like a heel. "How's Daffodil?" she asked. "She'll be fine, right?"

He nodded. "It's more a matter of watching her for signs of serious discomfort and then treating her, per the vet's instructions," he said. "Why don't we dig into those sandwiches and fries? You can tell the triplets a story, if you want."

"I do want," she said, putting the bags down by the door and hurrying over to the triplets. She knelt down and kissed each one on the head, getting a *ba* from Carson and gummy smiles from Chloe and Caleb, who was shaking his bear rattle. "I've really missed them. One minute I'm doing something so intensely, and then the next, not. It's like how Olivia described the empty nest." Her gaze was tender on the babies, and she looked like she might burst.

Oh, Savannah. That you adore the triplets was never the issue. He would always be grateful for how she'd helped him, how she'd cared for his children.

"I'm really glad you're here," he said. *Really glad. Because not only do I get to be with you just a little longer than I expected, you're not with what's-his-name.* He wanted to ask if she would be seeing the guy again, but Savannah's love life certainly wasn't his business.

He thought she'd allude to the two of them running into each other today, make a quip and he'd get a sense of whether she'd already moved way on from him, but she didn't. Hutch was jealous when he had no right to be.

"Me too," she said fast. She popped up and brought the bags over to the coffee table, eyeing the bounty he'd placed there. "Just in case we get bored, huh? Scrabble, Jenga, Pictionary." She smiled.

We have to do something to keep us busy in our downtime so that we don't talk about personal stuff, which always seems to lead to a kiss...and bed, he wanted to say, but he bit his tongue.

Savannah started taking out containers, the smell of delicious french fries filling the air. She brought hers over to the play mat and sat down "crisscross applesauce," the container beside her. She picked up a quarter of the club sandwich and took a bite. "Yum," she told them. "Just wait till you guys get old enough to have turkey clubs from the Bear Ridge Diner. So good."

He smiled and took a bite too, bringing his container over and sitting on the rocker by the sliding glass window. He listened as she told the triplets a story about a cheese omelet and a stack of pancakes who were best friends, chuckling at how ridiculous it was. The babies' eyes were beginning to droop despite the animated sound of her voice and the softly playing Christmas carols in the background. Within twenty minutes, the omelet and pancakes about to attend their first school dance, the triplets had fallen asleep.

"Oops," she said. "Maybe we should have put them in their bassinets and *then* told stories."

"Their naps were cut a little short—Caleb was fussing and woke up the other two. So I suppose they're all making up for the lost half hour." He stood up and undid Chloe's harness, gently taking her out. Savannah did the same with Caleb. They headed to the nursery, a light trail of Savannah's intoxicating perfume managing to permeate the air more than the fries. They got both babies down, Caleb iffy on the fuss-making, but he settled down pretty quickly once Savannah started singing one of her mangled Christmas carols. He went back for Carson and settled him in his bassinet, then gave each baby's head a soft caress.

They tiptoed out, grabbing their dinners and settling on the sofa. Hutch sat a good distance away, making sure he couldn't easily turn and kiss her.

"When will you have to go to the barn?" she asked, swiping a fry through the mound of ketchup she'd squeezed from the packets onto the side of the container.

"About twenty minutes. I'll give her medicine and stay for a while to make sure she's tolerating it. Then I'll check on her in another half hour."

"Poor Daffodil. I wonder if she'd say the sub sandwich was worth it."

He smiled. "Now no. Tomorrow when she's all better? Probably."

She took a sip of her soda, then set it back on the coffee table. "Oh, is that the family feud stuff?" she asked, gesturing at the legal file.

He nodded. "I've gone through about a quarter of it. There are a lot of old letters from the brothers, from their wives, from their children over the decades, but I didn't find anything about Helene. Nothing that would help me figure out how to have a skyward chat with ole Ernest and Harlan and let them know they can put the feud to rest."

"Can I sift through the letters?" she asked. "I love this kind of stuff."

"Sure," he said.

She took out a letter. "This is from Ernest to his brother." She read through it, eyes widening, barely stopping to look at the fry she was swiping through ketchup before popping it in her mouth, eyes glued to the page. "Wow, Ernest sure was mad at his brother."

"Same for Harlan. They argued about everything. According to a letter dated a few months before that one, they'd agreed to put their grievances down on paper as documentation."

As Savannah read another letter, taking another bite of her sandwich, he was drawn to her lips. Drawn to everything about her. Good thing he had to go right now. Because he had to do something about how the proximity to her was affecting him.

"I'll be back in a half hour," he said. "If you need me, just text."

"'Kay," she said, sliding a glance at him before returning her attention to the letter she was reading, this one from Ernest's wife to Harlan's wife.

"God, this is juicy stuff," she said.

He smiled. "See you in a bit."

She looked at him and held his gaze for a moment. The connection between them was so powerful that he almost felt the zap of it in his chest. She must have felt it too, because she put the letter down and looked away from him.

Maybe we can have a last night together, he thought. *She's here. I'm here. The babies are asleep. A last hurrah. Something to help put our brief romance to rest.*

Don't even think of suggesting it, jerk, he told himself as he headed to the door, grabbing his coat from the rack and shrugging into it.

He wouldn't. Not after pulling out the rug from under her *twice*.

Oh, but he wanted to.

Savannah sat on the sofa in Hutch's living room, sipping eggnog, which she couldn't get enough of, Christmas carols by various great old-timey singers playing softly in the background, and reading through the letters from the Family Feud file. There were so many from the generations, most ranch-business oriented, but many from brother to brother, from wife to wife. Nieces to aunts. Granddaughters to grandmothers. Hutch and Daniel's dad hadn't been a letter writer, but his parents had saved every card—birthday, Christmas, get well— that he'd sent, and there were a big stack of those.

Hutch had been gone a good twenty minutes. Savannah had just finished a particularly juicy letter from Vera Dawson, Ernest's wife, to Catherine Dawson, Harlan's wife. Vera had a list of grievances, from the "sharp" way Catherine had spoken to her oldest daughter, to how she'd butted into a conversation before church that past Sunday and answered for her and had gotten it wrong. No love lost between those two.

Savannah sipped her eggnog, about to grab the next letter when she heard a little cry. She couldn't tell which triplet it was—out of practice after just a day—but the baby must have soothed him- or herself back to sleep. She got up to stretch her legs and check on the trio anyway. All three were fast asleep, their little chests rising up and down.

Savannah stood over their bassinets, unable to move away, her love for these three little humans overwhelming. She was about to whisper to them what was on her mind, that she wished she could be part of this family, when she remembered that Hutch went nowhere without a baby monitor in his pocket. Phew. That would have been embarrassing.

She went back to the sofa and picked up the next letter. From Catherine Dawson's daughter, Dahlia, to her aunt Vera, Ernest's wife, in 1960.

Dear Aunt Vera,
It's a new year and a time to start fresh. I've always wished we were closer. Why do families always get in the way of each other? Or maybe it's just our family. I have a new beau and his huge family is close as can be. But I found out something today that touched me, and I think it'll have the same effect on you and my mother. I'm going to tell her right after I get this to the post office.

I went to see Helene Mayhew's cousin today. That's right—I just knocked right on her door and asked her if she knew anything about Helene and the Dawson brothers, which one she'd been

going to choose as her husband. And guess what
she told me? Something that, if the brothers had
each known, would have helped heal their rifts,
maybe even brought them closer.

Savannah gasped and put down her eggnog. She sat
up straight and kept reading.

Turns out that, unbeknownst to the other, both
Ernest and Harlan had gone to see Helene that
day. Each told her separately that he was with-
drawing his marriage proposal, that the triangle
had deepened the chasm between him and his
brother and it was destroying the family. There
were other problems between them than a gal, but
each told her that stepping away and letting the
other have Helene as his wife would be a good
start.

Apparently, Helene was furious that they were
making the choice for her and now she had no
one to choose between. She'd galloped off on
her horse and got thrown. Helene's cousin thinks
each brother blamed himself for that and resented
the other for having to be magnanimous when it
hadn't mattered.

I know my father loved my mother deeply and
that she was his true love. Same for Uncle Earnest—
I can plainly see that the few times I've been to visit.
Helene didn't come between the brothers after all.
They just both felt guilty and upset at doing the right
thing when it ended badly. Isn't that something? I

*wish Daddy was still alive so I could sit him and
Uncle Earnest down and tell them what each had
done for the other, but it's too late. Isn't that the way?*

Savannah couldn't wait to show Hutch the letter. This
was the smoking gun! The explanation that would settle
things for the brothers, let them rest in peace. Helene's
accident wasn't either of their faults. It wasn't both of
their faults. They were each being kind to the other, unbeknownst to them. But the tragedy ended up pulling
them apart even worse.

She read through a couple more letters postmarked
around the same time. The next generation of Dawsons
running the Dueling Dawsons Ranch had more beefs
with one another, and so the family feud had just kept
continuing. But Savannah did find a letter back from
Vera to her niece Dahlia thanking her for the information and that Ernest hadn't known that, and it surely
would have helped make peace between the brothers.
She'd hoped, anyway.

There it was.

She heard the key turning in the lock and bolted up
with the two letters, so excited to share them with Hutch.

He eyed her as he took off his coat and scarf and
stepped out of his boots. "Find a recipe for eggnog in
there or something? You look incredibly happy."

"I found it, Hutch. That smoking gun your father
wrote about on his list of Unfinished Business. You and
Daniel can make peace between Harlan and Ernest before Christmas after all!"

His mouth dropped open. "Really?" He came over and

took the letters, then sat down and read them. "Whoa. They both withdrew their marriage proposals without the other knowing. For the sake of the other, the ranch and the family. Amazing."

"And very sweet," she said.

He set the letters aside. "I'll tell Daniel when he gets back. Maybe we can go visit their grave sites and share the news."

"That's a really nice idea," she said.

"Once again, you're a Christmas miracle, Savannah." His gaze was on hers, then for a split second dropped to her lips, then back up to her eyes.

Hutch, Hutch, Hutch, she thought. *How am I leaving this house tomorrow morning? How am I leaving you behind to start the life I want when you're the man I want? The only man I can ever imagine wanting?*

She'd have to find a way. Today had been a start, and she'd take each day as it came.

"I was so excited about the letters that I didn't even ask you how Daffodil is," she said. "She's holding her own?"

He nodded. "She looks good, no sign of discomfort. I think she'll be okay by morning. I'll check on her a couple more times just to be safe. I hope my coming and going won't wake you up."

"As if I could sleep so easily," she said, feeling her eyes widen. She hadn't meant to say that aloud.

He looked at her for a moment. "Yeah, I know what you mean."

She couldn't drag her eyes off his handsome face, but she had to. "So maybe we should exchange presents now," she said, needing to ruin the moment. There could be *no* moment.

He was probably glad she had ruined it. He went over to the tree they'd decorated together and returned with a medium-sized gift.

"What is it?" she asked, touched that he'd gotten her something. From the size and feel of it, she'd say it was a hardcover book and she hoped it wasn't a biography of Eleanor Roosevelt or something completely impersonal like that.

"Open it and see," he said.

She ripped off the paper, her hand going to her heart. It *was* a hardcover book. Titled: *You're Gonna Be a Great Mama: For the New Mother, Single or Married, Biological or Adopted or In-between.*

"Perfect," she whispered. "Thank you." She wanted to run up to him and hug him.

He was frowning. "I hated seeing you on your date today, Savannah. But I'm glad you're going after what you want. You deserve everything. Everything."

So give me you, she wanted to say. But she didn't. They'd been through it over and over.

She reached into her gift bag and pulled out his present. "For you," she said, handing it to him.

He took it with a smile and sat a few feet away from her on the sofa. He gave it a gentle shake. "Hmm, no idea what it could be." He tore off the wrapping paper, moved the tissue paper and pulled out a navy sweatshirt embroidered with *Wyoming's Best Dad* on the front, three little cowboy hats under it, each with Caleb's, Carson's and Chloe's name embroidered on its brim. He held up the sweatshirt with a grin. "I love this. Maybe the best present I've ever gotten."

He moved to kiss her cheek, but she'd turned to face him at the same moment, and suddenly, their lips met. They pulled apart just an inch and looked at each other, and then she cupped his face with her hand and kissed him, leaning more into him.

He responded.

She inched away again. "Hutch. I'm here. You're here. The triplets are asleep. We have tonight. I vote for saying a meaningful goodbye. And then we can go our separate ways."

You can be the dad you want to be. I can be the mom I want to be. In due time, when I'm a bit more over you.

"A meaningful goodbye," he repeated. "I do like that. I'll carry it with me."

And then he slid a hand under her and picked her up, all five feet ten inches of her, and carried her into his bedroom, kissing her along the way.

He laid her down on his bed and covered her body with his, fingers entwined with hers over her head, kissing her mouth, her neck, her collarbone. Then he freed his hands to take off her sweater, then her jeans. She made quick work of his belt buckle and his own jeans.

And suddenly they were naked. She reveled in his appreciative gaze on her body, his mouth and hands following. She moaned and arched her back as his mouth explored her breasts, a hand inching lower down her torso. She was about to explode with pleasure but wanted to prolong it, so she got them turned so that she was on top and kissed her way from his mouth to his neck to his glorious chest and down, down, down to his manhood. He groaned and grabbed the sides of the bed.

And then he was reaching in his bedside table for a condom. She rolled it on and then straddled him, rocking with him in perfect harmony, meeting his passion, their gazes colliding in equal parts tenderness and desire for each other.

I love you, she thought before a crescendo started building. *I love you so much.*

They exploded together, their mouths fused, until she collapsed on him, both breathing hard, his arms tight around her.

I love you, she thought again, wishing with all her heart that this didn't have to end.

Chapter Fifteen

Hutch was in the barn before dawn, well before the triplets could even think about fussing their way into a new day. Leaving his warm, cozy bed with Savannah naked beside him had been very difficult, but he'd had to get out of the room before she opened her eyes when walking away from her—literally and figuratively—would kill him.

The good news was that Daffodil had made it through the night and showed no signs of colic. He'd been up with her twice, and dashing into the cold from the house to the barn had done wonders to wake him up—to his situation. Maybe going along with Savannah's idea for one last night together wasn't the smartest idea. Or maybe it was. He didn't see how it had made letting her go any easier.

When he got back to the house, Savannah was in the kitchen in her 2019 Blue Smoke rodeo T-shirt and jeans,

the triplets in their high chairs, Cheerios on their trays.
Their happy faces, their calls of *ba*, reminded him of
why he was saying goodbye to Savannah. He would be
the best father he could be. He'd be there for his children
except in cases of emergency, like last night. Anyway, it
wasn't like he and Savannah would work out anyway. If
his own wife could dump him while pregnant, anyone
could do anything. Savannah could fall for someone
else. She could change her mind about motherhood. She
could want something completely different. He couldn't
take another upheaval, not when these three precious
beings were counting on him.

He would let Savannah go.

She had their jars of baby food out and they passed
the time feeding them with small talk, about Daffodil,
about the worst Christmas presents they'd ever gotten,
about their favorite holiday traditions. As he burped
Carson, he was aware of an ache deepening in his chest.
Savannah would leave after breakfast. And that would
be that.

While he took the triplets into the living room, he
could hear her making coffee, and the scents of the special holiday blend brewing and cinnamon raisin bagels
toasting made his mouth water. She brought in a tray,
keeping up a stream of chatter to the triplets, avoiding
eye contact with him.

They had coffee and bagels with cream cheese, Savannah reaching out a hand to catch a rattle Chloe threw
before it could land in Carson's face. She was so good
with them. For a moment, he imagined her here always, sharing in his life, in their lives. But he'd seen

what adding something big into his life could do—take his time and attention from his children—and he couldn't do that.

"I got you three each a Christmas present," she said, looking a bit sad but clearly pasting a cheerful smile on her face. She brought over a bag and pulled out three wrapped gifts. "Carson, this one is for you." She unwrapped it and took out footed pj's with his name embroidered across the front. Chloe and Caleb received the same.

"Thank you," he said. "And they thank you."

She did look at him then, and he wondered if she might cry. He hoped not because he wouldn't be able to stand it; it would tear his heart apart even more.

Savannah took a deep breath. "I guess we had our meaningful goodbye, but all it did for me was remind me how truly meaningful this thing between us is," she said. "I love you, Hutch. I do and there's no getting away from it. So I'm telling you. Just in case."

He stared at her, everything inside him freezing. He couldn't have a relationship. Not now. Not for a long time. A year? Two years? He had to be on his own. For his children's sake and his own. "I… You mean a lot to me, Savannah. You know that. But…"

"But you can't. Or won't."

He nodded.

"Well," she said. "I guess this is goodbye, then." With that, she kissed each baby on the head, then grabbed her tote bag and ran out the door.

Taking a big part of his heart with him. Exactly what he was trying to avoid. Even when he tried to do the right thing, he messed up. His heart was supposed to be completely and firmly with the three in this room. Only.

Not a half hour after Savannah had left, he received a text from Allison. She missed the triplets too much to stay away a minute longer, and she and Ted had flown home a few days early. They'd arrived at the ranch with their glowing, tanned newlywed faces, and within five minutes, the triplets were out the door.

He wouldn't see Chloe, Caleb and Carson until Christmas night.

Allison hadn't said anything about upping her custody days, probably because she knew it was bad enough she was not only back early but also having most of the holiday with them. But he knew it was coming, and he'd stand firm. He'd decided that he would structure two set days off from the ranch to have the triplets with him, and then a third day in which he'd have to hire a sitter. But that would be just one day a week. He'd make this work for himself.

As he stood in his living room, the swings empty, the portable playpen empty, the silence unbearable, he went out to the barn to check on Daffodil one last time, surprised to find his brother in there. Daniel must have stopped home to change since he was in his work clothes, ready to take on the day.

"You're back?" Hutch asked. "How's Ethan?"

"Absolutely fine. He wears the bad cuts and stitches like a badge."

"Yup. I remember those days. So my nephew and Daffodil both made it through fine."

"Savannah in the house with the triplets?" Daniel asked. "We stopped at the bakery on the way home, and Olivia picked out a heap of things for you two to say thanks for stepping in. Both of you. I know you wanted to use the last few days full-time with the triplets on your own, but hey, you and Savannah make a great team."

A vision of Savannah's beautiful face and long red hair floated into his mind, her showing each triplet their new pj's with their names on the chest. He inwardly sighed. He should be grateful he'd be back at work today, because he needed to distract himself from thoughts of her. Hurting her.

"Actually, Savannah left about an hour ago," he said, the ache in his heart making him turn away for a moment to get ahold of himself.

"Oh? Where are the kiddos?" Daniel asked, looking around as if sure they must be asleep in their stroller somewhere in the barn.

"Allison and her new husband came back early since she missed the triplets too much. They're gone too." He shoved his hands in his pockets, then pulled them out and went over to the equipment locker for a rake. Might as well get to work. He could see Daniel peering at him. "This is what happens when you get married," Hutch said. "You wind up alone on Christmas Eve and most of Christmas, your triplets somewhere else. With their new stepfather."

"Well, you won't be alone. You'll come to our house. I'm sure you got the Dawson Family Guest Ranch Christmas party invitation—Olivia and I will be going over Christmas Day. The three of us will go together."

Hutch gave something of a nod. "Won't be the same, but I'd better get used to this. Do you know the divorce decree says we'll each have them on their birthdays every other year? Allison says we'll do joint birthday parties, but who the hell knows. Can you imagine not being with your kid on his first birthday?"

"Dad missed quite a few of my birthdays," Daniel said. "You know why? Not because of custody issues. Because like I said yesterday, he didn't give two flying figs. There's the difference, Hutch. One of you cares. One of you didn't. One of you is a great father, no matter how often you see your children, and one of you was negligent and made me—and probably you—feel like crap."

"Yeah, he missed a few of mine too," Hutch said, remembering how nothing would interfere with Lincoln's twice yearly trips—one to a ranching convention, one a hunting expedition with his rancher cronies.

"I'm not saying he didn't have his good points," Daniel said. "He drove three hours in the pouring rain to attend my college graduation. Do you remember about fifteen years ago, Olivia was in the hospital for almost a week, and not only did he bring her chicken soup from the diner every night she was there, but he had food sent over to the house. And he made sure to spend a little extra time with Ethan during that time. I hated how inconsistent he was, though. But at least I couldn't hate *him*."

Hutch thought about his father ordering those beautiful bassinets for the triplets, how he'd opened his home to Hutch—and yes, his heart—when Allison had turned his life upside down.

"I guess people are just multifaceted," Hutch said. "He had his good points and his bad ones, for sure."

"If you broke up with Savannah because you think the only way to be a good dad is to have limited things on your mind, you're in for a seriously rude awakening."

Hutch stopped raking in Daffodil's stall. "I do think that. I'm already stretched thin. I need to give my all to my kids and to the ranch. We just inherited this place. And I might have been the foreman the last ten years, but owning it is a whole other story."

"Savannah doesn't take your mind off what's important, Hutch. Quite the opposite."

Hutch shook his head. "You and Olivia had to take Chloe to the ER because I was on a date."

"Hutch, you're always going to need childcare or backup. You have a full-time job—actually, *two* twenty-four-hour jobs, really. Your kids and the ranch. A life partner doesn't *add* to the responsibility—a life partner *shares* in it. If I've learned one thing the past week it's that Olivia is everything to me."

But Hutch had thought he'd had a life partner and that had been blown to bits. He and Allison had made a deal, a practical arrangement, but he had *very* strong feelings for Savannah. If he lost her? He'd be a wreck. How could he risk that?

"What turned on the light bulb?" Hutch asked, genuinely curious.

"You did, actually."

Hutch gaped at his brother. "Me? What do you mean?"

"When I saw how you were in the ER, shutting Savannah out, something just finally clicked. And then when you said you ended things for the wrong reasons, in my humble opinion, I realized I'd been shutting Olivia out for a while now. Keeping her at a distance because…" He trailed off and stared at the straw spread on the floor of the stall.

"Because?" Hutch prodded gently.

"Because I've always been scared as hell that I'd lose her somehow. I think I was trying to convince myself I didn't need her so badly or care so much or love her that much, when of course I do. I've loved that woman since I was eighteen. I'm not saying you don't want to be a great dad, Hutch. But I am saying you broke up with Savannah because you're scared spitless of how you feel about her."

Hutch closed his eyes for a moment. He'd pretty much admitted that to himself. "I'm glad I could help," he said. "I actually mean that."

"Except I did the opposite of what you're doing. I know what I have in Olivia, and I'll be proving that to her every day from now on."

"You and I are at different points in our lives, Daniel. You've got a son in college. I have three in diapers. So look, I'm really happy for both of you. But our situations are different."

"Nope. They're not."

Hutch had to get off this subject.

"I guess you two won't be having a baby after all," Hutch said.

Daniel grinned. "Thank God, no. But had she pressed it, I most likely would be convinced."

"Huh, you really have changed."

"Nothing more important than love, Hutch. Nothing. I've always known that. But I took Olivia for granted. I won't make that mistake again. And you're taking for granted that you can live without Savannah, but you won't be able to. And who'll be stuck watching you mope around? Me. You love her, Hutch. Olivia and I can both see that."

He inwardly sighed. Daniel was going too far. He was all warm and fuzzy with this—wonderful—change in attitude and was trying to push it on Hutch. Not having his kids for the next few days *or* on Christmas Eve and most of Christmas Day would *suck*. Nothing would change that. When he did have them with him, he'd be 100 percent focused on them.

Hutch continued raking. "No one said anything about love."

Well, Savannah did. *I love you, Hutch. I do and there's no getting away from it. So I'm telling you. Just in case.*

"You can be a great dad and have the woman you love by your side, Hutch. That's a fact. Another fact—one of the reasons you fell in love with Savannah is probably due to the next fact, that she's so good with the triplets, that she adores them. You think down the road you're gonna find both of those things in one woman?"

"I'm not looking down the road. I'm focusing on now," Hutch said.

"It'll be fun watching Savannah date that blond guy with the BMW. You can read all about their wedding in the *Bear Ridge Weekly* next to your constant ads for sitters. Oh, and you can see her happily pregnant around town."

"Why don't we change the subject?" Hutch groused, trying to erase every one of those images that slammed into his mind. "I have the smoking gun. We can cross off the first item on Dad's list of Unfinished Business. And by Christmas, like he wanted."

"Oh yeah? So what's the story?"

He told Daniel about how Savannah had found the real story in the letters in the file while he'd been out in the barn with Daffodil.

Daniel laughed and shook his head. "So once again, Savannah to the rescue. You probably never would have found that letter or been interested in reading it."

Hutch had to admit that was true. "Yeah, probably. So do you want to visit Dad's grave site today and let him know? What we tell him will have old Ernest and Harlan making their peace not too far down from him in the family cemetery."

"We can tell them ourselves. Because then we'll know that we checked off the second thing on Dad's list. Thanks to it being on the list in the first place."

Hutch stared at Daniel. *Bring Hutch and Daniel closer together.* His shoulders unbunched some. "I guess he did do that."

"Well, we did. With a little help from the women in our lives. Dad just pushed it from afar."

The women in our lives... The woman who *used* to be in his life. A burst of sadness let loose in his chest to the point that he had to grip the post on the stall. He turned away for a moment. Savannah *was* a miracle and a gift—and he had sent her away. Not just from himself but from the triplets.

"Oh, and just so there are no secrets between us?" Daniel added.

Uh-oh. What was this?

"When I needed someone to cover me with Daffodil last night and this morning? I didn't actually call any of our cousins over at the Dawson Family Guest Ranch. I wanted to force you and Savannah together. Olivia thought it was a brilliant plan. It was the start of us coming back together."

"That was your idea?" Hutch asked. "I'm surprised."

"Like I said, I saw how miserable she seemed when you shut her out at the ER. And I saw how miserable you seemed when we ran into her on that date. So I figured I'd do some good at Christmastime." He shrugged.

Hutch smiled. "Sneaky. I like it." He and Savannah had had one last beautiful night because of that sneaky plan. He extended his hand, but Daniel pulled him into a hug.

Hutch could not have been more surprised.

"I've shut *you* out a long time," Daniel said. "Even though you've tried over the years to bring us closer. I'm sorry about that. I guess I've been through a lot of changes myself without even realizing it."

Hutch bear clapped his brother. "Yeah, me too."

"So maybe we should think about changing the name of the ranch," Daniel said, tipping up his Stetson. "The Dawson Brothers Ranch. For ole Ernest and Harlan and you and me. If Ethan and the triplets take over when we're old and gray, they can change it again to The Dawson Cousins Ranch. Changing the name can be a generational thing."

Hutch grinned. "I love it. Done."

"Good," Daniel said. "You've got a lot of hard thinking to do. So I'll go round up the herd. Don't screw up two people's Christmas," he added before walking out.

Huh. The miracles just never stopped coming.

"What do you think, Daffodil?" he asked. "Am I being a stubborn fool or just trying to do right by my kids and their legacy—this ranch?"

I'm not saying you don't want to be a great dad, Hutch. But I am saying you broke up with Savannah because you're scared spitless of how you feel about her.

Good thing he had a lot of time on his hands to do that hard thinking.

Chapter Sixteen

Christmas Eve dawned bright and sunny and cold, flurries coming down so beautifully that Savannah couldn't help but smile. She was at the town green, having just left the Santa hut and her former client Logan Winston, who'd brought his seven-year-old to see Santa, even though they'd had their visit with Santa a few days ago. Turned out adorable Cody had one last Christmas wish, and he'd whispered it in Savannah's ear.

"I want a baby brother or sister," Cody had said quite seriously. "Should I tell Santa?"

Savannah's heart had practically burst. "Definitely tell him." She had it on good authority that he'd get that wish since Logan's new wife, Annabel, Cody's mom, had recently found out they were expecting their second child. They planned to surprise Cody with the big news on Christmas morning.

She'd told Logan all about Hutch and the sad good-bye, and he had smiled and said, "Trust me, that man's gonna come banging down your door by Christmas Day. He's stubborn like me. He'll be back."

Savannah couldn't bear to hope so, but hope she did.

She sat down on the bench where she'd come upon Olivia just a week ago. So much had happened since. She tightened the fuzzy red scarf her niece had given her for Christmas around her neck; her sister's family tradition was that each family member could open one gift on Christmas Eve morning and the rest on Christmas Day morning. The scarf helped to make her feel like her family was with her, even though she felt so alone right now.

So sad.

But right now, you're just going to take life one day at a time, she reminded herself, a flake landing on her nose. *No rush to do anything. You're where you want and need to be—your hometown—and with your family.*

The Walsh crew would go over to her dad's house tonight for Christmas Eve, and she'd be surrounded by her dear relatives. Slowly, her heart would heal and she'd take the next steps for the life she wanted.

But Hutch's handsome face came into her mind, the triplets too with their big blue eyes and wispy brown hair and baby-shampoo scents. She wished she was with him, with them.

She lifted her chin against the yearning and looked toward the tree, the line for the Santa hut getting longer. Maybe she should wait in line to see Santa. Tell him what she so desperately wanted. Make a wish—just one more time.

She had Hutch on the brain so much she could swear he was walking toward her. Six foot two. Shoulders forever. His dark, thick hair covered with a brown Stetson, his brown leather barn coat, and a wool scarf wrapped around his neck.

Tears pricked her eyes.

"Savannah!" the man in the scarf called.

That was Hutch's voice.

That *was* Hutch coming toward her.

She stood up.

He jogged the rest of the way over to her. "Your sister Morgan told me where to find you. There's something I have to tell you."

"What's that?" she asked.

"That I love you too, Savannah Walsh. That I've loved you since the day you took my hand on the sidelines of the rodeo I blew seventeen years ago. That I've loved you—hard—ever since you came back into my life ten days ago."

She gasped. She surreptitiously gave herself a little pinch on her hand to make sure she wasn't dreaming, that he had really just said those words.

"I was afraid of how much I love you," he added. "I'm not anymore."

"I love you too, Hutch. So, so much."

"I'm so grateful for that. For *you*," he said, taking both her hands. "You only *add* to my life. I understand that now."

She wrapped her arms around his neck. "Wow, talk about a Christmas miracle."

He nodded. "My ex came back early and took the

triplets. And you know what? I hate that I won't be with them, but they're *here*," he said, touching a hand to his heart. "Just like you are."

She brought his hand over to her heart and held it there. "And just like you are here."

"I love you and I need you, Savannah. And I very much want our little ginger baby. Maybe this time next year, we'll be just getting the happy news that you're expecting."

"Oh, Hutch," she whispered, tears misting her eyes. "This is going to be a great Christmas after all."

He nodded and slung an arm over her shoulder. "How about I treat you to breakfast at the diner? Then I'd like to take you shopping for another Christmas present. An engagement ring. If you'll marry me, that is."

"Oh, I will *definitely* marry you," she said.

Her lifelong Christmas wish coming true.

* * * * *

*And don't miss out on these other
great Christmas romances:*

The Maverick's Holiday Delivery
By Christy Jeffries

Holiday at Mistletoe Cottage
By Nancy Robards Thompson

Their Convenient Christmas Engagement
By Catherine Mann

Available now from Harlequin Special Edition!

SPECIAL EXCERPT FROM

Sparks fly when beautiful PR expert Georgia
O'Neill brings an armful of stray kittens to veterinarian Mel Carter's small-town animal shelter. Mel has loved and lost before, and Georgia
is only in town short-term, so it makes sense to
ignore their mutual attraction. But as they open
up about their pasts, will they also open up to the
possibility of new love?

Read on for a sneak preview of
The Vet's Shelter Surprise,
the first book by debut author Elle Douglas.

Chapter One

"Now, you keep those claws away from my sleeve. This is cashmere," Georgia murmured to the first adorable, yet inconvenient ball of fluff that she gently separated from the rest of the kittens, all cuddled up beside their plump mother cat. She deposited it in the banker's box lined with dish towels as the little creature mewed and glared at her, then went in for the second, her hands protected by red oven mitts.

"Okay, okay, you'll all get your turn. I'm trying to help you here. Something tells me your fur likes water almost as much as my shoes do," she said, eyeing the soft brown suede of her brand-new ankle boots and shifting the umbrella wedged between her neck and shoulder. One by one, she moved the six kittens, the mother helping her by leaping into the box unassisted, nuzzling her babies and licking their foreheads as they jostled to be next to her.

Despite the rain, Georgia paused for a moment, taking in the sight of the mother cat's fierce love and protection, and her kittens' desperate battle for her affection and attention. While Georgia was no animal person, it was hard to deny how cute the little fluff balls were. They were adorable, but it would only get them so far. They'd soon realize they'd have to claw their own way forward in this world.

Only an hour ago, Georgia had discovered the cat and her kittens while taking the garbage out to the bins housed in the shed behind her aunt's lakefront cottage. Their gentle cries guided her to the dugout under the stairs leading to the shed, where the furry brood was nestled in a pile of dried-out leaves and twigs. The mother didn't appear to be feral; she was well-fed with a healthy gray coat. She was just a bit out of her element.

Just like Georgia.

Georgia had promised herself she would keep her phone confined in her aunt's old wooden bread box until at least 4:00 p.m. (happy hour—or not so happy, depending on what messages had come through in the meantime), but this was an emergency, right? What kind of person would she be, leaving those poor, defenseless animals out in the rain? Talk about bad press. And it wasn't like she was about to take them inside. Just the thought of vacuuming all that fur was all the permission she needed to free her phone. She'd braced herself for an onslaught of messages on her home screen, and was surprised to find that none had come through. Was she already irrelevant?

After a quick online search for the local animal shelter and a message left on their voice mail, Georgia had a purpose for the day. It wasn't glamorous, and it required her to drive in the rain, which she hated, but it was a welcome event; Georgia didn't do downtime. "Let's get you somewhere safe," she whispered to her box of kittens as she navigated around puddles to get to her car.

She placed the box in the back seat of her rented Audi, shut the back door, then paused. She opened the door again and strapped the seat belt across the box, congratulating herself on how well she was executing this small heroic act.

The GPS guided her the ten minutes it took to navigate the winding, tree-lined roads to reach the Sunset County Animal Shelter, where she planned to deliver her rescued strays, then get back to the business of her day, which so far included waking up early after yet another terrible sleep, drinking too much coffee, resisting looking at the news, getting dressed and made up for no one, and looking out the window waiting for something to happen. The rest of the day promised more of the same, so really, this little adventure might be the highlight.

The shelter, a small limestone structure with a steep gabled roof, sat at the top of Sunset County's Main Street, which led down to the shore of Hollyberry Lake, one of the four sparkling lakes in the charming but very dead Northern Ontario town. Out front, a sprawling garden of mums in every shade of red, yellow and orange were like a mirror reflection of the large red maples flanking the building, their branches swaying in the breeze overhead. The sign outside needed a fresh coat of paint and the windows were on the dustier side, but, for all its flaws, it exuded the same homespun charm that oozed from every pore of Sunset County, a stark contrast to the traffic jams and bright lights awaiting Georgia's return to Los Angeles. Whenever that would be.

The mother cat eyed Georgia warily as she unbuckled the seat belt and gathered the banker's box in her arms. "Trust me, you're better off here," Georgia said as she kicked the back door closed with her boot. She scolded herself for forgetting the umbrella in the car as she turned toward the front entrance, eager to shield the little kittens from the rain. She was capable, sure. But no one would ever mistake her for the nurturing type.

As she let herself in through the front gate, a red van across the street caught her eye, emblazoned with a Channel 4 News logo. Georgia froze as she watched a petite woman with long braids emerge from the front seat, and a camera operator pull his gear out from the back of the truck. Impossible. How had they found her? No one was supposed to have the slightest clue who she was in this teeny-tiny town in the middle of nowhere. Wasn't that why she'd taken a five-hour flight and driven north, to the last place on earth she'd ever be recognized? She'd only been there three days, and had barely left Nina's cottage.

With her heart in her throat and the box in her hands, Georgia bolted up the path and let herself in through the shelter door, then peered out the window past the Help Wanted sign (Help wanted? More like help needed!). The camera operator was fiddling with the mic on the reporter's lapel. Georgia gasped, her mind racing. As if she hadn't suffered enough of an invasion of her privacy over the last few weeks.

She stared intently at the news crew across the street, then almost jumped out of her skin when she heard a throat clearing behind her. "Can I help you?" a voice sounded from what felt like inches away.

Georgia spun around, colliding with a woman, causing her to tip the box sideways. She felt the mother and babies slide to the side of the box, and narrowly saved them from tumbling out by quickly shifting her arm to block them. Before she could even look up at the source of her surprise, she felt the box level in her arms as the woman in front of her helped steady it. "Whoa, whoa," she said. "Easy there."

One of the little kittens, a miniature orange-and-white puffball the size of a teacup, had gotten loose and had its claws stuck in her sleeve. Georgia allowed the woman to take the box while she cupped the kitten in her hand, gently dislodging its teeny-tiny claws from the threads of her sweater.

"Nice save," the woman said. Georgia cradled the kitten in her hands, steadying herself, and took in the stranger in front of her, a woman with the most intense brown eyes she'd ever seen and perfect wavy chestnut hair that fell just above her shoulders. She wore a white lab coat over a hunter green sweater and jeans, and looked at Georgia with a curious and amused expression. She peered inside the box. "Ah. I see someone didn't heed public health advice."

Georgia narrowed her eyes. "Excuse me?" The kitten moved in her hand. She looked down at the baby animal, who rubbed his little head on her wrist, then yawned, revealing a pink tongue not much bigger than a pencil eraser.

"Looks like he likes you," said the woman, as the mother cat made a squawking mewing noise. "But Mom's not too happy."

"Here," Georgia said. She placed the kitten back in the box in the woman's arms and looked up at her. "So, here they are."

The woman raised her eyebrows.

"I left a message earlier?" Georgia said.

"Not that I know of," the woman said, looking back in the box. "Seamus isn't here right now. He's the manager. He would have told you that you have to keep them."

"Well, these aren't mine. I found them."

She looked at Georgia quizzically. "Found them?"

"Under the porch out back of my aunt's house. I don't live here. I mean, I'm just in town for a bit. I don't know who these belong to." For someone who coached others in speaking for a living, Georgia felt her speech getting all muddled up in the woman's deep brown gaze. "And why would you be surprised?" She looked around the room. "You're an animal shelter, right?"

The woman looked away, then furrowed her brow. Georgia followed her gaze out to the street where the news team was still standing and remembered why she'd flown in there like a tornado.

"We're currently an animal shelter. We might be without a home soon, though." She studied the reporters, then looked at Georgia. "The county's plans to cut funding were just announced yesterday, and our regular fundraising won't be enough to cover the shortfall. Looks like the local news is reporting on the story."

A wave of relief washed over Georgia. Of course there were other things going on in the world other than her own personal, and very embarrassing, drama. For example, the undeniable electric charge pulsing through her from standing so close to this incredibly alluring woman. She steeled herself. If there was anything Georgia O'Neill was good at, it was keeping her cool. One recent lapse didn't negate that, right? "Okay, well, I'm very sorry to hear that, Doctor…"

"Melanie Carter. Mel. Don't apologize to me. I just check in on the animals once a week or so. It's my uncle Seamus who's losing. This place has been his life's work. Not to mention the animals." Mel was a tad cool in her demeanor, but at the mention of her uncle and the animals, Georgia thought she detected her expression softening.

"I'm Georgia O'Neill. What will happen to them?" Georgia asked. She looked behind Mel's shoulder to see a hallway that led to a series of rooms where she guessed the animals were kept.

"Nothing's set in stone yet. But we'll try to move them to another place a few counties over. So," she said, looking down at the box of kittens, "we're in no place to take in any new animals."

"What am I supposed to do with these?" Georgia asked, straightening her posture. The kittens were cute. But seeing Mel Carter, with her broad shoulders and narrow waist that suggested a regular fitness regimen, holding on to the box, inspecting the contents—well, that just about made her knees buckle.

Georgia felt Mel's eyes studying her. Was she sizing up her ability to care for another living thing? Or was that flicker in her eye something else? Georgia was suddenly glad she'd taken the time to get herself together that morning rather than giving in to the temptation of spending the rest of her day in her pajamas. Being locked in Mel Carter's—*Doctor* Mel Carter's—gaze was poking some serious holes in her trademark cool confidence.

"You'll have to take them with you," Mel said, and for a moment Georgia wanted nothing more than for the doctor to lay out more orders. She'd pretty much do anything Mel wanted her to, and maybe then some. "There's really no—"

Mel was interrupted by the door to the shelter opening behind Georgia, and a small gray-haired man coming through the entrance. His glasses were crooked and the laces on one shoe were untied, though it was unclear as to whether his disheveled state was situational or just a general way of being. He bumbled past Georgia without acknowledging her. "Melanie," he said. "How's my Checkers?"

"Just fine, Seamus. I gave her a dose of vitamin E mixed with selenium. She should be back to her old self before you know it."

"Thank you, Doctor. Now, what have we got here?" Georgia watched as Seamus peered into the box of kittens that she was apparently about to inherit. He let out a shout of glee. "It's Molly! Oh, the Harris family is going to be overjoyed. They've been worried sick about her. And look at these kittens. Beautiful."

Seamus turned and did a double take when he noticed Georgia. "Oh. Hello. Where did you find them? Not sure if you've noticed the posters all around town, but there are two young girls who have been beside themselves for weeks. Seems that they'd been trying to keep her inside, with her delicate condition and all, but one of them left the back door open after burning a batch of sugar cookies and Ms. Molly here couldn't resist an adventure. She's an outdoor cat, but she must have been chased or scared by something and lost her way."

Lost her way. Georgia and Molly had more in common than she'd initially thought. She was about to answer, when Mel cut in. "Georgia here found them under her porch and wanted to dump them off," she said.

Georgia's face went hot. "I found them under my aunt's porch. And I wasn't dumping them off. It's an animal shelter."

Mel's expression changed from skeptical to amused. "You're right." She smiled, and Georgia instinctively touched her neck, something she'd trained her clients not to do. It showed vulnerability. Weakness. Which was what Mel was making her feel. Mel peered back in the box. "It's just frustrating how many people don't neuter or spay their cats and aren't willing to care for the kittens."

"The Harris family will take good care. Now, why don't I call them?" Seamus said. "Finally, some good news today." He pulled back the curtain to look at the news truck driving away.

"I heard you might be losing some funding," Georgia said. "I'm really sorry." She paused, looking back at the kittens still in Mel's arms, and again had to gather herself. Someone gorgeous holding kittens? Come on. They made calendars out of this, didn't they? "I'd be happy to deliver them to the family. My day's pretty open." Another task. She was starting to feel like herself again.

Seamus nodded. "Wonderful. I'll go call them now." He looked at Mel. "They live just up on Russell Road. You're heading that direction, right? Why don't you show Georgia the way there?"

"Happy to," Mel said, but Georgia failed to detect any happiness in her response.

"Thanks," said Georgia. Dropping off a lost cat and her kittens to a family who thought they were gone forever? If only she could get that news crew to come back to get some footage of this. And maybe a shot or two of the gorgeous vet cradling some very adorable animals.

She watched as Mel grabbed her jacket from behind the reception desk. This was supposed to be a break from work. But all of a sudden, Mel Carter had Georgia's mind on overdrive.

Mel knew very well she should have thanked Georgia. Probably profusely, for going out of her way like she did. Heck, she'd been in the business long enough to know that some people were downright cruel to animals. It tapped into an anger deep inside her that propelled her to go to work every day. Taking care of those animals that were turned away, who were so humble and so brave despite their circumstances. Nothing deserved her attention more than that.

She'd once thought of going into oncology, or even dentistry, but she thanked her lucky stars every day that she'd had the instinct to pursue veterinary medicine. There were lots of great humans, but there were lots of downright rotten ones too. Mel knew that well enough, and every day tried to silence the voice in her head that told her she attracted the bad ones. So, she was more than fine to devote 100 percent of her energy to those beings that were 100 percent deserving of all the attention and care in the world.

Mel had never seen this Georgia woman before. She'd grown up in Sunset County and knew the whole town, as well as the seasonal cottagers. Not only had she never seen or heard of her, but she stuck out in a way that was intriguing but set off more than one alarm bell. Firstly, her smooth skin had a hint of a summer glow that wasn't common in these parts toward the end of October. Then there was the fairly impractical nature of her attire, which, granted, caused Mel's eyes to linger maybe a moment or two too long, but didn't align with the usual jeans and fleece pullovers sported by most in the area. Georgia appeared as though she'd stepped right out of the pages of one of those fashion magazines her sister Andie always had lying around her place, the ones Mel teased her for with their headlines of "How to Own It in the Bedroom and the Boardroom!" or "Get Clear Skin from the Inside Out!"

She held open the shelter door for Georgia, then followed her to the street. "You can follow me in your car. It's only a few minutes up the road." She looked at Georgia's Audi, which had a sticker from the car rental company on the bumper. "Hope you're not planning on staying in town too long. Those tires won't cut it up here once the snow comes."

Georgia fished her keys out of her purse. "The guy at the rental company told me they're 'all season.'"

Mel knew her last comment came across as unwelcoming. She'd been brought up better than that. "Where are you from?" she asked as Georgia unlocked her door and slid into the driver's seat. The car was definitely impractical. But she looked great behind the wheel.

"LA."

Now the tan made sense. "So, not much experience with winter."

"Actually, I grew up right outside of Chicago. I know the drill. I'll be gone by the time the bad weather comes." She flashed Mel a quick smile.

So she was just passing through. Most Sunset County cottagers came from Toronto, but every now and then someone visited from farther afield. "That's me," Mel said, nodding to her silver pickup truck. "I'll lead the way."

Through her rearview mirror as she buckled her seat belt, Mel watched as Georgia applied lipstick, for whatever reason, and ran her hand through her silky, toffee-colored hair. Mel cleared her throat and shook her head. She'd lead Georgia to the Harris place and then be on her way. One thing Mel had always shared with animals was a strong sense of instinct. And her instinct was telling her that Georgia might be drop-dead gorgeous, but she was trouble. And when it came to fight, flight or freeze, Mel knew enough by this time in her life that flight left you with fewer problems in the long run.

She guided Georgia through the winding roads just outside of the Sunset County downtown, then pulled into the long gravel driveway leading to the Harris home. The family, clearly having received Seamus's call, were all assembled on the front porch, waiting to welcome home their cherished pet. Hopefully they'd be ready to house six more. Mel slowed to a stop at the side of the driveway, and rolled down her window as Georgia pulled up beside her.

"Here we are," Mel said. "Take care."

"What, you're not coming up?" Georgia asked. "What if they have any questions? I have absolutely no idea how to care for kittens."

Mel considered. Georgia was right. She sighed, then shifted back into Drive. She'd stay for a few minutes to make sure the family was all set up to care for their new pets, then head back to her clinic in town to finish the pile of paperwork waiting for her. A tall, boring pile of paperwork. It felt like exactly the solution to how hyperaware she'd been feeling since Georgia O'Neill burst through the doors of the shelter, her magnetic energy awakening something in her that Mel had worked to stow away for the past three years. Ever since everything she believed in and the life she thought was a happy one turned out to be a complete sham. She had to get away from Georgia, despite a nagging desire to be closer to her side.

Mel navigated the rest of the way up the path to the

house. The two little girls were jumping up and down on the front porch, huge grins on their faces. She sat for a moment, watching as Georgia removed the box from her back seat—did she have a seat belt around it?—then proudly handed the box over to the girls, who at their parents' permission had run down from the porch, almost attacking Georgia. It was a pretty great scene. Mel struggled to keep herself from grinning, then got out of her truck.

"Molly!" the younger girl said, hoisting the mother cat out of the box and into her arms, as the other twin enveloped them both in a giant hug. "We thought you were gone forever."

One of the girls separated herself from the hug and peered into the box. "Mommy, Daddy, look at the kittens! They're so cute!" she exclaimed, carefully lifting one out of the box. "We're keeping them, right?"

"We'll see," said the dad. "Seven is a lot of cats in one house."

"Might be a bylaw infraction," Mel said. Georgia shot her a look. Well, someone had to be the practical one, right?

"I'm sure we can find a home for a few of these cuties," Mrs. Harris said, peering into the box. "We can't thank you enough for finding Molly. There've been a lot of tears around here."

"I'm just glad she found her way home," Georgia said, her eyes sparkling. Mel swallowed hard as Georgia trailed her hand through her hair, allowing it to cascade down her back in a perfect thickness that Mel could easily imagine running her fingers through.

Georgia reached in and picked up the same orange-and-white kitten that had gotten stuck in her sweater earlier. "You're home, little one," she cooed, nuzzling the miniature animal against her face. Mel breathed in sharply at the idea of touching her perfect, tanned skin. It was time to leave.

"He likes you," said one of the little girls to Georgia.

"Let us know if you want dibs on him. You can visit in the meantime," their dad said.

Georgia laughed. "Oh, not me. I'm just in town for a bit. Good luck finding homes for them, though."

After another minute of small talk and thank-yous, and a few instructions for care from Mel, the family waved goodbye and carried the box into their home, leaving Mel and Georgia standing outside together.

"There you go. Your noble deed for the day," Mel said. "Collecting some good karma."

"Ha!" Georgia said, rolling her eyes. "Don't I need it."

Mel didn't know what that meant, and had no intention of probing, but it confirmed her instincts about Georgia O'Neill. *Trouble.*

"All right, well, you enjoy your time with your aunt," Mel said, turning toward her truck.

"Actually, she passed last month. I'm just here—well, I'm helping sort a couple of things out with her estate."

Mel turned back. "Nanny?" she asked.

Georgia looked confused. "Her name was Nina. Nina Miller."

"We all—" Mel took a moment to gather herself.

"Everyone in town called her Nanny. She was like everyone's grandma."

"I didn't know that." She looked to the side when she said it. Had Georgia and her aunt been close? Maybe she just wasn't telling the truth. Mel had never been good at detecting a lie, a crucial flaw that had only resulted in her getting burned. Torched, actually.

Georgia's eyes flickered with sadness, and Mel softened. "Well, I'm sorry about your aunt. She was an amazing woman." Georgia's eyes welled up a bit. Mel had to get out of there. "Lots of helpful people in this town if you need anything." It was the truth. Mel had only left Sunset County for a while to go to university and then vet school, and the familiar workings of the small town, and the way people took care of one another, were close to Mel's heart.

Georgia was quiet, and Mel felt the pressure of her waiting for a better response, but she said nothing. She might have been raised to be polite, but she was no therapist.

"Okay, well, thanks for bringing me out here," Georgia said. "Good luck with the rest of the animals at the shelter." Once again, Mel felt the strong pull of the vulnerability that was showing through the cracks of Georgia's confident, self-assured presentation. She watched as Georgia got in her car, and Mel returned the quick wave she offered as she drove away.

Mel heaved a big sigh as she got back into her truck, forcing herself to relax. But the way she was feeling? It might take a bit more than some deep breathing to recover from being around Georgia. She was a spark. The type that Mel knew could blur her judgment.

If Mel had learned anything in the past few years, it was that there were all sorts of ways that life could pull the rug out from under you. And she needed to stay on solid ground.

Chapter Two

A small package was propped up at the door on the front porch of Aunt Nina's cottage. It could only be from one person. Despite Georgia's desire to remain as under the radar as possible for the next few weeks, she thought it prudent to let at least her best friend, Paulina, under strict secrecy, know the exact location of her hideout lest some terrible accident befall her.

So far, so good. She hadn't counted on being a hero in her first few days in town, but she had to admit she'd enjoyed seeing the looks on the young girls' faces when she'd returned Molly and the kittens.

And then there was Mel Carter. The veterinarian looked as though she'd walked out of a casting call for the role, every bit the "I'm not a doctor but I play one on TV" stereotype. Seriously. The woman was a knock-out, and it irritated Georgia to no end that her attempt to do a good deed went so unnoticed. Punished, even! That comment about her being too irresponsible to neuter her cat? If it weren't for her disarming, penetrating gaze, and the subtle swagger of her detached demeanor, Georgia might have had the wherewithal to bite back. It was a capacity that she was rarely without.

She sighed, picked up the package and brought it into the redwood-shingled cottage her aunt had lived in for the last thirty years, the one she'd left behind every time she'd traveled to visit Georgia and her parents in San Diego in Georgia's early childhood, or Evanston in her teens. Georgia's calendar had never afforded her the time off to travel to Nina's place, when summer enrichment programs, SAT prep and competitive tennis all began to take over her life, all in the name of following the carefully laid-out path her parents had designed for her. But she'd loved when her aunt visited. Nina was younger than her sister, Georgia's mother, by ten years, and took an interest in Georgia's life beyond her schoolwork and extracurricular achievements. A visit from Nina always promised frivolous fun, like trips to the soft-serve ice cream truck in town for breakfast, or hours-long games of Monopoly. Georgia could only imagine that there were some negotiations behind the scenes and some disapproval from her parents, who only put up with Nina's disregard for Georgia's usual routines because it allowed them to leave on research field trips without too much guilt.

Standing in the entrance of Nina's cottage, she felt the same sense of calm that her aunt had brought to any space she entered. It was a small structure, but immaculately maintained. The wood-paneled living room looked out over a small, tree-lined inlet of Robescarres Lake, which afforded some privacy from the passing speed-boats, canoes and kayaks. A bedroom sat to the left side of the living room, and to the right of the entrance was a small, bright kitchen edged with countertops that offered forest views wherever you were cooking.

So they called her Nanny. The fact that Mel knew her aunt wasn't surprising—Nina was very social, and could barely walk ten meters down the street without striking up a casual conversation with whoever happened to be walking by—but the way that Mel dropped her aunt's nickname so casually, as though Georgia should have known, summoned a lump in her throat that she was having a tough time swallowing.

She plopped down into the worn green corduroy couch that wasn't about to win any design awards, but felt like a perfect hug—the kind of couch you could spend a whole day on, reading paperback mysteries and drinking hot chocolate. She examined the box in her hands, laughing to herself at the name Paulina had addressed the box to: "Hurricane Georgia." Only Paulina could get away with that. With anyone else, it would be too soon.

Georgia winced when she recalled, for the millionth time, the event that had earned her that nickname. How could a mere thirty seconds threaten to tear down everything she'd worked for all these years? How long would she be the laughingstock of the industry, the bringer of the greatest irony: the PR rep who earned the worst PR of all time?

It had all happened three weeks earlier. Georgia had known the red-carpet gala fundraiser would be a challenging evening, but thought she could manage. Days before the event, she'd received notice that Nina had finally lost her battle with cancer. And that there were strict instructions that she didn't want any kind of funeral or end-of-life celebration. Georgia was grieving, hard, crumbling inside but doing everything in her power to hold it together for her job. She'd always been able to compartmentalize.

What she hadn't anticipated was the combination of that grief paired with the incredible amount of pressure she'd been feeling in the first three months of her new role as Brand Reputation and Issues Response Specialist at Herstein PR, one of the world's leading agencies—with offices in LA, London, Miami, Toronto and New York— and the company to which she'd committed every last ounce of her time and energy over the past several years.

Not only was Georgia starting to handle the major flubs of some of the firm's top clients, but by special request, she'd continued to rep a huge tennis star who loved Georgia and insisted she'd employ another firm if Georgia wasn't on her team. The athlete was one of the marquee guests of the charity event that evening. Georgia was accompanying her on the red carpet, and stuck by her side during interview after interview until one of the journalists had veered off of the agreed-upon script. Instead of being asked about her athletic prowess and many amazing achievements, both on the court and in her philanthropic work, the star athlete was questioned about her love life and her weight, which had recently gone up and was the subject of massive tabloid speculation—was she pregnant? Was she not? Georgia knew very well that she was not, and had been scrambling to figure out how to shut down the interview without causing a scene.

The pivotal moment came when the journalist asked an even more insulting question, insinuating that the tennis star's weight was the reason behind her recent catastrophic loss in the finals of the US Open.

Georgia didn't remember much, but the videos that went viral on social media immediately following the event quite easily filled in the memory gaps. Georgia first used her elbow to jostle the tennis star out of the way, preventing her from answering the question. Not only did she then proceed to give the reporter a piece of her mind (filled with expletives that Georgia had no idea were part of her vernacular), but in her expressive delivery she sent the tennis star's glass of red wine flying toward the journalist, who, as it turned out, was a former college badminton player and boasted tremendous reflexes, the type that allowed him to duck prior to being hit by the projectile refreshment.

As luck would have it, the multiple-Academy-Award-winning starlet who was hosting the event, Aurelia Martin, was wearing a stunning white Valentino gown and happened to be directly behind the journalist, engaged in an interview of her own, and was splattered from cheek to hip with Georgia's assault. And it was all. On. Video. From multiple angles. In a way that allowed news outlets to create a humiliating, almost 360-degree compilation of the footage, which then traveled to TikTok and Instagram and beyond, where millions of people had viewed the dramatic event, and Georgia's complete and utter humiliation.

And then there were the memes. Objectively, some of them were quite clever, and if Georgia hadn't been the subject of the jokes, she might have admired the tidal wave of fun at her expense. She'd always been in awe of the power of social media.

Her meltdown had resulted in the VP of the company mandating that Georgia take a "wellness pause" from her work. Once she'd wrapped her head around the forced exile, and the impact on what, until recently, had been a promising career trajectory, Georgia weighed her options. The company owned a villa in the Turks and Caicos, but the island would be teeming with their clients on holidays. She briefly toyed with the idea of one of those silent retreats in Colorado, or even just hiding under her duvet for a good long while, but when she received the call from the lawyer handling her aunt's estate, informing her that Nina had left everything to her, hiding out in the small Canadian town felt like the perfect move.

Her aunt wouldn't be there, but maybe being in her home, surrounded by her things, would give Georgia the assurance and guidance she needed to get back on her feet and recover from this fiasco. Nina had always been her guide, and as gutted as Georgia was that she was no longer there to lean on, she longed to at least feel her spirit. Not to mention that handling her aunt's estate would give her something productive to work on, even though in typical Nina style, everything was so well organized, and her place was so tidy and clutter-free, that there really wasn't much to do.

Georgia's parents, as always, were off in some far-flung location—was it Krabi province in Thailand this time?—conducting research on infectious disease ecology and evolution, and were happy to leave the task to their only child, who had seemed to gravitate to Nina more than them anyway.

Georgia's goal was to get the cottage on the market in the next week, in the sweet spot before the fall ended and the beginning of what she'd read was a slow winter real-estate market in Sunset County. By then, she'd be welcomed back to the office and could pick up where she'd left off, helping the brightest stars and athletes in LA manage their public personas.

She picked up the box she'd found on the front porch, peeled back the packing tape, then laughed as she opened the top flap to reveal the contents. Paulina knew her well. Nestled into some shredded paper threads was a bottle of her favorite red wine from the vineyard they loved in Sonoma, as well as a jar of Dr. Barbara Sturm face mask, a pair of furry hot-pink Gucci slippers and a note reading "Hope you find your zen place! xoxo—P."

She instinctively reached for her phone to text her friend and remembered that she had returned it to the bread box and vowed to keep it shut away until 4:00 p.m.

It was only one thirty.

Georgia contemplated the living room of the cottage, trying to decide her next move. She needed to do a bit of staging before putting the cottage on the market, but that could wait.

The energy that she'd been feeling since being in the presence of Mel Carter hadn't gone anywhere, and one of the first things she planned on doing once she freed her phone was going to be looking her up on the internet to see what she could find. Despite Mel's less-than-perfect manners, Georgia predicted she'd have a squeaky-clean online presence. But Georgia had a few more tricks up her sleeve, with a forensic accountant's level of scrutiny from working with her clients.

If anything, she could spend a few minutes studying any profile pictures she came across. Her pink lips. Those deep brown eyes that could make you forget it was a human necessity to breathe, and the easy way she tucked her dark, glossy waves behind her ear. Georgia shivered.

She had some serious energy to expend.

After changing into her running gear, she did a few stretches, then set out to the backcountry roads around Nina's cottage. She settled into a comfortable pace, inhaling the cool fall air that carried a faint hint of bonfire smoke but felt cleaner than any air she'd ever breathed. Georgia was used to hills near her place in Hollywood and found a sudden burst of energy that she gave in to, finally settling into her favorite part about jogging: the moment when her mind went completely blank, and her only focus was getting to the next imaginary goalpost she set for herself on the path ahead.

The roads on the outskirts of Sunset County had a wide gravel shoulder on each side, so Georgia felt safe even when the occasional car or motorcycle whizzed by. Every time a nagging thought or a flash to the last few weeks threatened to enter her consciousness, Georgia picked up the pace just a bit more, and the increased challenge helped to keep the intrusions at bay.

Her watch alerted her that she'd hit the five-kilometer mark. She slowed to a walk in front of a unique, modern-looking home that was a touch out of place compared to the other houses and cottages in the area. The wide glass windows reflected the trees around it in a way that allowed the forest to continue uninterrupted, as though the house was trying to camouflage itself.

She'd stopped to examine the building further when a big fluffy dog with black, white and golden fur came bounding across the yard to greet her at the fence. Georgia crouched down and extended her hand through an opening between the fence posts, allowing the dog to sniff her. Then she petted its soft head. Seemed she was becoming quite the animal whisperer.

"What's your name?" Georgia asked quietly, as the dog panted and licked her hands. The dog had the gentlest eyes she'd ever seen, as though it could peer right into someone's soul. The earnest, sweet animal in front of her gave her a small window into why people loved being in the presence of dogs.

Then again, they didn't necessarily smell terrific.

"I didn't peg you as an animal person," a voice called from closer to the house. A familiar voice, which was unusual in an unfamiliar town.

Georgia stood up, and her heart, which had just started to slow down in the brief break from running, immediately sped up again at the sight of Mel Carter, who was emerging from the front entrance of the house holding a dog leash and making her way toward Georgia. A hot blush burned her already red cheeks. "You live here?" Georgia asked. "Nice place."

"You seem surprised," Mel said, her eyes traveling over Georgia's tight running top and pants, sending a heat wave of desire coursing through her body as though Mel's gaze was a laser beam. Mel had also changed since Georgia had last seen her and was still wearing her faded jeans, but she'd swapped out her lab coat for a red-and-black houndstooth wool button-up, rolled up at the sleeves.

Georgia had to consciously resist the urge to touch her neck, or fix her shirt, or smooth her hair. "Well, it's a bit surprising. I mean, not that you live here. Just that of all the places in the area I could have stopped for a break in front of—"

"Franny here has that effect on people," Mel said, opening the gate and leashing up Franny before she could bound toward Georgia. "She's a bit of a neighborhood ambassador."

"She's very cute," Georgia said, taking a tentative step forward to pet Franny again. Franny leaped up, trying desperately to lick her cheek. Georgia laughed and scratched the dog behind her ears when she settled down. "Rescue, I'm assuming?"

"Yeah," said Mel. She squatted down to Franny's height, and immediately Franny turned back to Mel for more pets. "She's a Bernese mountain dog. A farmer down the road got really badly injured in a trailer accident. He's not walking anymore, so he had to give up the farm. I took her in a couple years ago." Mel stood up, and Franny immediately jumped up again, almost hugging her, then licked her cheek. "Okay, okay," she said. "We're going for a walk. Don't worry." She looked at Georgia. "So—how's it going at your aunt's place? I'm sure that's a big chore. Going through everything."

Georgia nodded. "Luckily she was a minimalist. And a bit of a neat freak. So, it's really not a lot of work. Just—" Despite herself, she found the words coming out of her mouth. "Just a bit hard to say goodbye. We were close."

Mel's expression softened, telling Georgia that she knew something about her pain. And for a moment, Georgia saw an opening, as though Mel was about to offer her help. Or invite her to walk together. There was a shimmer of warmth, a genuine connection.

"Well, good luck with everything. Let's go, Franny," Mel said, taking a step away from her, and suddenly the spell was broken and Georgia felt foolish for entertaining the idea that a woman she had met mere hours ago would have any interest in doing anything to help her. "You know your way home, right?"

"Yeah, for sure," Georgia said, adjusting her watch. Had she done something wrong? She knew some people didn't like to talk about death, but surely someone in the health-care profession would know very well that it was a fact of life, wouldn't they? And what about that current of electricity between them? There was no way Mel didn't feel it too.

She glanced over her shoulder to check the road before crossing and give a quick wave before resuming her jog, but Mel had already turned her back and was walking the other way. "Take care," Mel called, without turning around.

Georgia stared for a moment, then started back toward Nina's cottage. Mel had clearly missed the class on bedside manners at vet school.

Try as she might to get back into the same zone she'd found so effortlessly at the beginning of her run, Georgia had no luck. That look in Mel's eyes—the one that for the very briefest of moments made Georgia desperate to know what she was thinking—was burned in her brain, and no amount of pushing herself and letting the fatigue overtake her would make it go away.

She'd come to Sunset County seeking a quiet place to hide out while she settled her aunt's affairs, and where she could find some way back to being the woman she was: a kick-ass PR agent, on top of her game. An achiever. A woman who could hold it together in the most challenging of situations.

So far, Mel Carter and her strong frame, and her deep, penetrating eyes, were *not* helpful in this endeavor.

Not one bit.

As soon as Mel knew Georgia was long gone, back toward Robescarres Lake, she stopped for a moment and took a deep breath while Franny sniffed a fallen branch at the side of the road. She looked out into the thick forest to her right and shook her head.

She knew she'd been incredibly rude. And should have asked Georgia if she needed anything. Her aunt had just died, an aunt she was close to, and now she had to pack up her place. Of course, that would be a hard thing to do. Heck, extending a hand, even to a stranger, was the essence of living in a small town, and she'd had more than her share of offers to help after everything that had happened to her three years ago. Not that she'd asked for it, but there was something reassuring in knowing there were good people looking out for you.

Even knowing this, she couldn't bring herself to do it. Because as soon as Mel offered help, and as soon as Georgia said yes, well, then she was in trouble. Georgia O'Neill was the first woman since Breanne who'd made Mel feel as though she was no longer standing on solid ground. She'd given in to that feeling for Breanne, big-time, and was still raw from the ache of that loss. A loss on two counts, and it was sometimes hard to know which was worse.

In the first few days, it was Breanne's death. The agony of losing the woman she loved and the future she'd envisioned, a future that was so vivid and so promising that it seemed impossible that something so alive and real could be snuffed out in a moment.

And then the details of the car accident were confirmed, and her best friend since childhood came clean with what was going on. Mel learned the reason why Breanne was rushing to get home, on a rainy night, when the roads were slippery. Mel had called her to say she'd just landed a day early from a conference and was going to take her out for dinner. Knowing the truth turned her sorrow, which was infused with a deep disappointment, into fierce anger.

Instead of going home from the airport, Mel had traveled by taxi to the hospital, where Breanne was about to take her last breath. Mel would never forget running through the hallways of the ICU ward, dodging wheelchairs and beds and nurses muttering at her to slow down, moments away from getting to the love of her life, with her suitcase trailing behind her and a ring in her pocket.

She'd missed saying goodbye.

It hadn't even for a moment struck her as strange that her best friend, Lauren, was there. Given what they'd been through together growing up, from skinned knees, soccer championships and failed math tests as kids, to supporting Lauren through her mother's Parkinson's disease and Lauren seeing Mel through the stress of vet school, of course she'd be there when Mel needed her most.

It was days later, over a bottle of whiskey, in a moment when she felt like she had her best friend, basically her sister, by her side to help her through what would be an impossible road ahead, when Mel learned the truth.

Lauren had called on the way over. "Can we talk?" she'd said. Her voice was timid, restrained. Nothing like her usual easygoing, affable self.

"Yeah, sure," Mel had said, not in the mood for conversation but grateful for her friend's company. She was working on her speaking notes for Breanne's celebration of life, and was terrified by the idea of standing up in front of a crowd and trying to make it through the speech without losing it.

When she opened the door, Lauren stood holding a bottle of Jim Beam, dark circles under her teary eyes, which were avoiding any contact with Mel's.

Mel had pulled two rocks glasses from the cupboard and poured them each a measure. "I might need you up there with me," she said. "In case I can't make it all the way through."

When she'd turned back to look at Lauren, her head was in her hands, her body shaking with guttural sobs. "I'm sorry. Oh, God, Mel, I hate myself."

Without Lauren even saying another word, the pieces of the puzzle started to click together. They'd always gotten along well when the three of them hung out, which Mel loved. Lauren would sometimes bring dates when they went out for drinks or to the movies, but she'd never suspected that the easy banter and affection between Lauren and Breanne was anything more than her girlfriend and her best friend getting along well for her sake.

"It just…happened," Lauren had whispered.

Just *happened*. Like the sunrise. Like the tide going out. Like a sneeze you couldn't control. Mel's stomach lurched, her anger clouding and shaking her vision at the same time.

She sat stiff and humiliated as Lauren choked out the hideous details of the affair. It had started during the trip the three of them had planned to take to Algonquin Park. Mel came down with strep throat the day they were supposed to leave. She'd encouraged them to go on without her. Then Mel's late nights getting the clinic up and running had apparently facilitated future meetups. She listened as Lauren tried to absolve herself of her guilt. *We felt so terrible. We were planning to tell you the truth.* And again: *It just* happened.

When she'd looked down at the table in front of her, she could barely make out the jotted-down notes she'd been working on of ideas for what she was going to say about Breanne. The words staring back at her re-arranged themselves, accusing her of being a complete fool. "How could you?" she managed.

Lauren continued to sob silently.

Minutes passed as Mel let the truth sink in. "Leave" was all she could think of to say. It was the last word she'd ever said to Lauren.

Her life had seemed perfect. Then. The person who mattered to Mel the most was gone, and the other, while still alive, was dead to her. Lauren had begged for her forgiveness, and in the weeks that followed, persisted in trying to convince Mel that their friendship could be mended. It took a while, but Lauren finally relented.

Over the past three years, the pain and anger had gradually turned to resignation, and a commitment to never get duped again. She'd tried therapy, but there didn't seem to be much of a point. It couldn't help her go back in time.

Small-town life suited her. She had a purpose, people knew her enough to respect that she liked to keep a polite distance, and there was the steadiness that very little changed, save for the cottagers and the weekenders passing through—mostly couples on a short getaway.

It had been a long time since she'd faced that same feeling she'd experienced when she first met Breanne on their university campus, when life seemed kind and it was conceivable that she could be happy. And al-though Mel knew nothing about Georgia O'Neill, how long she'd be in town for or what that meant for her, that familiar feeling was undeniable and set off every signal in her body to get as far away from Georgia as possible, as quickly as possible. Georgia thinking Mel was rude was way better than the alternative.

Franny sniffed, and Mel realized she'd been standing still for several minutes, staring out into the crimson-and-amber tapestry of the forest. "Come on," she called, then whistled, which made Franny leap up, wagging her tail in a fit of excitement.

Mel let Franny off her leash and watched her bound down the forest trail chasing a chipmunk, blissfully living in the moment. Animals were simple. Uncomplicated. They gave you all their love, unconditionally, and wanted nothing in return.

But most of all, they were loyal.

Chapter Three

"Hurricane Georgia, huh?" Georgia said, flopping back onto the couch with her phone.

Paulina's big grin filled the phone screen, and her booming laugh rang through the speaker. The sight of her best friend immediately brought up Georgia's spirits. Paulina was wearing a fluorescent yellow button-up with a black lightning bolt print and sparkly red-rimmed glasses, which fit her self-ascribed "fabulous Indian Ms. Frizzle" aesthetic. "Come on. That was at least a category four," Paulina said.

"With the wreckage of a five. How are you?"

"Oh, you know. Grant's on the road right now. So I'm sleeping really well."

Georgia rolled her eyes, laughing. Paulina was in a new relationship with a semipro basketball player and loved to brag about his stamina, both on and off the court. "Miss you, though," Paulina said. "How are things there?"

"Well. I just finished organizing the apps on my phone by color, and I've watched at least two hours of dance videos on TikTok, so safe to say you might need to get up here ASAP."

"Wait, so what you're saying is you're actually taking a break?"

Georgia tilted the phone down so Paulina could see her outfit, a purple tie-dyed lounge set.

"Wait," Paulina said, "are you still in your pajamas? This is bad. I'm on my way."

"Yeah, right," Georgia said. As a senior associate at her law firm on a fast track to partner, Paulina was just as devoted to her job as Georgia. "It's been all right. I'm just... I'm restless." Georgia sighed and stared out the window to the lake, which was sparkling in the early-evening light. Two loons bobbed close to shore, slowly paddling through the green lily pads dotting the surface of the water. At least she wasn't the only one in town with nothing to do.

"You're a workaholic. Makes sense. But you need this time."

"I'm not a workaholic."

"And I'm not a coffee addict."

"Fine. I'm finding it a bit challenging. But these slippers are definitely helping." Georgia pointed her feet in the air and wiggled her toes.

"Why don't you sign up for an online course or something? You've always talked about learning Mandarin."

"Nah."

"Scrapbooking?"

"Stop."

"Part-time job?"

"Ha. I might be needing one. Maybe I'll update my résumé."

"Volunteer? I know you love to work. But what about putting in some hours somewhere, just because it's a good thing to do? And good for your mental health."

"Maybe. Anyway, thanks for calling. I'm going to go organize my cosmetics bag or something. I'll call you tomorrow."

"Don't forget to relax. Miss you!"

Georgia tossed her phone on the coffee table and stared up at the ceiling. Where had she put that wine Paulina sent?

After pouring herself a generous glass of cabernet sauvignon (she was here to relax, wasn't she?), Georgia threw a couple of logs on the fire and sat back in front of the crackling flames, the light and heat comforting her while the pink evening sky began to fade to dark.

Maybe Paulina was onto something. She didn't need a work visa to volunteer. And doing something productive that contributed to society would look really good to her bosses and show them she was ready and able to work again. Maybe she could volunteer at Nina's old school. She could handle a few hours of playing with kids, couldn't she? Entertain them with a few celeb stories?

A quick Google search of the school board's website quashed that idea. All volunteers were required to provide a vulnerable sector check, which would take time to come through.

Maybe there was some kind of charity race or big event in the area she could help promote. Another few minutes of Google searching revealed a fundraising bingo that was happening at the local Legion, but it was scheduled for that evening.

Georgia sipped her wine. She'd figure this out.

Ever since she was a child, she'd been trained to be calculated and confident in everything she did, every decision she made. She was the one friends came to for advice. Other parents used her as an example for their own children: "Why can't you be more like that Georgia O'Neill?" She wore it as a badge of honor. And lived in a state of perpetual fear that the badge could be stripped away at any moment.

The truth was, Georgia liked being on top. She loved working hard, and her parents might have laid out the expectations, but Georgia happily met them.

It wasn't until she was in her first year at university that she felt the full weight of her parents' grand plan, each step in her life carefully mapped out for her, likely before she was even born.

College prep school. Violin lessons. Summer enrichment programs at campuses across the country. An exchange in Spain. And right into premed at Northwestern, where her parents were professors and researchers and could meticulously advise her on her course selections, professors most likely to write her a glowing reference for med school, and volunteer jobs and research positions at Chicago's top hospitals.

A bigger curveball had likely never been thrown their way when, without telling them, Georgia had switched into modern languages with a minor in art history early in her second year. Georgia wasn't sure what had surprised them more: the one-eighty on her academic plan or her bringing home her first girlfriend at Thanksgiving.

And as always, Nina had been there to guide her through, taking her phone calls late into the night, talking for hours and helping her figure out the right thing to do. Not right for anyone else, but right for her and her alone.

And here she was, at a time when she should have been working to advance her career righting *other people's* wrongs, trying to figure out how to wipe her own slate clean and get back to the steady trajectory of success that was true to her heart and that she'd set in motion years ago.

Paulina was right. She should take this time here, in Sunset County, to rest and move beyond what had happened. It was a small part of her story, and it was time to get over it. She remembered that morning, when she'd thought the news truck was following her. When she'd peered out the shelter's window, past the Help Wanted sign.

The Help Wanted sign.

If there was anything the past twelve hours had taught Georgia, it was that she was an unexpected hit with animals. And how hard could it be, petting and cuddling kittens and puppies, racking up some volunteer hours and making a few well-curated social media posts that her bosses would hopefully see?

The shelter manager—what was his name? Samuel? Steven? Seamus. He seemed like a nice man. And someone who likely hadn't seen her video.

And then there was Mel Carter. She had to admit

that the idea of seeing Mel again wasn't an entirely un-pleasant one, even if she seemed a bit odd and prickly.

Either way, she could put up with Mel and her moods. Plus, she'd told Georgia she only worked there once a week.

She scrolled back in her call history and dialed the shelter's number. It was past business hours, so she left a voice mail. "Hello, Seamus, we met this morning," Georgia said. "Georgia O'Neill. I saw your Help Wanted sign when I came by with the kittens. And I'm ready to help." She concluded the message with her phone number and a promise to follow up if she didn't hear from him by noon the next day. It was always good practice to exert a little control over the situation.

Her dampened mood was slightly lifted by the idea of having something productive to do (the wine didn't hurt), and she sat back on the couch, watching the dancing flames in the fireplace, and for the first time since arriving in Sunset County, she felt something approaching relaxation.

It was so quiet at Nina's place, and so warm and comforting. No wonder her aunt was always calm.

She'd lock in the volunteer job in the morning, and then do some work organizing her aunt's things later in the day. For now, she was going to enjoy the moment.

Right after she did some internet searching for Dr. Mel Carter.

"You mean that woman who was in here yesterday? Who's clearly never held an animal in her life, never mind has no experience whatsoever?" Mel said, moments after Seamus shared that he'd hired a new volunteer, and she'd be coming by momentarily to fill out the volunteer information form. Through gritted teeth, Mel was trying to manage her tone; she hated speaking to her gentle and kind uncle in a confrontational way.

"We've had that sign up for weeks, and no luck," Seamus said. "My back is giving me so much trouble, I can't keep up with all the extra work. And she seems nice."

Mel clenched her jaw. How was it that the one person she was eager to avoid was now about to invade her workspace? To be fair, most of Mel's time was spent at her clinic down the street, but still. What was Georgia up to? She was supposed to be dealing with her aunt's estate, not volunteering on a whim to make Mel's days more difficult.

"Fine," Mel sighed. "Hope she knows what she's getting into, though. It's not glamorous work. And she seems a bit—" she thought about the sheen in Georgia's thick, shiny hair, the expensive-looking outfit she'd worn to the shelter, the pristine Audi "—high-maintenance."

"I'll give her the benefit of the doubt. It's not like anyone else is knocking down the door to help out."

Before Mel could respond, the door of the shelter flung open, and in strode Georgia, looking like a complete knockout in a pair of royal blue high-heeled shoes, a black leather jacket and oversize tortoiseshell sunglasses. Mel's annoyance melted away, and she steadied herself.

Georgia removed her sunglasses, revealing her hazel

eyes framed with long lashes—eyes like a doe, but Mel wasn't sure she had the animal's trademark innocence.

"Georgia, welcome," Seamus said, rushing to the door to greet her and shake her hand. "We're so happy that you're interested in helping us out." Seamus looked at Mel expectantly.

Mel cleared her throat, trying to recover from Georgia's sparkling entrance, which had all but bowled her over. "Hey, Georgia" was all she could muster.

Georgia didn't seem fazed. "I printed out the volunteer form at my aunt's place. So, here it is. All filled out." She grinned and passed the paper to Seamus.

"Thank you," Seamus said, surveying the form. "Now, let me just pop this in a file folder. Then I'll give you a tour of the facility."

Mel saw her chance to make an exit. "All right, then. I'll see you around," she said and turned to her uncle. "I'll be back on Thursday. Just call if you need anything." She watched Seamus stand up on a chair to open the top cabinet, then stop, bending over and crying out in pain.

"You okay?" Mel asked, rushing to Seamus's side.

"My back," Seamus said, groaning, then accepting Mel's hand to help him off the chair. "I've really got to get to the chiropractor."

"Slowly, slowly," Mel said as Seamus got back on solid ground, wincing and holding his lower back.

"Can I call someone for you?" said Georgia, her big eyes shining with concern. She was right there with Mel, holding Seamus's other hand.

"No, no, I just need to rest for a few minutes," he said. With both of their assistance, he sank into the office chair, then looked at Georgia. "This is why we need you here. I'm getting too old to manage things on my own." Mel bristled.

"Well, I'm glad to be of service," Georgia said.

"Melanie, you don't mind giving Georgia a quick tour of the facility before you leave, do you?"

Mind? Of course she minded. Every moment she spent in Georgia's presence was another moment she felt herself losing her bearings. The woman was bewitching.

"I can come back tomorrow, if you're busy…" Georgia said, and Mel saw an out, until she looked down at Seamus's expectant expression. The old man knew her all too well.

"Not at all," Mel said through gritted teeth. Fine. The universe was testing her. She'd take Georgia on a quick tour, make sure Seamus was okay to get home on his own, then get the heck out of there.

She glanced at Georgia's impractical, albeit incredibly sexy footwear. Was she trying to torture her? "Have you got any other shoes you can wear? A number of our animals are out back. It's dirty."

"Ugh, what was I thinking?" Georgia laughed. "Sorry. In my line of work, heels are pretty much the uniform. I'm sure I'll be fine."

Despite herself, Mel couldn't help but smile. This would be interesting. What line of work did she mean? Cocktail waitress? Runway model? Pageant queen? Not that Mel was a fashion expert, but in her mind, any job that required a woman to wear heels was woefully behind the times. And Georgia O'Neill didn't seem like the kind of woman to be coerced into doing anything she didn't want to. So, the heels had to be a matter of personal preference.

"All right. Follow me," Mel said, leading Georgia down the bright hallway toward the back room. Time to see how she'd do with their resident reptiles. "Right in here," she said, motioning to the open door at the end of the hall. "After you."

Heels clicking against the linoleum, Georgia breezed by, leaving the floral scent of her shampoo in her wake and causing Mel to take a deep breath before following her into the room. How was it that something as inane as hair soap could make her heartbeat rev up to double time, and make her palms sweat like a cold glass of lemonade on a hot day? It really had been too long.

Mel surveyed Georgia's reactions as she walked between the reptile tanks, silently peering into each one with a curious expression.

"Who's this one? What's his name?" she asked, pointing to the iguana.

"That's Sherbet. And she's a she," Mel said.

"Okay. Cute. And who's this?" Georgia pointed to the turtle.

"That's Pixie. Careful with that one. She almost took my finger off last time I fed her," she said. She followed Georgia to the gecko tank. "Lollipop is the brown-and-white one, and Gummy Bear is the yellow one." She waited for Georgia to approach the final tank, which housed a ball python snake named Slinky. Slinky was mellow and gentle, as well as nonvenomous, but Mel knew very few people who liked being in the presence

of his sort. Time to see how much Georgia really wanted
to volunteer at the shelter.

To Mel's surprise, Georgia scanned the tank and
tapped quietly on the glass. "A snake," she said matter-
of-factly.

"Slinky," said Mel. Georgia was full of surprises,
she was starting to realize. "Most people don't want to
go near him with a ten-foot pole."

"I lived outside the desert for a few years as a kid.
Place was teeming with snakes," she said. "Okay, next
stop?" Her sparkling hazel eyes ratcheted up Mel's heartbeat from double time to a full-on Ginger Rogers tap
dance.

Next stop was the bunny room. Mel was doomed.

Georgia followed Mel through the animal shelter,
meeting the different residents and trying to solicit the
little information Mel seemed willing to share. Mel was
curt with her explanations and checked her watch several times, and when Georgia asked her about her vet
clinic and how long she'd been operating it, Mel made
Georgia feel as though she'd asked for her blood type
and password to her online banking account. Wasn't
politeness supposed to be a thing in Canada?

She sensed that Mel had introduced her to Slinky the
snake to get a rise out of her. It had taken everything
in her to maintain her cool. The truth was, she hated
snakes. As a child, when her parents were visiting professors at UC San Diego, she refused to go on hikes with
them to Joshua Tree or Anza-Borrego because of what
she'd read about the local residents of the parks, and on

any trip to the zoo she'd skip the reptile pavilion. But she wasn't about to give Mel the satisfaction of seeing her as anything less than an animal lover in her first thirty minutes at the shelter. She needed this position.

Mel led her through the shelter's back door to the fenced-in outdoor space, where a series of pens with plywood roofs housed a variety of farm animals: a few goats, a potbellied pig, some ducks and a few others who must have been hiding in their homes.

"This is the outdoor crew," Mel said. "You'll mostly be feeding and watering them." She motioned for Georgia to follow her to the back pen. Dammit. The heels were definitely a mistake. Mel must have noticed her taking careful steps through the uneven gravel and sand, and extended her elbow for Georgia to grab on to. She paused for a moment, unsure about the sudden kind gesture, then placed her hand on Mel's forearm, grateful for the support and appreciative of the soft strength of it.

"She's not as cute as Slinky, but..." Mel pointed to a sandy-colored miniature horse with white hair, tucked in the back corner of its pen, with eyes so sad that Georgia instinctively wanted to take the animal into her arms. Snakes? No way. Horses? Now they were getting somewhere. "This is Taffy," Mel said, then whistled and grabbed a carrot from the bucket outside of Taffy's pen. The little horse trotted over slowly, looking up at Georgia with curiosity.

"She's beautiful," Georgia breathed, then looked around at the collection of farm animals quietly going about their business in their pens. "Wouldn't a local farmer want to take them in?"

Mel passed Georgia the carrot, and she accepted. Their hands brushed together, and the warmth of Mel's skin felt like her California sunshine on the most perfect of days. Georgia clutched the carrot, then looked sideways at Mel to find the woman examining her, chocolate-brown eyes pensive and deep, as though she was being tested. Georgia straightened her posture, and despite her heels digging into the gravel, took a few steps closer to Taffy's pen and extended the carrot to the horse, willing her to come closer.

"Some do," Mel said. "Depends on their backstory. Some of these were collected by the SPCA after a report of mistreatment. Others had to be given up by their owners once their farms were sold to developers. Lots of reasons why animals end up here," she said. "That one," Mel said, motioning to Taffy, "is infertile. Wouldn't sell at market. Not worth it for the breeder to house and feed her, so she got unloaded here." Mel's words carried a sharp sense of protectiveness.

"You poor thing," Georgia whispered, lightly running her hand over Taffy's soft head.

"She's gentle," Mel said. "Seamus is training her to be a therapy animal."

"I can see why."

"You're good with her," Mel said.

"You sound surprised." Georgia looked up to see if Mel's expression had changed, but it was still all business. She was a tough one to crack. But it wasn't Georgia's style to back down. "I was always jealous of the girls in my class who grew up on ranches," she said, remembering her peers who showed off their ribbons from horseback riding events during show-and-tell, or who spent their weekends riding the trails of the nearby canyons. In contrast, Georgia's weekends were spent doing reach-ahead math sessions with tutors and practicing the violin while her mother sat in the adjoining sitting room, tut-tutting every time Georgia made an error.

The idea of spending her day on a majestic horse, galloping beside a stream or across a palm oasis (high up and out of the reach of any snake, of course), was the stuff of many a daydream, and something she knew her mother and father would never go for.

"And you never went riding as a kid?" Mel asked.

"No," said Georgia. "My parents had my time pretty mapped out. But I plan on it, someday." She looked into Taffy's eyes, charmed by the animal's innocence and gentle nature. Maybe she could convince Seamus to keep her on Taffy duty.

Mel hadn't said a word, and Georgia looked to her side to see if she was still there. What had moments ago been an untrusting expression was now the slightest bit tender, as though she actually cared what Georgia had to say, and maybe, just maybe, was interested in hearing more.

Georgia paused for a moment, then opened her mouth, ready to continue, when Mel cleared her throat loudly, then checked her watch. "Well, gotta run," she said, looking away from Georgia, then starting back toward the shelter. She stopped, then turned back. "Need my help getting back?" she said, gesturing toward her heels, which were now covered in dirt.

"I'm okay," Georgia said. What had she done wrong?

"I'm just going to spend a few more minutes out here looking around. You go ahead."

"All right. I'm going to help Seamus out and lock up, so you can exit through the gate. See you around," Mel said, beelining back to the building.

"Wait," Georgia called, just before Mel could leave. She turned around, and Georgia took in her tall, lean body and the way her jeans hugged her hips perfectly. "You haven't told me which one is your favorite."

Mel raised her eyebrows, then chuckled. "I don't play favorites," she said. "You look long enough in any of their eyes and you'll find something to love." With that, she disappeared through the door, leaving Georgia outside with her new charges.

She stood in the quiet of the shelter's outdoor space and considered what Mel said, and the notion of having to look for something in someone to love. Was that how it worked? Didn't love come easy, effortlessly, not like something you set out to do?

Not that she was looking to Mel Carter as the authority on all things love. The woman didn't exactly have warm and fuzzy written all over her.

But that intent, searching look in her eyes, quietly observing, was leading Georgia to believe that there was a lot more under the surface, and maybe something that she was keeping hidden from the world. Georgia prided herself on her ability to read people. To know when they were telling the truth, when they were lying, when they were afraid. It was part of why she was so good at her work. But with Mel? It was challenging.

Now she was working with her. Would Mel ever reveal

anything about herself to her? The idea was intriguing, and just a bit nerve-racking.

You're here for a few weeks. A month, tops, she reminded herself. In that amount of time, how much of someone could you really know?

Don't miss
The Vet's Shelter Surprise *by Elle Douglas,*
available November 2023 wherever
Harlequin Special Edition books
and ebooks are sold.

www.Harlequin.com